"Auster cons … people, possessed b … ss their ideas in creative ways." —… Review

"The latest and arguably most user-friendly among the whip-smart fiction canon of Paul Auster." —*The Boston Globe*

"Exquisitely crafted, surprisingly tender . . . A story grounded in the potent emotions of love, loss, regret and vengeance, and the painful reality of current day calamities like evictions and bankruptcies."
—Jane Ciabattari, NPR.org, "Books We Like"

"Resonate[s] with a warm acknowledgment of the tests and limitations of age and the vibrancy of experience . . . A lovely ride." —*Elle*

"A swift-moving, character-driven narrative . . . explores guilt, luck, and our enduring need for human contact and a sense of belonging. Powerful . . . Readers might find their one regret is seeing the book end."
—*Richmond Times-Dispatch*

"A haymaker of a contemporary American novel, realistic and serious as your life." —*The Milwaukee Journal Sentinel*

"Auster doesn't repair his characters so much as he curates and bears witness to their brokenness, holding each flawed life up to the light with great tenderness and compassion . . . A surprising novel." —*Cleveland Plain Dealer*

"*Sunset Park* [is] a novel about the difficulty of finding redemption in a world defined by loss."
—*Los Angeles Times*

"As remarkable as are Auster's skill and experience, this kind of writing—this kind of ending—takes another, rarer attribute: tremendous courage." —*The Seattle Times*

"Unexpectedly searing . . . *Sunset Park*'s prodigal-son tale is somberly poignant, a study of how deeply the urge to connect runs." —Salon.com

"Auster has delivered an emotionally appealing book about the varieties of modern love . . . The son-father story is in fact the warmest line of narrative Auster has ever written."
—*Dallas News*

"Captivating . . . This is classic Auster."
—*Minneapolis Star Tribune*

"With a plot that encompasses war in the Middle East, economic recession, and the perils of the publishing industry, a contemporary vitality distinguishes the latest from the veteran author. . . . Sure to please Auster fans and likely to attract new readers as well."
—*Kirkus Reviews* (Starred Review)

"Passionately literary . . . every element is saturated with implication as each wounded, questing character's story illuminates our tragic flaws and profound need for connection, coherence, and beauty. In a time of daunting crises and change, Auster reminds us of lasting things, of love, art, and 'the miraculous strangeness of being alive.'"
—*Booklist* (Starred Review)

"Auster deftly balances minute details that evoke New York City, post-financial meltdown, with marvelously drawn characters . . . This should be the novel that brings him a broader readership." —*Library Journal* (Starred Review)

Also By Paul Auster

NOVELS

The New York Trilogy (City of Glass, Ghosts, The Locked Room)
In the Country of Last Things
Moon Palace
The Music of Chance
Leviathan
Mr. Vertigo
Timbuktu
The Book of Illusions
Oracle Night
The Brooklyn Follies
Travels in the Scriptorium
Man in the Dark
Invisible

NONFICTION

The Invention of Solitude
The Art of Hunger
Why Write?
Hand to Mouth
The Red Notebook
Collected Prose

SCREENPLAYS

Three Films: Smoke, Blue in the Face, Lulu on the Bridge
The Inner Life of Martin Frost

POETRY

Collected Poems

ILLUSTRATED BOOKS

The Story of My Typewriter (with Sam Messer)
Auggie Wren's Christmas Story (with Isol)
City of Glass (adapted by Paul Karasik and David Mazzucchelli)

EDITOR

The Random House Book of Twentieth-Century French Poetry
I Thought My Father Was God and Other True Tales from NPR's National Story Project
Samuel Beckett: The Grove Centenary Edition

SUNSET PARK

PAUL AUSTER

PICADOR

A FRANCES COADY BOOK
HENRY HOLT AND COMPANY
NEW YORK

For information on Picador Reading Group Guides and titles, please contact Picador.
Phone: 1-646-307-5259
Fax: 212-253-9627
E-mail: readinggroupguides@picadorusa.com

ISBN: 0-312-84088-2
EAN: 978-0-312-84088-4

First published in the United States by Henry Holt and Company.

First Picador Paperback Edition: May 2011

10 9 8 7 6 5 4 3 2 1

SUNSET PARK

MILES HELLER

1

For almost a year now, he has been taking photographs of abandoned things. There are at least two jobs every day, sometimes as many as six or seven, and each time he and his cohorts enter another house, they are confronted by the things, the innumerable cast-off things left behind by the departed families. The absent people have all fled in haste, in shame, in confusion, and it is certain that wherever they are living now (if they have found a place to live and are not camped out in the streets) their new dwellings are smaller than the houses they have lost. Each house is a story of failure—of bankruptcy and default, of debt and foreclosure—and he has taken it upon himself to document the last, lingering traces of those scattered lives in order to prove that the vanished families were once here, that the ghosts of people he will never see and never know are still present in the discarded things strewn about their empty houses.

The work is called trashing out, and he belongs to a four-man crew employed by the Dunbar Realty Corporation, which subcontracts its "home preservation" services to the local banks that now own the properties in question. The sprawling flatlands of south Florida are filled with these orphaned structures, and because it is in the interest of the banks to resell them as quickly as possible, the vacated houses must be cleaned, repaired, and made ready to be shown to prospective buyers. In a collapsing world of economic ruin and relentless, ever-expanding hardship, trashing out is one of the few thriving businesses in the area. No doubt he is lucky to have found this job. He doesn't know how much longer he can bear it, but the pay is decent, and in a land of fewer and fewer jobs, it is nothing if not a good job.

In the beginning, he was stunned by the disarray and the filth, the neglect. Rare is the house he enters that has been left in pristine condition by its former owners. More often there will have been an eruption of violence and anger, a parting rampage of capricious vandalism—from the open taps of sinks and bathtubs overflowing with water to sledgehammered, smashed-in walls or walls covered with obscene graffiti or walls pocked with bullet holes, not to mention the ripped-out copper pipes, the bleach-stained carpets, the piles of shit deposited on the living room floor. Those are extreme examples, perhaps, impulsive acts triggered by the rage of the dispossessed, disgusting but understandable statements of despair, but even if he is not always gripped by revulsion when he enters a house, he never opens a door without a feeling of dread. Inevitably, the first thing to contend with is the smell, the onslaught of sour air rushing into his nostrils, the ubiquitous, commingled aromas of mildew, rancid milk, cat litter, crud-caked toilet bowls, and food rotting on the kitchen counter. Not even fresh air pouring in through open windows can wipe out the smells; not even the tidiest, most circumspect removal can erase the stench of defeat.

Then, always, there are the objects, the forgotten possessions, *the abandoned things*. By now, his photographs number in the thousands, and among his burgeoning archive can be found pictures of books, shoes, and oil paintings, pianos and toasters, dolls, tea sets, and dirty socks, televisions and board games, party dresses and tennis racquets, sofas, silk lingerie, caulking guns, thumbtacks, plastic action figures, tubes of lipstick, rifles, discolored mattresses, knives and forks, poker chips, a stamp collection, and a dead canary lying at the bottom of its cage. He has no idea why he feels compelled to take these pictures. He understands that it is an empty pursuit, of no possible benefit to anyone, and yet each time he walks into a house, he senses that the things are calling out to him, speaking to him in the voices of the people who are no longer there, asking him to be looked at one last time before they are carted away. The other members of the crew make fun of him for this obsessive picture taking, but he pays them no heed. They are of little account in his opinion, and he despises them all. Brain-dead Victor, the crew boss; stuttering, chatterbox Paco; and fat, wheezing Freddy—the three musketeers of doom. The law says that all salvageable objects above a certain value must be handed over to the bank, which is obliged to return them to their owners, but his co-workers grab whatever they please and never give it a second thought. They consider him a fool for turning his back on these spoils—the bottles of whiskey, the radios, the CD players, the archery equipment, the dirty magazines—but all he wants are his pictures—not things, but the pictures of things. For some time now, he has made it his business to say as little as possible when he is on the job. Paco and Freddy have taken to calling him El Mudo.

He is twenty-eight years old, and to the best of his knowledge he has no ambitions. No burning ambitions, in any case, no clear idea of what building a plausible future might entail for him. He knows that he will not stay in Florida much longer, that the moment is coming when he will feel the need to move on again, but until that need ripens into a necessity to act, he is content to remain in the present and not look ahead. If he has accomplished anything in the seven and a half years since he quit college and struck out on his own, it is this ability to live in the present, to confine himself to the here and now, and although it might not be the most laudable accomplishment one can think of, it has required considerable discipline and self-control for him to achieve it. To have no plans, which is to say, to have no longings or hopes, to be satisfied with your lot, to accept what the world doles out to you from one sunrise to the next—in order to live like that you must want very little, as little as humanly possible.

Bit by bit, he has pared down his desires to what is now approaching a bare minimum. He has cut out smoking and drinking, he no longer eats in restaurants, he does not own a television, a radio, or a computer. He would like to trade in his car for a bicycle, but he can't get rid of the car, since the distances he must travel for work are too great. The same applies to the cell phone he carries around in his pocket, which he would dearly love to toss in the garbage, but he needs it for work as well and therefore can't do without it. The digital camera was an indulgence, perhaps, but given the drear and slog of the endless trash-out rut, he feels it is saving his life. His rent is low, since he lives in a small apartment in a poor neighborhood, and beyond spending money on bedrock necessities, the only luxury he allows himself is buying books, paperback books, mostly novels, American novels, British novels, foreign novels in translation, but in the end books are not luxuries so much as necessities, and reading is an addiction he has no wish to be cured of.

If not for the girl, he would probably leave before the month was out. He has saved up enough money to go anywhere he wants, and there is no question that he has had his fill of the Florida sun—which, after much study, he now believes does the soul more harm than good. It is a Machiavellian sun in his opinion, a hypocritical sun, and the light it generates does not illuminate things but obscures them—blinding you with its constant, overbright effulgences, pounding on you with its blasts of vaporous humidity, destabilizing you with its miragelike reflections and shimmering waves of nothingness. It is all glitter and dazzle, but it offers no substance, no tranquillity, no respite. Still, it was under this sun that he first saw the girl, and because he can't talk himself into giving her up, he continues to live with the sun and try to make his peace with it.

Her name is Pilar Sanchez, and he met her six months ago in a public park, a purely accidental meeting late one Saturday afternoon in the middle of May, the unlikeliest of unlikely encounters. She was sitting on the grass reading a book, and not ten feet away from her he too was sitting on the grass reading a book, which happened to be the same book as hers, the same book in an identical soft-cover edition, *The Great Gatsby,* which he was reading for the third time since his father gave it to him as a present on his sixteenth birthday. He had been sitting there for twenty or thirty minutes, inside the book and therefore walled off from his surroundings, when he heard someone laugh. He turned, and in that first, fatal glimpse of her, as she sat there smiling at him and pointing to the title of her book, he guessed that she was even younger than sixteen, just a girl, really, and a little girl at that, a small adolescent girl wearing tight, cut-off shorts, sandals, and a skimpy halter top, the same clothes worn by every half-attractive girl throughout the lower regions of hot, sun-spangled Florida. No more than a baby, he said to himself, and yet there she was with her smooth, uncovered limbs and alert, smiling face, and he who rarely smiles at anyone or anything looked into her dark, animated eyes and smiled back at her.

Six months later, she is still underage. Her driver's license says she is seventeen, that she won't be turning eighteen until May, and therefore he must act cautiously with her in public, avoid at all costs doing anything that might arouse the suspicions of the prurient, for a single telephone call to the police from some riled-up busybody could easily land him in jail. Every morning that is not a weekend morning or a holiday morning, he drives her to John F. Kennedy High School, where she is in her senior year and doing well, with aspirations for college and a future life as a registered nurse, but he does not drop her off in front of the building. That would be too dangerous. Some teacher or school official could catch sight of them in the car together and raise the alarm, and so he glides to a halt some three or four blocks before they reach Kennedy and lets her off there. He does not kiss her good-bye. He does not touch her. She is saddened by his restraint, since in her own mind she is already a full-grown woman, but she accepts this sham indifference because he has told her she must accept it.

Pilar's parents were killed in a car wreck two years ago, and until she moved into his apartment after the school year ended last June, she lived with her three older sisters in the family house. Twenty-year-old Maria, twenty-three-year-old

Teresa, and twenty-five-year-old Angela. Maria is enrolled in a community college, studying to become a beautician. Teresa works as a teller at a local bank. Angela, the prettiest of the bunch, is a hostess in a cocktail lounge. According to Pilar, she sometimes sleeps with the customers for money. Pilar hastens to add that she loves Angela, that she loves all her sisters, but she's glad to have left the house now, which is filled with too many memories of her mother and father, and besides, she can't stop herself, but she's angry at Angela for doing what she does, she considers it a sin for a woman to sell her body, and it's a relief not to be arguing with her about it anymore. Yes, she says to him, his apartment is a shabby little nothing of a place, the house is much bigger and more comfortable, but the apartment doesn't have eighteen-month-old Carlos Junior in it, and that too is an immense relief. Teresa's son isn't a bad child as far as children go, of course, and what can Teresa do with her husband stationed in Iraq and her long hours at the bank, but that doesn't give her the right to pawn off babysitting duties on her kid sister every other day of the week. Pilar wanted to be a good sport, but she couldn't help resenting it. She needs time to be alone and to study, she wants to make something of herself, and how can she do that if she's busy changing dirty diapers? Babies are fine for other people, but she wants no part of them. Thanks, she says, but no thanks.

He marvels at her spirit and intelligence. Even on the first day, when they sat in the park talking about *The Great Gatsby,* he was impressed that she was reading the book for herself and not because a teacher had assigned it at school, and then, as the conversation continued, doubly impressed when she began to argue that the most important character in the book was not Daisy or Tom or even Gatsby himself but Nick Carraway. He asked her to explain. Because he's the one who tells the story, she said. He's the only character with his feet on the ground, the only one who can look outside of himself. The others are all lost and shallow people, and without Nick's compassion and understanding, we wouldn't be able to feel anything for them. The book depends on Nick.

If the story had been told by an omniscient narrator, it wouldn't work half as well as it does.

Omniscient narrator. She knows what the term means, just as she understands what it is to talk about *suspension of disbelief, biogenesis, antilogarithms,* and *Brown v. Board of Education.* How is it possible, he wonders, for a young girl like Pilar Sanchez, whose Cuban-born father worked as a letter carrier all his life, whose three older sisters dwell contentedly in a bog of humdrum daily routines, to have turned out so differently from the rest of her family? Pilar wants to know things, she has plans, she works hard, and he is more than happy to encourage her, to do whatever he can to help advance her education. From the day she left home and moved in with him, he has been drilling her on the finer points of how to score well on the SATs, has vetted every one of her homework assignments, has taught her the rudiments of calculus (which is not offered by her high school), and has read dozens of novels, short stories, and poems out loud to her. He, the young man without ambitions, the college dropout who spurned the trappings of his once privileged life, has taken it upon himself to become ambitious for her, to push her as far as she is willing to go. The first priority is college, a good college with a full scholarship, and once she is in, he feels the rest will take care of itself. At the moment, she is dreaming of becoming a registered nurse, but things will eventually change, he is certain of that, and he is fully confident that she has it in her to go on to medical school one day and become a doctor.

She was the one who proposed moving in with him. It never would have occurred to him to suggest such an audacious plan himself, but Pilar was determined, at once driven by a desire to escape and enthralled by the prospect of sleeping with him every night, and after she begged him to go to Angela, the major breadwinner of the clan and therefore the one with the final word on all family decisions, he met with the oldest Sanchez girl and managed to talk her into it. She was reluctant at first, claiming that Pilar was too young and inexperienced to consider such a momentous step. Yes, she knew her sister was in love with him, but she didn't approve of that love because of the difference in their ages, which meant that sooner or later he would grow bored with his adolescent plaything and leave her with a broken heart. He answered that it would probably end up being the reverse, that he would be the one left with a broken heart. Then, brushing aside all further talk of hearts and feelings, he presented his case in purely practical terms. Pilar didn't have a job, he said, she was a drag on the family finances, and he was in a position to support her and take that burden off their hands. It wasn't as if he would be abducting her to China, after all. Their house was only a fifteen-minute walk from his apartment, and they could see her as often as they liked. To clinch the bargain, he offered them presents, any number of things they craved but were too strapped to buy for themselves. Much to the shock and jeering amusement of the three clowns at work, he temporarily reversed his stance on the do's and don'ts of trash-out etiquette, and over the next week he calmly filched an all-but-brand-new flat-screen TV, a top-of-the-line electric coffeemaker, a red tricycle, thirty-six films (including a boxed collector's set of the *Godfather* movies), a professional-quality makeup mirror, and a set of crystal wineglasses, which he duly presented to Angela and her sisters as an expression of his gratitude. In other words, Pilar now lives with him because he bribed the family. He bought her.

Yes, she is in love with him, and yes, in spite of his qualms and inner hesitations, he loves her back, however improbable that might seem to him. Note here for the record that he is not someone with a special fixation on young girls. Until now, all the women in his life have been more or less his own age. Pilar therefore does not represent an embodiment of some ideal female type for him—she is merely herself, a small piece of luck he stumbled across one afternoon in a public park, an exception to every rule. Nor can he explain to himself why he is attracted to her. He admires her intelligence, yes, but that is finally of scant importance, since he has admired the intelligence of other women before her without feeling the least bit attracted to them. He finds her pretty, but not exceptionally pretty, not beautiful in any objective way (although it could also be argued that every seventeen-year-old girl is beautiful, for the simple reason that all youth is beautiful). But no matter. He has not fallen for her because of her body or because of her mind. What is it, then? What holds him here when everything tells him he should leave? Because of the way she looks at him, perhaps, the ferocity of her gaze, the rapt intensity in her eyes when she listens to him talk, a feeling that she is entirely present when they are together, that he is the only person who exists for her on the face of the earth.

Sometimes, when he takes out his camera and shows her his pictures of the abandoned things, her eyes fill up with tears. There is a soft, sentimental side to her that is almost comic, he feels, and yet he is moved by that softness in her, that vulnerability to the aches of others, and because she can also be so tough, so talkative and full of laughter, he can never predict what part of her will surge forth at any given moment. It can be trying in the short run, but in the long run he feels it is all to the good. He who has denied himself so much for so many years, who has been so stolid in his abnegations, who has taught himself to rein in his temper and drift through the world with cool, stubborn detachment has slowly come back to life in the face of her emotional excesses, her combustibility, her mawkish tears when confronted by the image of an abandoned teddy bear, a broken bicycle, or a vase of wilted flowers.

The first time they went to bed together, she assured him she was no longer a virgin. He took her at her word, but when the moment came for him to enter her, she pushed him away and told him he mustn't do that. The *mommy hole* was off-limits, she said, absolutely forbidden to male members. Tongues and fingers were acceptable, but not members, under no condition at any time, not ever. He had no idea what she was talking about. He was wearing a condom, wasn't he? They were protected, and there was no need to worry about anything. Ah, she said, but that's where he was wrong. Teresa and her husband always believed in condoms too, and look what happened to them. Nothing was more frightening to Pilar than the thought of becoming pregnant, and she would never risk her fate by trusting in one of those iffy rubbers. She would rather slit her wrists or jump off a bridge than get herself knocked up. Did he understand? Yes, he understood, but what was the alternative? The *funny hole,* she said. Angela had told her about it, and he had to admit that from a strictly biological and medical standpoint it was the one truly safe form of birth control in the world.

For six months now, he has abided by her wishes, restricting all member penetration to her funny hole and putting nothing more than tongue and fingers in her mommy hole. Such are the anomalies and idiosyncrasies of their love life, which is nevertheless a rich love life, a splendid erotic partnership that shows no signs of abating anytime soon. In the end, it is this sexual complicity that binds him fast to her and holds him in the hot nowhere-land of ruined and empty houses. He is bewitched by her skin. He is a prisoner of her ardent young mouth. He is at home in her body, and if he ever finds the courage to leave, he knows he will regret it to the end of his days.

2

He has told her next to nothing about himself. Even on the first day in the park, when she heard him speak and understood that he came from somewhere else, he didn't tell her that the somewhere else was New York City, the West Village in Manhattan to be precise, but vaguely answered that his life had begun *up north*. A bit later, when he started the SAT drills and introduced her to calculus, Pilar quickly learned that he was more than just an itinerant trash-out worker, that he was in fact a highly educated person with a nimble mind and a love of literature so vast and so informed that it made her English teachers at John F. Kennedy High look like impostors. Where had he gone to school? she asked him one day. He shrugged, not wanting to mention Stuyvesant and the three years he had spent at Brown. When she continued to press him, he looked down at the floor and muttered something about a small state college in New England. The following week, when he gave her a novel written by Renzo Michaelson, who happened to be his godfather, she noticed that it had been published by a company called Heller Books and asked him if there was any connection. No, he said, it's just a coincidence, Heller turns out to be a fairly common name. This prompted her to ask the simple, altogether logical next question about which Heller family he happened to belong to. Who were his parents, and where did they live? They're both gone, he replied. Gone as in dead and gone? I'm afraid so. Just like me, she said, her eyes suddenly filling with tears. Yes, he answered, just like you. Any brothers and sisters? No. I'm an only child.

Lying to her in this way has spared him the discomfort of having to talk about things he has been struggling to avoid for years. He doesn't want her to know that six months after he was born his mother walked out on his father and divorced him to marry another man. He doesn't want her to know that he has not seen or spoken to his father, Morris Heller, founder and publisher of Heller Books, since the summer after his third year at Brown. Least of all does he want her to know anything about his stepmother, Willa Parks, who married his father twenty months after the divorce, and nothing, nothing, nothing about his dead stepbrother, Bobby. These matters do not concern Pilar. They are his own private business, and until he finds an exit from the limbo that has encircled him for the past seven years, he will not share them with anyone.

Even now, he can't be sure if he did it on purpose or not. There is no question that he pushed Bobby, that the two of them were arguing and he pushed him in anger, but he doesn't know if the push came before or after he heard the oncoming car, which is to say, he doesn't know if Bobby's death was an accident or if he was secretly trying to kill him. The entire story of his life hinges on what happened that day in the Berkshires, and he still has no grasp of the truth, he still can't be certain if he is guilty of a crime or not.

It was the summer of 1996, roughly one month after his father had given him *The Great Gatsby* and five other books for his sixteenth birthday. Bobby was eighteen and a half and had just graduated from high school, having squeaked through by the skin of his teeth in no small part thanks to the efforts of his stepbrother, who had written three final term papers for him at the cut-rate price of two dollars per page, seventy-six dollars in all. Their parents had rented a house outside Great Barrington for the month of August, and the two boys were on their way to spend the weekend with them. He was too young to drive, Bobby was the one with the license, and therefore it was Bobby's responsibility to check the oil and fill the tank before they left—which, needless to say, he failed to do. About fifteen miles from the house, traveling along a twisty, hilly, back-country road, the car ran out of gas. He might not have become so angry if Bobby had shown some remorse, if the dim-witted slacker had taken the trouble to apologize for his mistake, but true to form, Bobby found the situation hilarious, and his first response was to burst out laughing.

Cell phones existed back then, but they didn't have one, which meant they had to get out of the car and walk. It was a hot, oppressively humid day, with squadrons of gnats and mosquitoes swarming around their heads, and he was in a foul temper, irritated by Bobby's moronic nonchalance, by the heat and the bugs, by having to walk down that crummy, narrow little road, and before long he was lashing out at his stepbrother, calling him names, trying to provoke a fight. Bobby kept shrugging him off, however, refusing to respond to his insults. Don't get worked up over nothing, he said, life is full of unexpected turns, maybe something interesting would happen to them because they were on this road, maybe, just maybe, they would discover two beautiful girls around the next bend, two completely naked beautiful girls who would take them into the woods and make love to them for sixteen straight hours. Under normal circumstances, he would laugh whenever Bobby started talking like that, fall willingly under the spell of his stepbrother's inane prattle, but nothing was normal about what was happening just then, and he was in no mood to laugh. It was all so idiotic, he wanted to punch Bobby in the face.

Whenever he thinks about that day now, he imagines how differently things would have turned out if he had been walking on Bobby's right instead of his left. The shove would have pushed him off the road rather than into the middle of it, and that would have been the end of the story, since there wouldn't have been a story, the whole business would have amounted to less than nothing, a brief outburst that would have been forgotten in no time at all. But there they were, for no special reason arrayed in that particular left-right tandem, he on the inside, Bobby on the outside, walking along the shoulder of the road in the direction of the oncoming traffic, of which there was none, not a single car, truck, or motorcycle for ten minutes, and after he'd been haranguing Bobby nonstop for those ten minutes, his stepbrother's jocular indifference to their plight slowly turned into peevishness, then belligerence, and a couple of miles after they started out, the two of them were shouting at each other at the top of their lungs.

How often had they fought in the past? Countless times, more times than he is able to remember, but there was nothing unusual about that, he feels, since brothers always fight, and if Bobby wasn't his flesh-and-blood brother, he nevertheless had been there for the full span of his conscious life. He was two years old when his father married Bobby's mother and the four of them started living together under the same roof, which necessarily makes it a time beyond recall, a period now wholly expunged from his mind, and therefore it would be legitimate to say that Bobby had always been his brother, even if that wasn't strictly the case. There had been the customary squabbles and conflicts, then, and because he was the younger by two and a half years, his body had received the bulk of the punishment. A dim recollection of his father stepping in to pull a screaming Bobby off him one rainy day somewhere in the country, of his stepmother scolding Bobby for *playing too rough,* of kicking Bobby in the shins when he yanked a toy out of his hands. But it hadn't been all war and combat, there had been lulls and truces and good times as well, and beginning when he was seven or eight, meaning when Bobby was nine or ten or eleven, he can remember actively liking his brother, perhaps even loving him, and that he was liked and perhaps even loved in return. But they were never close, not close in the way some brothers are, even fighting, antagonistic brothers, and no doubt that had something to do with the fact that they belonged to an artificial family, a constructed family, and each boy's deepest loyalty was reserved for his own parent. It wasn't that Willa had been a bad mother to him or that his father had been a bad father to Bobby. Quite the reverse. The two adults were steadfast allies, their marriage was solid and remarkably free of trouble, and each one bent over backward to give the other's kid every benefit of the doubt. But still, there were invisible fault lines, microscopic fissures to remind them that they were a patched-together entity, something not completely whole. The matter of Bobby's name, for example. Willa was Willa Parks, but her first husband, who had died of cancer at thirty-six, was Nordstrom, and Bobby was Nordstrom as well, and because he had been Nordstrom for the first four and a half years of his life, Willa had been reluctant to change it to Heller. She felt Bobby might be confused, but more to the point, she couldn't bring herself to wipe out the last traces of her first husband, who had loved her and was dead through no fault of his own, and to deprive his son of his name would have made her feel that he was being killed for a second time. The past, then, was part of the present, and the ghost of Karl Nordstrom was the fifth member of the household, an absent spirit who had left his mark on Bobby—who was both a brother and not a brother, both a son and not a son, both a friend and a foe.

They lived under the same roof, but apart from the fact that their parents were husband and wife, they had little in common. By temperament and outlook, by inclination and behavior, by all the measures used to gauge who and what a person is, they were different, deeply and unalterably different. As the years went by, each drifted off into his own separate sphere, and by the time they were bumping along through early adolescence, they rarely intersected anymore except at the dinner table and on family outings. Bobby was bright, quick, and funny, but he was an atrocious student who detested school, and because he was a reckless and defiant mischief maker on top of that, he was labeled *a problem*. By contrast, his younger stepbrother consistently earned the highest grades in his class. Heller was quiet and withdrawn, Nordstrom was extroverted and rambunctious, and each thought the other was going about the business of life in the wrong way. To make matters worse, Bobby's mother was a professor of English at NYU, a woman with a passion for books and ideas, and how difficult it must have been for her son to listen to her praise Heller for his academic achievements, exult at his acceptance by Stuyvesant, and talk to him over dinner about goddamned bloody *existentialism.* By fifteen, Bobby had turned into a serious pothead, one of those glassy-eyed high school stoners who puke their stomachs out at weekend parties and make small drug deals to keep themselves in extra cash. Stick-in-the-mud Heller, bad-boy Nordstrom, and never the twain could meet. Verbal attacks were occasionally delivered from each side, but the physical fighting had stopped—largely due to the mysteries of genetics. When they found themselves on that road in the Berkshires twelve years ago, the sixteen-year-old Heller stood a couple of centimeters below six feet and weighed one hundred and seventy pounds. Nordstrom, derived from scrawnier stock, was five-eight and weighed one forty-five. The mismatch had canceled all potential bouts. For some time now, they had belonged in different divisions.

What were they arguing about that day? What word or sentence, what series of words or sentences had so enraged him that he lost control of himself and pushed Bobby to the ground? He can't remember clearly. So many things were said during that argument, so many accusations flew back and forth between them, so many buried animosities came roiling to the surface in so many gusts of vehemence and vindictiveness that he has trouble pinpointing the one particular phrase that set him off. At first, it was all quite childish. Irritation on his part over Bobby's negligence, yet one more botch in a long line of botches, how could he be so stupid and careless, look at the mess you've gotten us into now. On Bobby's part, irritation over his brother's tight-assed response to a minor inconvenience, his sanctimonious rectitude, the know-it-all superiority he'd been busting his balls with for years. Boys' stuff, hotheaded adolescent boys' stuff, nothing terribly alarming. But then, as they continued going at each other and Bobby warmed up to the battle, the dispute reached a deeper, more resonant level of bitterness, the nether lode of bad blood. It became the family then and not just the two of them. It was about how Bobby resented being the outcast of the holy four, how he couldn't stand his mother's attachment to Miles, how he'd had it up to here with the punishments and groundings that had been meted out to him by heartless, vengeful adults, how he couldn't bear to listen to another word about academic conferences and publishing deals and why this book was better than that book—he was sick of it all, sick of Miles, sick of his mother and stepfather, sick of everyone in that stinking household, and he couldn't wait to be gone from there and off at college next month, and even if he flunked out of college, he was through with them and wouldn't be coming back. Adios, assholes. Fuck Morris Heller and his goddamned son. Fuck the whole fucking world.

He can't remember which word or words pushed him over the edge. Perhaps it isn't important to know that, perhaps it will never be possible to remember which insult from that rancorous spew of invective was responsible for the shove, but what is important, what counts above all else, is to know if he heard the car coming toward them or not, the car that was suddenly visible after rounding a sharp curve at fifty miles an hour, visible only when it was already too late to prevent his brother from being hit. What is certain is that Bobby was shouting at him and he was shouting back, telling him to stop, telling him to shut up, and all through that insane shouting match they were continuing to walk down the road, oblivious to everything around them, the woods to their left, the meadow to their right, the hazy sky above them, the birds singing in every pocket of the air, finches, thrushes, warblers, all those things had disappeared by then, and the only thing left was the fury of their voices. It seems certain that Bobby didn't hear the approaching car—or else he wasn't concerned by it, since he was walking on the shoulder of the road and didn't feel he was in danger. But what about you? Miles asks himself. Did you know or didn't you know?

It was a hard, decisive shove. It knocked Bobby off balance and sent him staggering onto the road, where he fell down and cracked his head against the asphalt. He sat up almost immediately, rubbing his head and cursing, and before he could climb to his feet, the car was mowing him down, crushing the life out of him, changing all their lives forever.

That is the first thing he refuses to share with Pilar. The second thing is the letter he wrote to his parents five years after Bobby's death. He had just finished his junior year at Brown and was planning to spend the summer in Providence, working as a part-time researcher for one of his history professors (nights and weekends in the library) and a full-time deliveryman for a local appliance store (installing air conditioners, lugging TVs and refrigerators up narrow flights of stairs). A girl had recently entered the picture, and since she lived in Brooklyn, he played hooky from his research job one weekend in June and drove down to New York to see her. He still had the keys to his parents' apartment on Downing Street, his old bedroom was still intact, and ever since he'd left for college the arrangement was that he could come and go as he pleased, with no obligation to announce his visits. He started out late on Friday after finishing work at the appliance store and didn't enter the apartment until well past midnight. Both of his parents were asleep. Early the next morning, he was awakened by the sound of their voices coming from the kitchen. He climbed out of bed, opened the door of his room, and then hesitated. They were speaking more loudly and more urgently than usual, there was an anguished undertow in Willa's voice, and if they weren't exactly quarreling (they rarely quarreled), something important was taking place, some crucial business was being settled or hashed about or reexamined, and he didn't want to interrupt them.

The proper response would have been to go back into his room and shut the door. Even as he stood in the hallway listening to them, he knew he had no right to be there, that he must and should withdraw, but he couldn't help himself, he was too curious, too eager to find out what was going on, and so he didn't budge, and for the first time in his life he eavesdropped on a private conversation between his parents, and because the conversation was largely about him, it was the first time he had ever heard them, had ever heard anyone, talk about him behind his back.

He's different, Willa was saying. There's an anger and a coldness in him that frighten me, and I hate him for what he's done to you.

He hasn't done anything to me, his father answered. We might not talk as much as we used to, but that's normal. He's almost twenty-one. He has his own life now.

You used to be so close. That's one of the reasons why I fell in love with you—because of how well you loved that little boy. Remember baseball, Morris? Remember all those hours you spent in the park teaching him how to pitch?

The golden days of yore.

And he was good, too, wasn't he? I mean really good. Starting pitcher on the varsity team his sophomore year. He seemed so happy about it. And then he turned around and quit the team the next spring.

The spring after Bobby died, remember. He was a bit of a mess then. We all were. You can't really blame him for that. If he didn't want to play baseball anymore, that was his business. You talk about it as if you think he was trying to punish me. I never felt that for a second.

That was when the drinking started, wasn't it? We didn't find out until later, but I think it started then. The drinking and the smoking and those crazy kids he used to run around with.

He was trying to imitate Bobby. They might not have gotten along very well, but I think Miles loved him. You watch your brother die, and after that a part of you wants to become him.

Bobby was a happy-go-lucky fuckup. Miles was the grim reaper.

I'll admit there was a certain lugubrious quality to his carryings-on. But he always did well at school. Through thick and thin, he always managed to pull down good grades.

He's a bright boy, I won't dispute that. But cold, Morris. Hollowed out, desperate. I shudder to think about the future . . .

How often have we talked about this? A hundred times? A thousand times? You know his story as well as I do. The kid had no mother. Mary-Lee walked out when Miles was six months old. Until you came on board, he was raised by Edna Smythe, the luminous, legendary Edna Smythe, but still, she was just a nanny, it was just a job, which means that after those first six months he never had the real thing. By the time you entered his life, it was probably too late.

So you understand what I'm talking about?

Of course I do. I've always understood.

He couldn't bear to listen anymore. They were chopping him into pieces, dismembering him with the calm and efficient strokes of pathologists conducting a postmortem, talking about him as if they thought he was already dead. He slipped back into the bedroom and quietly shut the door. They had no idea how much he loved them. For five years he had been walking around with the memory of what he had done to his brother on that road in Massachusetts, and because he had never told his parents about the shove and how deeply he was tormented by it, they misread the guilt that had spread through his system as a form of sickness. Maybe he was sick, maybe he did come across as a shut-down, thoroughly unlikable person, but that didn't mean he had turned against them. Complex, high-strung, infinitely generous Willa; his open-hearted, genial father—he hated himself for having caused them so much sorrow, so much unnecessary grief. They looked on him now as a walking dead man, as someone without a future, and as he sat down on the bed and considered that futureless future hovering dimly before him, he realized that he didn't have the courage to face them again. Perhaps the best thing for all concerned would be to remove himself from their lives, to disappear.

Dear Parents, he wrote the next day, Forgive the abruptness of my decision, but after finishing yet another year of college, I find myself feeling a little burned out on school and think a pause might do me some good. I've already told the dean that I want to take a leave of absence for the fall semester, and if that turns out to be insufficient, for the spring semester as well. I'm sorry if this disappoints you. The one bright spot is that you won't have to worry about paying my tuition for a while. Needless to say, I don't expect any money from you. I have work and will be able to support myself. Tomorrow, I'm taking off for L.A. to visit my mother for a couple of weeks. After that, as soon as I settle in wherever I happen to wind up living, I will be in touch. Hugs and kisses to you both, Miles.

It's true that he left Providence the following morning, but he didn't go to California to see his mother. He settled in somewhere. Over the past seven-plus years he has settled in at any number of new addresses, but he still hasn't been in touch.

3

It is 2008, the second Sunday in November, and he is lying in bed with Pilar, flipping through the *Baseball Encyclopedia* in search of odd and amusing names. They have done this once or twice in the past, and it counts heavily for him that she is able to see the humor in this absurd enterprise, to grasp the Dickensian spirit locked inside the two thousand seven hundred pages of the revised, updated, and expanded 1985 edition, which he bought for two dollars at a used bookstore last month. He is roaming among the pitchers this morning, since he always gravitates toward the pitchers first, and before long he stumbles upon his first promising find of the day. Boots Poffenberger. Pili scrunches up her face in an effort not to laugh, then shuts her eyes, then holds her breath, but she can't resist for more than a few seconds. The air comes bursting out of her in a tornado of yelps, screeches, and firecracker guffaws. When the fit subsides, she tears the book from his hands, accusing him of having made it up. He says: I would never do that. Games like this aren't fun unless you take them seriously.

And there it is, sitting in the middle of page 1977: Cletus Elwood "Boots" Poffenberger, born July 1, 1915, in Williamsport, Maryland, a five-foot-ten-inch right-hander who played two years with the Tigers (1937 and 1938) and one year with the Dodgers (1939), compiling a career record of sixteen wins and twelve losses.

He continues on through Whammy Douglas, Cy Slapnicka,

Noodles Hahn, Wickey McAvoy, Windy McCall, and Billy McCool. On hearing this last name, Pili groans with pleasure. She is smitten. For the rest of the morning, he is no longer Miles. He is Billy McCool, her sweet and beloved Billy McCool, ace of the staff, ace in the hole, her ace of hearts.

On the eleventh, he reads in the paper that Herb Score has died. He is too young to have seen him pitch, but he remembers the story his father told about the night of May 7, 1957, when a line drive off the bat of Yankee infielder Gil McDougald hit Score in the face and put an end to one of the most promising careers in baseball history. According to his father, who was ten years old at the time, Score was the best left-hander anyone had ever seen, possibly even better than Koufax, who was also pitching then but didn't come into his own until several years later. The accident occurred exactly one month before Score's twenty-fourth birthday. It was his third season with the Cleveland Indians, following his rookie-of-the-year performance in 1955 (16–10, 2.85 earned run average, 245 strikeouts) and an even more impressive performance the next year (20–9, 2.53 earned run average, 263 strikeouts). Then came the pitch to McDougald on that chilly spring night at Municipal Stadium. The ball knocked Score down *as if he'd been shot by a rifle* (his father's words), and as his motionless body lay crumpled on the field, blood was pouring from his nose, mouth, and right eye. The nose was broken, but more devastating was the injury to the eye, which was hemorrhaging so badly that most people feared he would lose it or be blinded for life. In the locker room after the game, McDougald, utterly distraught, promised to quit baseball *if Herb loses the sight in his eye.* Score spent three weeks in a hospital and missed the rest of the season with blurred vision and depth-perception difficulties, but the eye eventually healed. When he attempted a comeback the next season, however, he was no longer the same pitcher. The sting in his fastball was gone, he was wild, he couldn't strike anyone out. He struggled for five years, won only seventeen games in fifty-seven starts, and then packed it in and went home.

Reading the obituary in the *New York Times,* he is astonished to learn that Score was a cursed man from the beginning, that the 1957 accident was only one of many mishaps that plagued him throughout his life. In the words of obit writer Richard Goldstein: *When he was three, he was struck by a bakery truck, which severely injured his legs. He missed a year of school with rheumatic fever, broke an ankle slipping on a wet locker-room floor and separated his left shoulder slipping on wet outfield grass while in the low minor leagues.* Not to speak of hurting his left arm during the comeback year of 1958, being gravely injured in a car crash in 1998, and suffering a stroke in 2002, from which he never fully recovered. It doesn't seem possible for a man to have encountered so much bad luck in the course of a single lifetime. For once, Miles is tempted to call his father, to chat with him about Herbert Jude Score and the imponderables of fate, the strangeness of life, the what-ifs and might-have-beens, all the things they used to talk about so long ago, but now isn't the time, if there ever is a time it mustn't begin with a long-distance phone call, and consequently he fights off the impulse, holding on to the story until he is with Pilar again that evening.

As he reads the obituary to her, he is alarmed by the sadness that washes over her face, the depth of misery emanating from her eyes, her downturned mouth, the dejected droop of her shoulders. He can't be certain, but he wonders if she isn't thinking about her parents and their abrupt and terrible deaths, the bad luck that took them from her when she was still so young, still so much in need of them, and he regrets having brought up the subject, feels ashamed of himself for having caused her this hurt. To lift her spirits, he tosses the paper aside and launches into another story, another one of the many stories his father used to tell him, but this one is special, it was folklore around the house for years, and he hopes it will erase the gloom from her eyes. Lucky Lohrke, he says. Has she ever heard of him? No, of course not, she answers, smiling ever so slightly at the sound of the name. Another baseball player? Yes, he replies, but not a very distinguished one. A utility infielder for the Giants and Phillies in the late forties and early fifties, a career .240 hitter, of no particular interest except for the fact that this fellow, Jack Lohrke, a.k.a. Lucky, is the mythic embodiment of a theory of life that contends that not all luck is bad luck. Consider this, he says. While serving in the army during World War II, not only did he survive the D-day invasion and the Battle of the Bulge, but one afternoon, in the thick of combat, he was marching along with four other soldiers, two on either side of him, when a bomb exploded. The four other soldiers were killed instantly, but Lohrke walked through without a scratch. Or this, he continues. The war ends, and Lucky is about to get on a plane that will fly him back home to California. At the last moment, a major or a colonel shows up, pulls rank on him, takes his seat, and Lucky is bumped from the flight. The plane takes off, the plane crashes, and everyone on board is killed.

This is a true story? Pilar asks.

One hundred percent true. If you don't believe me, look it up.

You know the weirdest things, Miles.

Wait. There's still one more to go. It's nineteen forty-six, and Lucky is back on the West Coast, playing baseball in the minor leagues. His team is on the road, traveling by bus. They stop somewhere for lunch, and a call comes for the manager, telling him that Lucky has been promoted to a higher league. Lucky has to report to his new team right away, on the double, and so rather than get back on the bus with his old team, he gathers up his belongings and hitchhikes home. The bus continues, it's a long trip, hours and hours of driving, and in the middle of the night it starts to rain. They're high up in the mountains somewhere, surrounded by darkness, wetness, and the driver loses control of the wheel, the bus goes tumbling into a ravine, and nine players are killed. Awful. But our little man has been spared again. Think of the odds, Pili. Death comes looking for him three times, and three times he manages to escape.

Lucky Lohrke, she whispers. Is he still alive?

I think so. He'd be well into his eighties by now, but yes, I think he's still with us.

Some days after that, Pilar finds out the scores of her SATs. The news is good, as good or better than he hoped it would be. With her unbroken run of A's in high school and these results from the test, he is convinced she will be accepted by any college she applies to, any college in the country. Ignoring his oath about not eating in restaurants, he takes her to a celebratory dinner the next night and struggles throughout the meal not to touch her in public. He is so proud of her, he says, he wants to kiss every inch of her body, to gobble her up. They discuss the various possibilities in front of her, and he urges her to think about leaving Florida, to take a stab at some of the Ivy League schools up north, but Pilar is reluctant to consider such a step, she can't imagine being so far away from her sisters. You never know, he tells her, things could change between now and then, and it won't do any harm to try—just to see if you can get in. Yes, she answers, but the applications are expensive, and it doesn't make sense to throw away money for no reason. Don't worry about the money, he says to her. He will pay. She mustn't worry about anything.

By the end of the following week, she is up to her neck in forms. Not just from the state universities in Florida, but from Barnard, Vassar, Duke, Princeton, and Brown as well. She fills them out, composes all the required essays (which he reads over but does not alter or correct, since no alterations or corrections are necessary), and then they return to life as they once knew it, before the college madness began. Later that month, he receives a letter from an old friend in New York, one of the boys from the gang of *crazy kids* he used to run around with in high school. Bing Nathan is the only person from the past he still writes to, the only person who has known each one of his many addresses over the years. At first, he was mystified by his willingness to make this exception for Bing, but after he had been gone for six or eight months, he understood that he couldn't cut himself off completely, that he needed at least one link to his old life. It isn't that he and Bing have ever been particularly close. The truth is that he finds Bing somewhat off-putting, at times even obnoxious, but Bing looks up to him, for unknown reasons he has attained the status of exalted figure in Bing's eyes, and that means Bing can be trusted, relied upon to keep him informed about any changes on the New York front. That is the nub of it. Bing was the one who told him about his grandmother's death, the one who told him about his father's broken leg, the one who told him about Willa's eye operation. His father is sixty-two years old now, Willa is sixty, and they aren't going to live forever. Bing has his ear to the ground. If anything happens to either one of them, he will be on the phone the next minute.

Bing reports that he is now living in an area of Brooklyn called Sunset Park. In mid-August, he and a group of people took over a small abandoned house on a street across from Green-Wood Cemetery and have been camped out there as squatters ever since. For reasons unknown, the electricity and the heat are still functioning. That could change at any second, of course, but for now it appears there is a glitch in the system, and neither Con Ed nor National Grid has come to shut off the service. Life is precarious, yes, and each morning they wake up to the threat of immediate and forcible eviction, but with the city buckling under the pressure of economic hard times, so many government jobs have been lost that the little band from Sunset Park seems to be flying under the municipal radar, and no marshals or bailiffs have shown up to kick them out. Bing doesn't know if Miles is looking for a change, but one of the original members of the group has recently left town, and a room is available for him if he wants it. The previous occupant was named Millie, and to replace Millie with Miles seems alphabetically coherent, he says. *Alphabetically coherent.* Another example of Bing's wit, which has never been his strong point, but the offer seems genuine, and as Bing goes on to describe the other people who are living there (a man and two women, a writer, an artist, and a graduate student, all in their late twenties, all poor and struggling, all with talent and intelligence), it is clear that he is trying to make a move to Sunset Park sound as attractive as possible. Bing concludes that at last word all was well with Miles's father and that Willa left for England in September, where she will be spending the academic year as a visiting professor at Exeter University. In a brief postscript he adds: Think it over.

Does he want to return to New York? Has the moment finally come for the wayward son to crawl home and put his life together again? Six months ago, he probably wouldn't have hesitated. Even one month ago, he might have been tempted to consider it, but now it is out of the question. Pilar has claimed dominion over his heart, and the mere thought of going off without her is unbearable to him. As he folds up Bing's letter and puts it back in the envelope, he silently thanks his friend for having clarified the issue in such stark terms. Nothing matters anymore except Pilar, and when the time is right, meaning when a little more time has passed and she has reached her next birthday, he will ask her to marry him. It is far from clear that she will accept, but he has every intention of asking her. That is his answer to Bing's letter. Pilar.

The problem is that Pilar is more than just Pilar. She is a member of the Sanchez family, and even if her relations with Angela are somewhat strained at the moment, Maria and Teresa are as close to her as ever. All four girls are still grieving over the loss of their parents, and strong as Pilar's attachment to him might be, her family still comes first. After living with him since June, she has forgotten how determined she was to fly out of the nest. She has become nostalgic for the old days, and not a week goes by now when she doesn't stop by the house to visit with her sisters at least twice. He stays out of it and accompanies her only rarely, as little as possible. Maria and Teresa are polite and innocuous motormouths, unobjectionable but boring company for more than an hour at a stretch, and Angela, who is anything but boring, rubs him the wrong way. He doesn't like how she keeps looking at him, scrutinizing him with that odd combination of contempt and seductiveness in her eyes, as if she can't quite believe her baby sister has snagged him—not that she has any interest in him herself (how could anyone be interested in a grubby trash-out worker?), but it's the principle of the thing, since reason dictates that he should be attracted to her, the beautiful woman, whose job in life is to be a beautiful woman and make men fall for her. That is bad enough, but he still carries around the memory of the bribes he paid her last summer, the countless stolen presents he showered on her every day for a week, and even if it was all to a good purpose, he couldn't help feeling revolted by her avidity, her inexhaustible craving for those ugly, stupid things.

On the twenty-seventh, he allows Pilar to talk him into going to the Sanchez house for Thanksgiving dinner. He does it against his better judgment, but he wants to make her happy, and he knows that if he stays behind he will do nothing but sulk in the apartment until she returns. For the first hour, all goes reasonably well, and he is startled to discover that he is actually enjoying himself. As the four girls prepare the meal in the kitchen, he and Maria's boyfriend, a twenty-three-year-old auto mechanic named Eddie, go into the backyard to keep an eye on little Carlos. Eddie turns out to be a baseball fan, a well-read and knowledgeable student of the game, and in the aftermath of Herb Score's recent death, they fall into a conversation about the tragic destinies of various pitchers from decades past.

It begins with Denny McLain of the Detroit Tigers, the last man to win thirty games and no doubt the last one who ever will, the top pitcher in America from 1965 to 1969, whose career was destroyed by compulsive gambling binges and a penchant for choosing mobsters as his closest friends. Gone from the scene by the time he was twenty-eight, he later went to prison for drug trafficking, embezzlement, and racketeering, gorged himself up to a titanic three hundred and thirty pounds, and returned to prison for six years in the nineties for stealing two and a half million dollars from the pension fund of the company he worked for.

He did it to himself, Eddie says, so I can't feel no pity for him. But think of a guy like Blass. What the hell happened to him?

He is referring to Steve Blass, who played for the Pittsburgh Pirates from the mid-sixties to the mid-seventies, a consistent double-digit winner, pitching star of the 1971 World Series, who went on to have his best season in 1972 (19–8, 2.49 earned run average), and then, following the end of that season, on the last day of the year, Roberto Clemente, his future Hall of Fame teammate, was killed in a plane crash on his way to deliver emergency relief packages to the survivors of an earthquake in Nicaragua. The next season, Blass could no longer throw strikes. His once excellent control was gone, he walked batter after batter—eighty-four in eighty-eight innings—and his record dropped to 3–9 with a 9.85 earned run average. He tried again the next year, but after one game (five innings pitched, seven batters walked), he quit the game for good. Was Clemente's death responsible for Blass's sudden downfall? No one knows for certain, but according to Eddie, most people in baseball circles tend to believe that Blass was suffering from something called survivor's guilt, that his love for Clemente was so great he simply couldn't go on after his friend was killed.

At least Blass had seven or eight good years, Miles says. Think about poor Mark Fidrych.

Ah, Eddie replies, Mark "the Bird" Fidrych, and then the two of them launch into a eulogy for the brief and flamboyant career of the out-of-nowhere sensation who dazzled the country for the space of a few miraculous months, the twenty-one-year-old boy who was perhaps the most lovable person ever to play the game. No one had seen his like before—a pitcher who talked to the ball, who got down on his knees and smoothed out the dirt on the mound, whose entire fidgety being seemed to be electrified by constant jolts of hectic, nervous energy—not a man so much as a perpetual motion machine in the shape of a man. For one season he was dominant: 19–9, a 2.34 earned run average, starting pitcher for the American League in the All-Star game, rookie of the year. A few months later, he damaged the cartilage in his knee while horsing around in the outfield during spring training, and then, even worse, tore up his shoulder just after the start of the regular season. His arm went dead, and just like that, the Bird was gone—from pitcher to ex-pitcher in the blink of an eye.

Yes, Eddie says, a sad case, but nothing to compare with what happened to Donnie Moore.

No, nothing to compare, says Miles, nodding in agreement.

He is old enough to have lived through the story himself, and he can still remember the stunned expression in his father's eyes when he looked up from his newspaper at breakfast twenty years ago and announced that Moore was dead. Donnie Moore, a relief pitcher with the California Angels, was brought in to shut down a ninth-inning rally by the Boston Red Sox in the fifth game of the 1986 American League Championship Series. The Angels were ahead by a run, on the verge of winning their first pennant, but with two outs and a runner on first base, Moore delivered one of the most unfortunate pitches ever thrown in the annals of the sport—the one that Boston outfielder Dave Henderson knocked out of the park for a home run, the one that turned the course of the game and led to the Angels' defeat. Moore never recovered from the humiliation. Three years after throwing that life-altering pitch, by then out of baseball, dogged by financial and marital difficulties, perhaps certifiably insane, Moore got into an argument with his wife in the presence of their three children. He pulled out a gun, fired three nonfatal shots into his wife's body, and then turned the gun on himself and blew his brains out.

Eddie looks at Miles and shakes his head in disbelief. I don't get it, he says. What he did wasn't no worse than what Branca did when he threw that pitch to Thomson in fifty-one. But Branca didn't kill himself, did he? He and Thomson are buddies now, they go around the country signing goddamned baseballs together, and whenever you see a picture of them they're smiling at each other, two old coots without a care in the world. Why isn't Donnie Moore out there signing balls with Henderson instead of lying in his grave?

Miles shrugs. It's a question of character, he says. Every

man is different from every other man, and when rough things happen, each man reacts in his own way. Moore cracked. Branca didn't.

He finds it soothing to talk about these things with Eduardo Martinez in the late afternoon light of this Thanksgiving Thursday, and even if the subject matter could be considered somewhat grim—stories about failure, disappointment, and death—baseball is a universe as large as life itself, and therefore all things in life, whether good or bad, whether tragic or comic, fall within its domain. Today they are examining instances of despair and blighted hope, but the next time they meet (assuming they meet again), they could fill an afternoon with scores of funny anecdotes that would make their stomachs hurt from laughing so hard. Eddie strikes him as an earnest, well-meaning kid, and he is touched that Maria's new boyfriend has donned a jacket and tie for this holiday visit to the Sanchez household, that he is sporting a fresh haircut, and that the air is filled with the smell of the cologne he has put on for the occasion. The boy is pleasant company, but just as useful as *pleasant* is the simple fact that Eddie is there, that he has been given a male ally in this country of women. When they are called in for dinner, Eddie's presence at the table seems to neutralize Angela's hostility toward him, or at least deflect her attention from him and reduce the number of challenging looks he normally receives from her. There is another person to look at now, another stranger to be sized up and judged, to be deemed worthy or unworthy of yet another younger sister of hers. Eddie seems to be passing the test, but it puzzles Miles that Angela hasn't bothered to arrange a date of her own for the evening, that she is apparently without a boyfriend. Teresa's husband is far away, of course, and he fully expected her to be without a male companion, but why hasn't Angela invited a man to join them? Maybe Miss Beautiful doesn't like men, he thinks. Maybe her work at the Blue Devil cocktail lounge has soured her on the whole business.

Sergeant Lopez has not been home for ten months, and the meal begins with a silent prayer for his continued safety.

A few seconds after they begin, everyone looks up as Teresa sniffs back a sudden onrush of tears. Pilar, who is sitting next to her, puts her arm around Teresa's shoulder and kisses her on the cheek. He looks down at the tablecloth again and resists addressing his thoughts to God. God has nothing to do with what is happening in Iraq, he says to himself. God has nothing to do with anything. He imagines George Bush and Dick Cheney being lined up against a wall and shot, and then, for Pilar's sake, for the sake of everyone there, he hopes that Teresa's husband will be lucky enough to make it back in one piece.

He is beginning to think he will get through this trial without any unpleasantness from Angela. They have polished off several courses by now, everyone is attacking the dessert, and afterward, as a gesture of goodwill, he will offer to do the dishes, do them by himself with no help from anyone, and once he has washed and dried the innumerable plates and glasses and utensils, once he has scrubbed the pots and pans and put everything back in the cupboards, he will go out to the living room and fetch Pilar, telling them that it's late, that he has to work tomorrow, and off they'll go, just the two of them, slipping out of the house and climbing into his car before another word can be spoken. An excellent plan, perhaps, but the moment Angela finishes the last forkful of her pumpkin pie (no Cuban food today, everything strictly American, from the big bird with the stuffing in it to the cranberry sauce and the gravy and the sweet potatoes and the traditional dessert), she puts down her fork, removes the napkin from her lap, and stands up. I need to talk to you, Miles, she says. Let's go out back where we can be alone, okay? It's very important.

It isn't important. It isn't the least bit important. Angela is feeling deprived, that's all it is. Christmas is coming soon, and she wants him to help her out again. What does she mean by that? he asks. Stuff, she says. Like what he did for her this summer. Impossible, he tells her, it's against the law to steal, and he doesn't want to lose his job.

You did it for me once, she says. There's no reason why you can't do it again.

I can't, he repeats. I can't risk getting into trouble.

You're full of shit, Miles. Everybody does it. I hear stories, I know what's been going on. Those trash-out jobs are like walking into a department store. Grand pianos, sailboats, motorcycles, jewelry, all kinds of expensive stuff. The workers pinch everything they can lay their hands on.

Not me.

I'm not asking for a sailboat. And what do I need a piano for when I can't even play? But nice stuff, you know what I mean? Good stuff. Stuff that will make me happy.

You're knocking on the wrong door, Angela.

You're really a stupid guy, aren't you, Miles?

Come to the point. I assume you're trying to tell me something, but all I hear is static.

Have you forgotten how old Pilar is?

You're not serious . . .

No?

You wouldn't dare. She's your own sister, remember?

One call to the cops, and you're toast, my friend.

Cut it out. Pilar would spit in your face. She'd never talk to you again.

Think about the stuff, Miles. Pretty stuff. Big mounds of pretty stuff. It's a lot better than thinking about jail, isn't it?

In the car on the way home, Pilar asks what Angela wanted to talk to him about, but he avoids telling her the truth, not wanting her to know how much contempt he feels for her sister, how profoundly he despises her. He mutters something about Christmas, a secret plan the two of them have been cooking up together that involves the whole family, but he can't breathe a word because Angela has made him promise to keep quiet about it until further notice. This seems to satisfy Pilar, who grins at the prospect of whatever good thing is in store for them, and by the time they are halfway back to their apartment, they are no longer talking about Angela, they are discussing their impressions of Eddie. Pilar finds him *sweet* and not at all bad-looking, but she wonders if he is smart enough for Maria—to which he offers no comment. In his mind, the question is whether Maria is smart enough for Eddie, but he isn't about to offend Pilar by insulting her sister's intelligence. Instead, he reaches out his right hand and begins stroking her hair, asking her what she thinks of the book he gave her this morning, *Dubliners*.

He goes back to work the next day, convinced that Angela's threat is nothing more than a bluff, a nasty little piece of theater designed to break down his resistance and get him to start stealing for her again. He isn't going to fall for such a mindless, transparent trick, and over his dead body will he give her a single thing—not even a toothpick, not even a used paper napkin, not even one of Paco's farts.

On Sunday afternoon, Pilar goes to the Sanchez house to spend a couple of hours with her sisters. Again, he has no wish to join her and remains in the apartment to prepare their dinner while she is gone (he is the one who shops and cooks for them), and when Pilar returns at six o'clock, she tells him that Angela asked her to remind him not to forget about their deal. She says she can't wait forever, Pilar adds, repeating her sister's words with a confused, questioning look in her eyes. What in the world does she mean by that? she asks. Nothing, he says, dismissing this new threat with a curt shake of the head. Absolutely nothing.

Two more days of work, three more days of work, four more days of work, and then, late on Friday, just after wrapping up the final trash-out operation of the week, as he walks away from yet another empty house and heads for his car across the street, he spots two men leaning against the front and back doors of the red Toyota, two large men, one Anglo and the other Latino, two very large men who look like defensive tackles or professional bodybuilders or nightclub bouncers, and if they are bouncers, he thinks, perhaps they are employed by an establishment called the Blue Devil. The wisest course of action would be to turn and run, but it is already too late, the men have already seen him approaching, and if he runs now, he will only make things worse for himself, since it is altogether certain that they will catch up to him in the end. It's not that he is a small person or that he shies away from fights. He stands at six-two now, he weighs one hundred and eighty-seven pounds, and after years of working at jobs that have asked more from his body than his mind, he is in better than passable condition—well built, muscular, strong. But not as strong as either one of the two men waiting for him, and because they are two and he is one, he can only hope the men are here to talk and not to demonstrate their fighting skills.

Miles Heller? the Anglo asks.

What can I do for you? he replies.

We have a message from Angela.

Why doesn't she give it to me herself?

Because you don't listen to her when she talks to you. She thought you might pay more attention if we delivered the message for her.

All right, I'm listening.

Angela is pissed off, and she's beginning to lose her patience. She says you have one more week, and if you don't come through for her by then, she's going to pick up the phone and make that call. You got it?

Yes, I've got it.

Are you sure?

Yes, yes, I'm sure.

Are you sure you're sure?

Yes.

Good. But just to make sure you don't forget you're sure, I'm going to give you a little present. Like one of those strings you tie around your finger when you want to remember something. You know what I'm talking about?

I think so.

Without warning, the man hauls off and punches him in the gut. It is a cannonball of a punch, a punch so colossal in its force and so devastating in its effect that it knocks him to the ground, and as he is knocked to the ground the air is knocked out of his lungs, and along with the air that comes bursting through his windpipe there also comes the entire contents of his stomach, his lunch and his breakfast, remnant particles from last night's dinner, and everything that was inside him a moment ago is now outside him, and as he lies there puking and gasping for breath and clutching his belly in pain, the two large men walk off to their car, leaving him alone in the street, a wounded animal felled by that single blow, a man wishing he were dead.

An hour later, Pilar knows everything. The bluff was not a bluff, and therefore he can no longer hold out on her. They are suddenly in a dangerous spot, and it is essential for her to know the truth. She cries at first, finding it impossible to believe that her sister could act like this, threatening to put him in jail, willing to ruin her happiness for the sake of a few measly things, none of it makes any sense to her. It's not the things, he says. The things are only an excuse. Angela doesn't like him, she's been against him from the start, and Pilar's happiness means nothing to her if that happiness is connected to him. He doesn't understand why she should feel such animosity, but there it is, it's a fact, and they have no choice but to accept it. Pilar wants to jump into the car, drive over to the house, and slap Angela across the face. That's what she deserves, he says, but you can't do it now. You have to wait until after I'm gone.

It is a horrible solution, an unthinkable solution, but the only one left to them under the circumstances. He must leave the state. There is no alternative. He must get out of Florida before Angela picks up the phone and calls the police, and he mustn't come back until the morning of May twenty-third, when Pilar turns eighteen. He is tempted to ask her to marry him right then and there, but too many things are happening at once, they are both miserable and overwrought, and he doesn't want to pressure her or confuse her, to complicate an already complicated business when so little time is left.

He tells her that a friend has a room for him somewhere in Brooklyn. He gives her the address and promises to call every day. Since going back to the family house is out of the question now, she will remain in the apartment. He writes out a check to cover six months' rent in advance, signs over the title of his car to her, and then takes her to the bank, where he shows her how to use the automated teller machine. There are twelve thousand dollars in his account. He withdraws three thousand for himself and leaves the remaining nine thousand for her. After slipping the bank card into her hand, he puts his arm around her as they walk out into the blaze of the midafternoon sun. It is the first time he has touched her in public, and he does it consciously, as an act of defiance.

He packs a small bag with two changes of clothes, his camera, and three or four books. He leaves everything else where it is—to convince her that he will be coming back.

Early the next morning, he is sitting on a bus headed for New York.

4

It is a long, tedious trip, more than thirty hours from start to finish, with close to a dozen stopovers ranging from ten minutes to two hours, and from one leg of the journey to the next the seat adjacent to his is variously occupied by a round, wheezing black woman, a sniffing Indian or Pakistani man, a bony, throat-clearing white woman of eighty, and a coughing German tourist of such indeterminate aspect that he can't tell whether the person sitting next to him is a woman or a man. He says nothing to any of them, keeping his nose in his book or pretending to sleep, and every time there is a break in the journey he scampers out of the bus and calls Pilar.

In Jacksonville, the longest stopover of the trip, he works his way through two fast-food hamburgers and a large bottle of water, chewing and swallowing with care, since his stomach muscles are still exceedingly tender from the punch that knocked him down on Friday. Yes, the pain is just as effective as a string you tie around your finger, and the large man with the stone fist was right to assume he wouldn't forget it. After finishing his snack, he wanders over to the terminal kiosk, where everything from licorice sticks to condoms are for sale. He buys several newspapers and magazines, stocking up on additional reading material in case he wants a pause between books during the hundreds of miles still ahead. Two and a half hours later, as the bus is approaching Savannah, Georgia, he opens the *New York Times,* and on the second page of the arts section, in a column of squibs about upcoming events and the doings of well-known personalities, he sees a small picture of his mother. It is not unusual for him to come across pictures of his mother. It has been happening to him for as long as he can remember, and given that she is a well-known actress, it is only natural that her face should turn up frequently in the press. The short article in the *Times* is of special interest to him, however. Having spent most of her life working in movies and television, his mother is returning to the New York stage after an absence of ten years to appear in a production that will be opening in January. In other words, there is a better than even chance that she is already in New York rehearsing her role, which means that for the first time in how many years, in how many long, excruciating centuries, both his mother and father will be living in New York at the same moment, which is the selfsame moment when their son will find himself there as well. How odd. How terribly odd and incomprehensible. No doubt it means nothing, nothing whatsoever, and yet why now, he asks himself, why did he choose to go back now? Because he didn't choose. Because the choice was made for him by a large fist that knocked him down and commanded him to run from Florida to a place called Sunset Park. Just another roll of the dice, then, another lottery pick scooped out of the black metal urn, another fluke in a world of flukes and endless mayhem.

Half his life ago, when he was fourteen years old, he was out walking with his father, just the two of them, without Willa or Bobby, who were off somewhere else that day. It was a Sunday afternoon in late spring, and he and his father were walking side by side through the West Village, on no particular errand, he remembers, just walking for the sake of walking, out in the air because the weather was especially fine that day, and after they had been strolling for an hour or an hour and a half, they sat down on a bench in Abingdon Square. For reasons that escape him now, he started asking his father questions about his mother. How and where they met, for example, when they were married, why they hadn't stayed married, and so on. He saw his mother only twice a year, and on his last visit to California he had asked her similar questions about his father, but she hadn't wanted to talk about it, she had brushed him off with a brief sentence or two. The marriage was a mistake from the start. His father was a decent man, but they were wrong for each other, and why bother to go into it now? Perhaps that was what prompted him to interrogate his father that Sunday afternoon in Abingdon Square fourteen years ago. Because his mother's answers had been so unsatisfactory, and he was hoping his father would be more receptive, more willing to talk.

He first saw her onstage, his father said, undaunted by the question, speaking without bitterness, in a neutral tone from the first sentence to the last, no doubt thinking that his son was old enough to know the facts, and now that the boy had asked the question, he deserved a straight and honest answer. Curiously enough, the theater wasn't far from where they were sitting now, his father said, the old Circle Rep on Seventh Avenue. It was October 1978, and she was playing Cordelia in a production of *King Lear,* a twenty-four-year-old actress named Mary-Lee Swann, a glorious name for an actress in his opinion, and she gave a moving performance, he was stirred by the strength and groundedness of her interpretation, which bore no resemblance to the saintly, simpering Cordelias he had seen in the past. *What shall Cordelia speak? Love, and be silent.* She delivered those words with a self-questioning hesitation that seemed to open up her very insides to the audience. An extraordinary thing to behold, his father said. Utterly heartbreaking.

Yes, his father seemed willing to talk, but the story he told that afternoon was vague, ever so vague and difficult to follow. There were details, of course, the recounting of various incidents, starting with that first night when his father went out for drinks after the play with the director, who was an old friend of his, along with a few members of the cast, Mary-Lee among them. His father was thirty-two at the time, unmarried and unattached, already the publisher of Heller Books, which had been in operation for five years and was just beginning to gain momentum, largely because of the success of Renzo Michaelson's second novel, *House of Words*. He told his son that the attraction was immediate on both sides. An unexpected congruency, perhaps, in that she was a country girl from a backwater in central Maine and he was a lifelong New Yorker, born into a modicum of wealth whereas she came from little or nothing, the daughter of a man who worked as the manager of a hardware store, and yet there they were, making eyes at each other across the table in that little bar off Sheridan Square, he with his two university degrees and she with a high school diploma and a stint at the American Academy of Dramatic Arts, a waitress between roles, a person without interest in books whereas publishing books was his life's work, but who can penetrate the mysteries of desire, his father said, who can account for the unbidden thoughts that rush through a man's mind? He asked his son if he understood. The boy nodded, but in fact he understood nothing.

He was blinded by her talent, his father continued. Anyone who could perform as she had in that demanding, delicate role must have had a greater depth of heart and a wider range of feeling than any of the women he had known in the past. But pretending to be a person and actually being a person were two different things, weren't they? The wedding took place on March 12, 1979, less than five months after their first meeting. Five months after that, the marriage was already in trouble. His father didn't want to bore him by reciting a litany of their disputes and incompatibilities, but what it came down to was this: they loved each other, but they couldn't get along. Did that make any sense to him?

No, it made no sense to him at all. The boy was utterly confused by then, but he was too afraid to admit it to his father, who was making every effort to treat him as an adult, but he wasn't up to the job that day, the world of adults was unfathomable to him at that point in his life, and he couldn't grasp the paradox of love and discord coexisting in equal measure. It had to be one or the other, love or not-love, but not love and not-love at the same time. He paused for a moment to collect his thoughts, and then he asked the only question that seemed relevant to him, the only question that had any pertinent meaning. If they disliked each other so much, why did they have a baby?

It was going to rescue them, his father said. That was the plan, in any case: make a child together and then hope the love they would inevitably feel for their son or daughter would arrest the disenchantment that was growing between them. She was happy about it at first, his father said, they were both happy about it, but then—. His father abruptly cut himself off in midsentence, looked away for a moment as he shifted mental gears, and finally said: She wasn't prepared to be a mother. She was too young. I shouldn't have pushed her into it.

The boy understood that his father was trying to spare his feelings. He couldn't come out and bluntly declare that his mother hadn't wanted him, could he? That would have been too much, a blow that no person could ever fully absorb, and yet his father's silence and sympathetic evasion of the brute particulars amounted to an admission of that very fact: his mother had wanted no part of him, his birth was a mistake, there was no tenable reason for him to be alive.

When had it started? he wondered. At what point had her early happiness turned into doubt, antipathy, dread? Perhaps when her body began to change, he thought, when his presence inside her began to show itself to the world and it was too late to ignore the bulging extrusion that now defined her, not to speak of the alarm caused by the thickening of her ankles and the spreading of her bottom, all the extra weight that was distorting her once slender, ravishing self. Was that all it was—a fit of vanity? Or was it fear that she would lose ground by having to take time off from work just when she was being offered better, more interesting roles, that she was disrupting her progress at the worst possible moment and might never get back on track? Three months after she gave birth to him (July 2, 1980), she auditioned for the lead in a film to be directed by Douglas Flaherty, *Innocent Dreamer.* She got the part, and three months after that she headed for

Vancouver, British Columbia, leaving her infant son in New York with his father and a live-in baby nurse, Edna Smythe, a two-hundred-pound Jamaican woman of forty-six who went on working as his nanny (and later Bobby's too) for the next seven years. As for his mother, that role launched her career in films. It also brought her a new husband (Flaherty, the director) and a new life in Los Angeles. No, his father said when the boy asked the question, she didn't fight for custody. She was *torn apart,* his father explained, quoting what she had said to him at the time, *giving up Miles was the toughest, most awful decision she had ever made,* but under the circumstances, *there didn't seem to be anything else she could do.* In other words, his father said to him that afternoon in Abingdon Square, she ditched us. You and me both, kid. She gave us the old heave-ho, and that was that.

But no regrets, he quickly added. No second thoughts or morbid exhumations of the past. His marriage to Mary-Lee hadn't worked out, but that didn't mean it could be called a failure. Time had proved that the real purpose of the two years he spent with her was not about building a sustainable marriage, it was about creating a son, and because that son was the single most important creature in the world for him, all the disappointments he'd endured with her had been worth it—no, more than worth it, absolutely necessary. Was that clear? Yes. On that point, the boy did not question what his father was saying to him. His father smiled, then put his arm around his shoulder, drew him in toward his chest, and kissed him on the top of his head. You're the apple of my eye, he said. Never forget that.

It was the only time they talked about his mother in this way. Both before and after that conversation fourteen years ago, it was largely a matter of practical arrangements, scheduling phone calls, buying plane tickets to California, reminding him to send birthday cards, figuring out how to coordinate his school holidays with his mother's acting jobs. She might have disappeared from his father's life, but lapses and inconsistencies notwithstanding, she remained a presence in his. From the very beginning, then, he was the boy with two mothers. His real mother, Willa, who had not given birth to him, and his blood mother, Mary-Lee, who played the role of exotic stranger. The early years do not exist anymore, but going back to when he was five or six years old, he can remember flying across the country to see her, the unaccompanied minor indulged by stewardesses and pilots, sitting in the cockpit before takeoff, drinking the sweet sodas he was rarely allowed to have at home, and the big house up in the hills above Los Angeles with the hummingbirds in the garden, the red and purple flowers, the junipers and mimosas, the cool nights after warm, light-flooded days. His mother was so terribly pretty back then, the elegant, lovely blonde who was sometimes referred to as the second coming of Carroll Baker or Tuesday Weld, but more gifted than they were, more intelligent in her choice of roles, and now that he was growing up, now that it was evident to her that she would not be having any more children, she called him her little prince, her precious angel, and the same boy who was the apple of his father's eye was anointed the peach of his mother's heart.

She never knew quite what to make of him, however. There were considerable amounts of goodwill, he supposed, but not much knowledge, not the kind of knowledge Willa had, and consequently he seldom felt that he was standing on solid ground with her. From one day to the next, from one hour to the next, she could turn from ebullience to distraction, from joking affability to withdrawn, irritable silence. He learned to be on his guard with her, to prepare himself for these unpredictable shifts, to savor the good moments while they lasted but not to expect them to last very long. She was usually between jobs when he visited, and that might have added to the anxiety that seemed to permeate the household. The telephone would start ringing early in the morning, and then she would be talking to her agent, to a producer, to a director, to a fellow actor, or else accepting or refusing to be interviewed or photographed, to appear on television, to present this or that award, not to mention where to have dinner that night, what party to go to next week, who said what about whom. It was always calmer when Flaherty was around. Her husband helped smooth out the rough patches and keep her nighttime drinking under control (she tended to get a bit slurry when he was off on a job somewhere), and because he had a child of his own from an earlier marriage, his stepfather had a better feel for what he was thinking than his own mother did. His daughter's name was Margie, Maggie, he can't remember now, a girl with freckles and chubby knees, and they sometimes played together in the garden, squirting each other with the hose or staging pretend tea parties as they acted out various bits from the Mad Hatter scene in *Alice in Wonderland.* How old was he then? Six years old? Seven years old? When he was eight or nine, Flaherty, a transplanted Englishman with no interest in baseball, took it upon himself to drive them out to Chavez Ravine one night to watch the Dodgers play against the Mets, his hometown team, the club he pulled for through good years and bad. He was an amiable sort, old Flaherty, a man with much to recommend him, but when Miles returned to California six months later, Flaherty was gone, and his mother was going through her second divorce. Her new man was Simon Korngold, a producer of low-budget independent films, and against all odds, considering her record with his father and Douglas Flaherty, he is still her man today after seventeen years of marriage.

When he was twelve, she came into his room and asked him to take off his clothes. She wanted to see how he was *developing,* she said, and he reluctantly obliged her by stripping down to his bare skin, sensing that it wasn't within his power to turn down her request. She was his mother, after all, and no matter how frightened or embarrassed he felt to be standing naked in front of her, she had a right to see her son's body. She looked him over quickly, told him to turn around in a circle, and then, fixing her eyes on his genitals, she said: Promising, Miles, but still a long way to go.

When he was thirteen, after a year of tumultuous changes, to both his inner self and his physical self, she made the same request. He was sitting by the pool this time, wearing nothing but a bathing suit, and although he was even more nervous and hesitant than he had been the previous year, he stood up, peeled down the top of his trunks, and gave her a glimpse of what she wanted to see. His mother smiled and said: The little fellow isn't so little anymore, is he? Watch out, ladies. Miles Heller is in town.

When he was fourteen, he flatly said no. She looked somewhat disappointed, he felt, but she didn't insist. It's your call, kid, she said, and then she left the room.

When he was fifteen, she and Korngold threw a party at their house, a large, clamorous party with over a hundred guests, and even though many familiar faces were there, actors and actresses he had seen in films and on television, famous actors, all of them good actors, people who had either moved him or made him laugh many times over the years, he couldn't stand the noise, the sound of all those chattering voices was making him ill, and after doing his best for more than an hour, he stole upstairs to his room and lay down on the bed with a book, his book of the moment, whatever book it happened to be, and he remembers thinking that he much preferred to spend the rest of the evening with the writer of that book than with the thunderous mob downstairs. After fifteen or twenty minutes, his mother burst into the room with a drink in her hand, looking both angry and a little smashed. What did he think he was doing? Didn't he know there was a party going on, and how dare he walk out in the middle of it? So-and-so was here, and so-and-so was here, and so-and-so was here, and who gave him the right to insult them by going upstairs to read a goddamned *book*? He tried to explain that he wasn't feeling well, that he had a bad headache, and what difference did it make anyway if he wasn't in the mood to stand around yakking with a bunch of grown-ups? You're just like your father, she said, growing more and more exasperated. A bred-in-the-bone sourpuss. You used to be such a fun kid, Miles. Now you've turned into a pill. For some reason, he found the word *pill* deeply funny. Or perhaps it was the sight of his mother standing there with a vodka tonic in her hand that amused him, his flustered, irate mother insulting him with baby words like *sourpuss* and *pill,* and all of a sudden he started to laugh. What's so funny? she asked. I don't know, he answered, I just can't help myself. Yesterday I was your peach, and today I'm a pill. To tell you the truth, I don't think I'm either one. At that moment, which was no doubt his mother's finest moment, her expression changed from one of anger to mirth, changed from one to the other in a single instant, and suddenly she was laughing too. Fuck me, she said. I'm acting like a real bitch, aren't I?

When he was seventeen, she promised to come to New York for his high school graduation, but she never showed up. Curiously, he didn't hold it against her. After Bobby's death, things that had once mattered to him no longer mattered at all. He figured she had forgotten. Forgetting is not a sin—it is simple human error. The next time he saw her, she apologized, bringing up the subject before he had a chance to mention it, which he never would have done in any case.

His visits to California became less frequent. He was in college now, and during the three years he spent at Brown he went out there only twice. There were other meetings, however, lunches and dinners in New York restaurants, several long telephone conversations (always at her initiative), and a weekend together in Providence with Korngold, whose decade of steadfast loyalty to her had made it impossible for him to feel anything but admiration for the man. In some ways, Korngold reminded him of his father. Not in looks or affect or bearing, but in the work he did, which was scrambling to make small, worthwhile films in a world of mega-junk, just as his father was scrambling to publish worthwhile books in a world of fads and weightless ephemera. His mother was well into her forties by then, and she seemed more comfortable with herself than she'd been at the summit of her beauty, less involved in the intrigues of her own life, more open to others. During that weekend in Providence, she asked him if he'd thought about what he wanted to do after graduation. He wasn't sure, he said. One day he was convinced he would become a doctor, the next day he was tilting toward photography, and the day after that he was planning to go into teaching. Not writing or publishing? she asked. No, he didn't think so, he said. He loved to read books, but he had no interest in making them.

Then he vanished. His mother had nothing to do with the impetuous decision to turn on his heels and run, but once he left Willa and his father, he left her as well. For better or worse, it had to be that way, and it has to be that way now. If he goes to see his mother, she will immediately contact his father and tell him where he is, and then everything he has struggled to accomplish over the past seven and a half years will have been for naught. He has turned himself into a black sheep. That is the role he has willed himself to play, and he will go on playing it even in New York, even as he wanders back to the edge of the flock he left behind. Will he dare to go to the theater and knock on his mother's dressing room door? Will he dare to ring the bell of the apartment on Downing Street? Possibly, but he doesn't think so—or at least he can't think about it now. After all this time, he still doesn't feel quite ready.

Just north of Washington, as the bus enters the final leg of the trip, snow begins to fall. They are moving into winter now, he realizes, the cold days and long nights of his boyhood winters, and suddenly the past has turned into the future. He closes his eyes, thinking about Pilar's face, running his hands over her absent body, and then, in the darkness behind his lids, he sees himself as a black speck in a world made of snow.

BING NATHAN AND COMPANY

Bing Nathan

He is the warrior of outrage, the champion of discontent, the militant debunker of contemporary life who dreams of forging a new reality from the ruins of a failed world. Unlike most contrarians of his ilk, he does not believe in political action. He belongs to no movement or party, has never once spoken out in public, and has no desire to lead angry hordes into the streets to burn down buildings and topple governments. It is a purely personal position, but if he lives his life according to the principles he has established for himself, he feels certain that others will follow his example.

When he talks about the world, then, he is referring to his world, to the small, circumscribed sphere of his own life, and not to the world-at-large, which is too large and too broken for him to have any effect on it. He therefore concentrates on the local, the particular, the nearly invisible details of quotidian affairs. The decisions he makes are necessarily small ones, but small does not always mean unimportant, and day after day he struggles to adhere to the fundamental rule of his discontent: to stand in opposition to things-as-they-are, to resist the status quo on all fronts. Since the war in Vietnam, which began nearly twenty years before he was born, he would argue that the concept known as *America* has played itself out, that the country is no longer a workable proposition, but if anything continues to unite the fractured masses of this defunct nation, if American opinion is still unanimous about any one idea, it is a belief in the notion of progress. He contends that they are wrong, that the technological developments of the past decades have in fact only diminished the possibilities of life. In a throwaway culture spawned by the greed of profit-driven corporations, the landscape has grown ever more shabby, ever more alienating, ever more empty of meaning and consolidating purpose. His acts of rebellion are petty ones, perhaps, peevish gestures that accomplish little or nothing even in the short run, but they help to enhance his dignity as a human being, to ennoble him in his own eyes. He takes it for granted that the future is a lost cause, and if the present is all that matters now, then it must be a present imbued with the spirit of the past. That is why he shuns cell phones, computers, and all things digital—because he refuses to participate in new technologies. That is why he spends his weekends playing drums and percussion in a six-man jazz group—because jazz is dead and only the happy few are interested in it anymore. That is why he started his business three years ago—because he wanted to fight back. The Hospital for Broken Things is located on Fifth Avenue in Park Slope. Flanked by a laundromat on one side and a vintage clothing shop on the other, it is a hole-in-the-wall storefront enterprise devoted to repairing objects from an era that has all but vanished from the face of the earth: manual typewriters, fountain pens, mechanical watches, vacuum-tube radios, record players, wind-up toys, gumball machines, and rotary telephones. Little matter that ninety percent of the money he earns comes from framing pictures. His shop provides a unique and inestimable service, and every time he works on another battered artifact from the antique industries of half a century ago, he goes about it with the willfulness and passion of a general fighting a war.

Tangibility. That is the word he uses most often when discussing his ideas with his friends. The world is tangible, he says. Human beings are tangible. They are endowed with bodies, and because those bodies feel pain and suffer from disease and undergo death, human life has not altered by a single jot since the beginning of mankind. Yes, the discovery of fire made man warmer and put an end to the raw-meat diet; the building of bridges enabled him to cross rivers and streams without getting his toes wet; the invention of the airplane allowed him to hop over continents and oceans while creating new phenomena such as jet lag and in-flight movies—but even if man has changed the world around him, man himself has not changed. The facts of life are constant. You live and then you die. You are born out of a woman's body, and if you manage to survive your birth, your mother must feed you and take care of you to ensure that you go on surviving, and everything that happens to you from the moment of your birth to the moment of your death, every emotion that wells up in you, every flash of anger, every surge of lust, every bout of tears, every gust of laughter, everything you will ever feel in the course of your life has also been felt by everyone who came before you, whether you are a caveman or an astronaut, whether you live in the Gobi Desert or the Arctic Circle. It all came to him in a sudden, epiphanic burst when he was sixteen years old. Paging through an illustrated book about the Dead Sea scrolls one afternoon, he stumbled across some photographs of the things that had been unearthed along with the parchment texts: plates and eating utensils, straw baskets, pots, jugs, all of them perfectly intact. He studied them carefully for several moments, not quite understanding why he found these objects so compelling, and then, after several more moments, it finally came to him. The decorative patterns on the dishes were identical to the patterns on the dishes in the window of the store across the street from his apartment. The straw baskets were identical to the baskets millions of Europeans use to shop with today. The things in the pictures were two thousand years old, and yet they looked utterly new, utterly contemporary. That was the revelation that changed his thinking about human time: if a person from two thousand years ago, living in a far-flung outpost of the Roman Empire, could fashion a household item that looked exactly like a household item from today, how was that person's mind or heart or inner being any different from his own? That is the story he never tires of repeating to his friends, his counterargument to the prevailing belief that new technologies alter human consciousness. Microscopes and telescopes have permitted us to see more things than ever before, he says, but our days are still spent in the realm of normal sight. E-mails are faster than posted letters, he says, but in the end they're just another form of letter writing. He reels off example after example. He knows he drives them crazy with his conjectures and opinions, that he bores them with his long, nattering harangues, but these are important issues to him, and once he gets started, he finds it difficult to stop.

He is a large, hulking presence, a sloppy bear of a man with a full brown beard and a gold stud in his left earlobe, an inch under six feet tall but a wide and waddling two hundred and twenty pounds. His daily uniform consists of a pair of sagging black jeans, yellow work boots, and a plaid lumberjack shirt. He changes his underwear infrequently. He chews his food too loudly. He has been unlucky in love. Of all the things he does in life, playing the drums gives him the most pleasure. He was a boisterous child, a noisemaker of undisciplined exuberance and clumsy, scattershot aggression, and when his parents presented him with a drum set on his twelfth birthday, hoping his destructive urges might take a new form, their hunch proved correct. Seventeen years later, his collection has grown from the standard kit (snare drums, tom-toms, side drum, bass drum, suspended cymbals, hi-hat cymbals) to include more than two dozen drums of various shapes and sizes from around the world, among them a murumba, a batá, a darbuka, an okedo, a kalangu, a rommelpot, a bodhrán, a dhola, an ingungu, a koboro, a ntenga, and a tabor. Depending on the instrument, he plays with sticks, mallets, or hands. His percussion closet is stocked with standbys such as bells, gongs, bull-roarers, castanets, clappers, chimes, washboards, and kalimbas, but he has also performed with chains, spoons, pebbles, sandpaper, and rattles. The band he belongs to is called Mob Rule, and they average two or three gigs a month, mostly in small bars and clubs in

Brooklyn and lower Manhattan. If they earned more money, he would gladly drop everything and spend the rest of his life touring the world with them, but they barely earn enough to cover the costs of their rehearsal space. He loves the harsh, dissonant, improvised sound they create—shit-kicking funk, as he sometimes calls it—and they are not without their loyal followers. But there aren't enough of them, not nearly enough, and so he spends his mornings and afternoons in the Hospital for Broken Things, putting frames around movie posters and mending relics that were built when his grandparents were children.

When Ellen Brice told him about the abandoned house in Sunset Park this past summer, he saw it as an opportunity to put his ideas to the test, to move beyond his invisible, solitary attacks on the system and participate in a communal action. It is the boldest step he has yet taken, and he has no trouble reconciling the illegality of what they are doing with their right to do it. These are desperate times for everyone, and a crumbling wooden house standing empty in a neighborhood as ragged as this one is nothing if not an open invitation to vandals and arsonists, an eyesore begging to be broken into and pillaged, a menace to the well-being of the community. By occupying that house, he and his friends are protecting the safety of the street, making life more livable for everyone around them. It is early December now, and they have been squatting there for close to four months. Because it was his idea to move there in the first place, and because he was the one who picked the soldiers of their little army, and because he is the only one who knows anything about carpentry, plumbing, and electric wiring, he is the unofficial leader of the group. Not a beloved leader, perhaps, but a tolerated leader, for they all know the experiment would fall apart without him.

Ellen was the first person he asked. Without her, he never would have set foot in Sunset Park and discovered the house, and therefore it seemed only fitting to give her the right of first refusal. He has known her since they were small children, when they went to elementary school together on the

Upper West Side, but then they lost contact for many years, only to find out seven months ago that they were both living in Brooklyn and were in fact not terribly distant Park Slope neighbors. She walked into the Hospital one afternoon to have something framed, and although he didn't recognize her at first (could anyone recognize a twenty-nine-year-old woman last seen as a girl of twelve?), when he wrote down her name on the order form he instantly understood that this was the Ellen Brice he had known as a boy. Strange little Ellen Brice, all grown up now and working as a real estate agent for a firm on Seventh Avenue and Ninth Street, an artist in her spare time in the same way he is a musician in his spare time, although he has the semblance of a career and she does not. That first afternoon in the shop, he blundered in with his usual friendly, tactless questions and soon learned that she was still unmarried, that her parents had retired to a coastal town in North Carolina, and that her sister was pregnant with twin boys. His first meeting with Millie Grant was still six weeks in the future (the same Millie who is about to be replaced by Miles Heller), and because he and Ellen were both officially available, he asked her out for a drink.

Nothing came of that drink, nor of the dinner he invited her to three nights later, but there had been nothing between them as children and that continued to be the case in adulthood as well. They were both at loose ends, however, and even if romance was not in the picture, they went on seeing each other from time to time and began to build a modest friendship. It didn't matter to him that she hadn't liked the Mob Rule concert she attended (the clanging chaos of their work was not for everyone), nor was he unduly concerned that he found her drawings and paintings dull (meticulous, well-executed still lifes and cityscapes that lacked all flair and originality, he felt). What counted was that she seemed to enjoy listening to him talk and that she never turned him down when he called. Something in him responded to the sense of loneliness that enveloped her, he was touched by her quiet goodness and the vulnerability he saw in her eyes, and yet the more their friendship advanced, the less he knew what to make of her. Ellen was not an unattractive woman. Her body was trim, her face was pleasant to look at, but she projected an aura of anxiety and defeat, and with her too pale skin and flat, lusterless hair, he wondered if she wasn't mired in some sort of depression, living out her days in an underground room at the Hotel Melancholia. Whenever he saw her, he did everything in his power to make her laugh—with mixed results.

Early in the summer, on the same scorching day that Pilar Sanchez moved in with Miles Heller down in southern Florida, a crisis broke out up north. The lease on the storefront that housed the Hospital for Broken Things was about to expire, and his landlord was demanding a twenty percent rent increase. He explained that he couldn't afford it, that the extra monthly charges would drive him out of business, but the prick refused to budge. The only solution was to leave his apartment and find a cheaper place somewhere else. Ellen, who worked in the rental division of her real estate company on Seventh Avenue, told him about Sunset Park. It was a rougher neighborhood, she said, but it wasn't far from where he was living now, and rents were a half or a third of the rents in Park Slope. That Sunday, the two of them went out to explore the territory between Fifteenth and Sixty-fifth streets in western Brooklyn, an extensive hodgepodge of an area that runs from Upper New York Bay to Ninth Avenue, home to more than a hundred thousand people, including Mexicans, Dominicans, Poles, Chinese, Jordanians, Vietnamese, American whites, American blacks, and a settlement of Christians from Gujarat, India. Warehouses, factories, abandoned waterfront facilities, a view of the Statue of Liberty, the shut-down Army Terminal where ten thousand people once worked, a basilica named Our Lady of Perpetual Help, biker bars, check-cashing places, Hispanic restaurants, the third-largest Chinatown in New York, and the four hundred and seventy-eight acres of Green-Wood Cemetery, where six hundred thousand bodies are buried, including those of Boss Tweed, Lola Montez, Currier and Ives, Henry Ward Beecher, F.A.O. Schwarz, Lorenzo Da Ponte, Horace

Greeley, Louis Comfort Tiffany, Samuel F. B. Morse, Albert Anastasia, Joey Gallo, and Frank Morgan—the wizard in *The Wizard of Oz.*

Ellen showed him six or seven listings that day, none of which appealed to him, and then, as they were walking along the edge of the cemetery, they turned at random down a deserted block between Fourth and Fifth avenues and saw the house, a dopey little two-story wooden house with a roofed-over front porch, looking for all the world like something that had been stolen from a farm on the Minnesota prairie and plunked down by accident in the middle of New York. It stood between a trash-filled vacant lot with a stripped-down car in it and the metal bones of a half-built mini–apartment building on which construction had stopped more than a year ago. The cemetery was directly across the way, which meant there were no houses lining the other side of the street, which further meant that the abandoned house was all but invisible, since it was a house on a block where almost no one lived. He asked Ellen if she knew anything about it. The owners had died, she said, and because their children had been delinquent in paying the property taxes for several years running, the house now belonged to the city.

A month later, when he made up his mind to do the impossible, to risk everything on the chance to live in a rent-free house for as long as it took the city to notice him and give him the boot, he was stunned when Ellen accepted his offer. He tried to talk her out of it, explaining how difficult it would be and how much trouble they might be getting themselves into, but she held her ground, saying yes meant yes, and why bother to ask if he wanted her to say no?

They broke in one night and discovered that there were four bedrooms, three small ones on the top floor and a larger one below, which was part of an extension built onto the back of the house. The place was in lamentable condition, every surface coated with dust and soot, water stains streaking the wall behind the kitchen sink, cracked linoleum, splintered floorboards, a team of mice or squirrels running relay races under the roof, a collapsed table, legless chairs, spiderwebs dangling from ceiling corners, but remarkably enough not one broken window, and even if the water from the taps spurted out brown, looking more like English Breakfast tea than water, the plumbing was intact. Elbow grease, Ellen said. That's all it was going to take. A week or two of scrubbing and painting, and they would be in business.

He spent the next several days looking for people to fill the last two bedrooms, but no one from the band was interested, and as he went down the list of his other friends and acquaintances, he discovered that the idea of living as a squatter in an abandoned house did not have the broad appeal he had supposed it would. Then Ellen happened to talk to Alice Bergstrom, her old college roommate, and learned that she was about to be kicked out of her rent-controlled sublet in Morningside Heights. Alice was a graduate student at Columbia, already well into her dissertation, which she hoped to finish within a year, and moving in with her boyfriend was out of the question. Even if they had wanted to live together, it wouldn't have been possible. His apartment was the smallest of small, postage-stamp studios, and there simply wasn't enough space for two people to work in there at the same time. And they both needed to work at home. Jake Baum was a fiction writer, until now exclusively a writer of short stories (some of them published, most of them not), and he barely managed to scrape by on the salary he earned from his part-time teaching job at a community college in Queens. He had no money to lend Alice, could offer no help in her search for a new apartment, and since Alice herself was nearly broke, she didn't know where to turn. Her fellowship came with a small stipend, but it wasn't enough to live on, and even with her part-time job at the PEN American Center, where she worked for the Freedom to Write Program, she was subsisting on a diet of buttered noodles, rice and beans, and an occasional egg sandwich. After hearing out the story of her friend's predicament, Ellen suggested that she have a talk with Bing.

The three of them met at a bar in Brooklyn the following night, and after ten minutes of conversation he was convinced that Alice would make a worthy addition to the group. She was a tall, big-boned Scandinavian girl from Wisconsin with a round face and meaty arms, a person of heft and seriousness who also happened to have a quick mouth and a sharp sense of humor—a rare combination, he felt, which made her a shoo-in from the word go. Just as important, he liked the fact that she was Ellen's friend. Ellen had proven herself to be an admirable sidekick, for reasons he would never understand she had taken on his mad, quixotic venture as her own, but he still worried about her, was still troubled by the closed-in, unabated sadness that seemed to accompany her wherever she went, and he was heartened to see how she loosened up in Alice's presence, how much happier and more animated she looked as the three of them sat there talking in the bar, and he hoped that sharing the house with her old friend would be good medicine for her.

Before he met Alice Bergstrom, he had already met Millie Grant, but it took him several weeks after that night in the bar to screw up his courage and ask her if she had any interest in taking over the fourth and last bedroom. He was in love with her by then, in love with her in a way he had never loved anyone in his life, and he was too frightened to ask her because the thought that she might turn him down was more than he could bear. He was twenty-nine years old, and until he ran into Millie after a Mob Rule gig at Barbès on the last day of spring, his history with women had been one of absolute, unending failure. He was the fat boy who never had a girlfriend in school, the bumbling naïf who didn't lose his virginity until he was twenty, the jazz drummer who had never picked up a stranger in a club, the dumbbell who bought blow jobs from hookers when he was feeling desperate, the sex-starved moron who jerked off to pornography in the darkness of his bedroom. He knew nothing about women. He had less experience with women than most adolescent boys. He had dreamed of women, he had chased after women, he had declared his love to women, but again and again he had been rebuffed. Now, as he was about to take the biggest gamble of his life, as he stood on the brink of illegally occupying a house in Sunset Park and perhaps landing in jail, he was going into it with a team composed entirely of women. His hour of triumph had come at last.

Why did Millie fall for him? He doesn't quite know, cannot be sure of anything when it comes to the murky realms of attraction and desire, but he suspects it might be connected to the house in Sunset Park. Not the house itself, but the plan to move in there, which was already turning around in his head by the time he met her, already mutating from whim and vague speculation into a concrete decision to act, and he must have been burning with his idea that night, emitting a shower of mental sparks that surrounded him like a magnetic field and charged the atmosphere with a new and vital energy, an irresistible force, as it were, making him more attractive and desirable than usual perhaps, which could have been the reason why she was drawn to him. Not a pretty girl, no, not by the conventional standards that define prettiness (nose too sharp, left eye veering off slightly, too thin lips), but she had a terrific head of wiry red hair and a lithe, fetching body. They wound up in bed together that night, and when he understood that she wasn't put off by his shaggy, overly round *corpus horrendous,* he asked her out to dinner the following night, and they wound up in bed again. Millie Grant, a twenty-seven-year-old part-time dancer, part-time restaurant hostess, born and raised in Wheaton, Illinois, a girl with four small tattoos and a navel ring, an advocate of numerous conspiracy theories (from the Kennedy assassination to the 9/11 attacks to the dangers of the public drinking-water system), a lover of loud music, a nonstop talker, a vegetarian, an animal rights activist, a vivacious, tightly sprung piece of work with a quick temper and a machine gun laugh—someone to hold on to for the long haul. But he couldn't hold on to her. He doesn't understand what went wrong, but after two and a half months of communal living in the house, she woke up one morning and declared that she was going to San Francisco to join a new dance company. She had auditioned for them in the spring, she said, had been the last person cut, and now that one of the dancers was pregnant and had been forced to drop out, she had been hired. Sorry, Bing. It was nice while it lasted and all that, but this was the chance she'd been waiting for, and she'd be a fool not to jump at it. He didn't know whether to believe her or not, whether *San Francisco* was simply a term that meant *good-bye* or if she was really going there. Now that she is gone, he wonders if he performed well enough in bed with her, if he was able to satisfy her sexually. Or, just the opposite, if she felt he was too interested in sex, if all his dirty talk about the bizarre couplings he had witnessed in porno films had finally driven her away. He will never know. She has not been in touch since the morning she left the house, and he is not expecting to hear from her again.

Two days after Millie's departure, he wrote to Miles Heller. He got a little carried away, perhaps, claiming there were four people in the house rather than three, but four was a better number than three somehow, and he didn't want Miles to think that his great anarchist insurrection had been whittled down to his own paltry self and a pair of women. In his mind, the fourth person was Jake Baum, the writer, and while it's true that Jake comes around to visit Alice once or twice a week, he is not a permanent member of the household. He doubts that Miles will care one way or the other, but if he does care, it will be easy enough to invent some fib to account for the discrepancy.

He loves Miles Heller, but he also thinks that Miles is insane, and he is glad his friend's lonesome cowboy act is finally coming to an end. Seven years ago, when he received the first of the fifty-two letters Miles has written to him, he didn't hesitate to call Morris Heller and tell him that his son wasn't dead as everyone had feared but working as a short-order cook in a diner on the South Side of Chicago. Miles had been missing for over six months by then. Just after his disappearance, Morris and Willa had asked Bing over to their apartment to question him about Miles and what he thought could have happened to him. He will never forget how Willa broke down in tears, never forget the anguished look on Morris's face. He had no suggestions to offer that afternoon, but he promised that if he ever heard from Miles or heard anything about him, he would contact them at once. He has been calling them for seven years now—fifty-two times, once after every letter. It grieves him that Morris and Willa have not jumped on a plane and flown off to any of the several spots where Miles has parked his bones—not to drag him back, necessarily, but just to see him and force him to explain himself. But Morris says there is nothing to be done. As long as the boy refuses to come home, they have no option but to wait it out and hope he will eventually change his mind. Bing is glad that Morris Heller and Willa Parks are not his parents. No doubt they are both good people, but they are just as stubborn and crazy as Miles.

Alice Bergstrom

No one is watching them. No one cares that the empty house is now occupied. They have settled in.

When she took the plunge and decided to join forces with Bing and Ellen last summer, she imagined they would be forced to live in the shadows, slinking in and out the back door whenever the coast was clear, hiding behind blackout shades to prevent any light from seeping through the windows, always afraid, always looking over their shoulders, always expecting the boom to fall on them at any moment. She was willing to accept those conditions because she was desperate and felt she had no choice. She had lost her apartment, and how can a person rent a new apartment when the person in question doesn't have the money to pay for it? Things would be easier if her parents were in a position to help, but they are barely getting by themselves, living on their Social Security checks and clipping coupons out of the newspaper in a perpetual hunt for bargains, sales, gimmicks, any chance to shave a few pennies from their monthly costs. She was anticipating a grim go of it, a scared and mean little life in a broken-down shithole of a house, but she was wrong about that, wrong about many things, and even if Bing can be intolerable at times, pounding his fist on the table as he subjects them to another one of his dreary exhortations, slurping his soup and smacking his lips and letting crumbs fall into his beard, she misjudged his intelligence, failed to realize that he had worked out a thoroughly sensible plan. No skulking around, he said. Acting as if they didn't belong there would only alert the neighborhood to the fact that they were trespassers. They had to operate in broad daylight, hold their heads high, and pretend they were the legitimate owners of the house, which they had bought from the city for next to nothing, yes, yes, at a shockingly low price, because they had spared them the expense of having to demolish the place. Bing was right. It was a plausible story, and people accepted it. After they moved in last August, there was a brief fluster of curiosity about their comings and goings, but that passed soon enough, and by now the short, sparsely populated block has adjusted to their presence. No one is watching them, and no one cares. The old Donohue place has finally been sold, the sun continues to rise and set, and life goes on as if nothing ever happened.

For the first few weeks, they did what they could to make the rooms habitable, diligently attacking all manner of blight and decay, treating each small task as if it were a momentous human endeavor, and bit by bit they turned their wretchedly inadequate pigsty into something that might, with some generosity, be classified as a hovel. It is far from comfortable there, countless inconveniences impinge on them every day, and now that the weather has turned cold, bitter air rushes in on them through a thousand cracks in the walls and embrasures, forcing them to bundle up in heavy sweaters and put on three pairs of socks in the morning. But she doesn't complain. Not having to pay rent or utility bills for the past four months has saved her close to thirty-five hundred dollars, and for the first time in a long while she can breathe without feeling her chest tighten up on her, without feeling that her lungs are about to explode. Her work is moving forward, she can see the end looming on the far horizon, and she knows that she has the stamina to finish. The window in her room faces the cemetery, and as she writes her dissertation at the small desk positioned directly below that window, she often stares into the quiet of Green-Wood's vast, rolling ground, where more than half a million bodies are buried, which is roughly the same number as the population of Milwaukee, the city where she was born, the city where most of her family still lives, and she finds it strange, strange and even haunting, that there are as many dead lying under that ground across from her window as the number of people living in the place where her life began.

She isn't sorry that Millie is gone. Bing is in shock, of course, still staggered by his girlfriend's abrupt exit from the house, but she feels the group will be better off without that fractious, redheaded storm of gripes and thoughtless digs, she of the unwashed dinner plates and the blaring radio, who nearly pulverized poor, fragile Ellen with her comments about her drawings and paintings. A man named Miles Heller will be joining them tomorrow or the day after. Bing says he is hands down the smartest, most interesting person he has ever known. They met when they were teenagers apparently, all the way back in the early years of high school, so their friendship has gone on long enough for Bing to have some perspective on what he is saying—which is rather extreme in her opinion, but Bing is often given to hyperbole, and only time will tell if Señor Heller measures up to this powerful endorsement.

It is a Saturday, a gray Saturday in early December, and she is the only person in the house. Bing left an hour ago to rehearse with his band, Ellen is spending the day with her sister and the little twins on the Upper West Side, and Jake is in Montclair, New Jersey, visiting his brother and sister-in-law, who have just had a child as well. Babies are popping out all over, in every part of the globe women are huffing and heaving and disgorging fresh battalions of newborns, doing their bit to prolong the human race, and at some point in the not-too-distant future she hopes to put her womb to the test and see if she can't contribute as well. All that remains is choosing the right father. For close to two years, she felt that person was Jake Baum, but now she is beginning to have doubts about Jake, something seems to be crumbling between them, small daily erosions have slowly begun to mar their patch of ground, and if things continue to deteriorate, it won't be long before entire shorelines are washed away, before whole villages are submerged under water. Six months ago, she never would have asked the question, but now she wonders if she has it in her to carry on with him. Jake was never an expansive person, but there was a gentleness in him that she admired, a charming, ironical approach to the world that comforted her and made her feel they were well matched, comrades under the skin. Now he is pulling away from her. He seems angry and dejected, his once lighthearted quips have taken on a new edge of cynicism, and he never seems to tire of denigrating his students and fellow teachers. LaGuardia Community College has turned into Pifflebum Tech, Asswipe U, and the Institute for Advanced Retardation. She doesn't like to hear him talk that way. His students are mostly poor, working-class immigrants, attending school while holding down jobs, never an easy proposition as she damned well knows, and who is he to make fun of them for wanting an education? With his writing, it's more or less the same story. A flood of caustic remarks every time another piece is rejected, an acid contempt for the literary world, an abiding grudge against every editor who has failed to recognize his gifts. She is convinced that he has talent, that his work has been progressing, but it is a small talent in her eyes, and her expectations for his future are equally small. Perhaps that is part of the problem. Perhaps he senses that she doesn't believe in him enough, and in spite of all the pep talks she has given him, all the long conversations in which she has cited the early struggles of one important writer after another, he never seems to take her words to heart. She doesn't blame him for feeling frustrated—but does she want to spend the rest of her life with a frustrated man, a man who is rapidly becoming a failure in his own eyes?

She mustn't exaggerate, however. More often than not, he is kind to her, and he has never once hinted that he is weary of their affair, has never once suggested that they break it off. He is still young, after all, not yet thirty-one, which is extremely young for a fiction writer, and if his stories keep improving, chances are that something good will happen, a success of one kind or another, and with that turn his spirits would undoubtedly improve as well. No, she can weather his disappointments if she has to, that isn't the problem, she can put up with anything as long as she feels he is solidly with her, but that is precisely what she doesn't feel anymore, and even if he seems content to glide along with her out of old habits, the reflex of old affections, she is becoming ever more certain, no, *certain* is probably too strong a word for it, she is becoming ever more willing to entertain the idea that he has stopped loving her. It isn't anything he ever says. It's the way he looks at her now, the way he has been looking at her for the past few months, without any noticeable interest, his eyes blank, unfocused, as if looking at her were no different from looking at a spoon or a washcloth, a speck of dust. He rarely touches her anymore when they are alone, and even before she moved to the house in Sunset Park, their sex life was in precipitous decline. That is the crux of it, without question the problem begins and ends there, and she blames herself for what has happened, she can't help believing that the fault rests entirely on her shoulders. She was always a big person, always bigger than the other girls at school—taller, broader, more robust, more athletic, never chubby, never overweight for her size, just big. When she met Jake two and a half years ago, she was five feet ten inches tall and weighed one hundred and fifty-seven pounds. She is still five-ten, but now she weighs one-seventy. Those thirteen pounds are the difference between a strong, imposing woman and a mountain of a woman. She has been dieting ever since she landed in Sunset Park, but no matter how severely she limits her intake of calories, she has not managed to lose more than three or four pounds, which she always seems to gain back within a day or two. Her body repulses her now, and she no longer has the courage to look at herself in the mirror. I'm fat, she says to Jake. Again and again she says it, I'm fat, I'm fat, unable to stop herself from repeating the words, and if she is repulsed by the sight of her own body, imagine what he must feel when she takes off her clothes and climbs into bed with him.

The light is fading now, and as she stands up from her bed to switch on a lamp, she tells herself that she must not cry, that only weaklings and imbeciles feel sorry for themselves, and therefore she must not feel sorry for herself, for she is neither a weakling nor an imbecile, and she knows better than to think that love is simply a question of bodies, the size and shape and heft of bodies, and if Jake can't cope with his somewhat overweight, furiously dieting girlfriend, then Jake can go to hell. A moment later, she is sitting at her desk. She turns on the laptop, and for the next half hour she vanishes into her work, reading over and correcting the newest passages from her dissertation, which were written this morning.

Her subject is America in the years just after World War II, an examination of the relations and conflicts between men and women as shown in books and films from 1945 to 1947, mostly popular crime novels and commercial Hollywood movies. It is a broad terrain for an academic study, perhaps, but she couldn't picture herself spending years of her life comparing rhyme schemes in Pope and Byron (one of her friends is doing that) or analyzing the metaphors in Melville's Civil War poetry (another friend is doing that). She wanted to take on something larger, something of human importance that would engage her personally, and she knows she is working on this subject because of her grandparents and her great-uncles and great-aunts, all of whom participated in the war, lived through the war, were changed forever by the war. Her argument is that the traditional rules of conduct between men and women were destroyed on the battlefields and the home front, and once the war was over, American life had to be reinvented. She has limited herself to several texts and films, the ones that feel most emblematic to her, that expose the spirit of the time in the clearest, most forceful terms, and she has already written chapters on *The Air-Conditioned Nightmare* by Henry Miller, the brutal misogynism of Mickey Spillane's *I, the Jury,* the virgin-whore female split presented in Jacques Tourneur's film noir *Out of the Past,* and has carefully dissected a bestselling anti-feminist tract called *Modern Woman: The Lost Sex.* Now she is about to begin writing on William Wyler's 1946 film, *The Best Years of Our Lives,* a work that is central to her thesis and which she considers to be the national epic of that particular moment in

American history—the story of three men broken by war and the difficulties they confront when they return to their families, which is the same story that was being lived out by millions of others at the time.

The entire country saw the film, which won the Academy Award for best picture, best director, best leading actor, best supporting actor, best editor, best original score, and best adapted screenplay, but while most critics responded with enthusiasm (*some of the most beautiful and inspiriting demonstrations of human fortitude that we have had in films,* wrote Bosley Crowther of the *New York Times*), others were less impressed. Manny Farber trashed it as *a horse-drawn truckload of liberal schmaltz,* and in his long, two-part review published in the *Nation,* James Agee both condemned and praised *The Best Years of Our Lives,* calling it *very annoying in its patness, its timidity*, and then concluded by saying: *Yet I feel a hundred times more liking and admiration for the film than distaste or disappointment.* She agrees that the movie has its faults, that it is often too tame and sentimental, but in the end she feels its virtues outweigh its deficits. The acting is strong throughout, the script is filled with memorable lines (*Last year it was kill Japs, this year it's make money; I think they ought to put you in mass production; I'm in the junk business, an occupation for which many people feel I'm well qualified by training and temperament*), and the cinematography by Gregg Toland is exceptional. She pulls out her copy of Ephraim Katz's *Film Encyclopedia* and reads this sentence from the William Wyler entry: *The revolutionary deep-focus shot perfected by Toland enabled Wyler to develop his favorite technique of filming long takes in which characters appear in the same frame for the duration of entire scenes, rather than cutting from one to another and thus disrupting intercharacter relationships.* Two paragraphs down, at the end of a brief description of *The Best Years of Our Lives,* the author remarks that the film contains *some of the most intricate compositions ever seen on celluloid.* Even more important, at least for the purposes of the dissertation she is writing, the story concentrates on precisely those elements of male-female conflict that most interest her. The men no longer know how to act with their wives and girlfriends. They have lost their appetite for domesticity, their feel for home. After years of living apart from women, years of combat and slaughter, years of grappling to survive the horrors and dangers of war, they have been cut off from their civilian pasts, crippled, trapped in nightmare repetitions of their experiences, and the women they left behind have become strangers to them. So the film begins. Peace has broken out, but what in God's name happens now?

She owns a small television set and a DVD player. Because there is no cable hookup in the house, the television doesn't receive normal broadcasts, but she can watch films on it, and now that she is about to begin her chapter on *The Best Years of Our Lives,* she feels she should take another look at it, have one last run-through before getting down to work. Night has fallen now, but as she settles onto her bed to begin watching, she turns off the lamp in order to study the film in total darkness.

It is deeply familiar to her, of course. After four or five viewings, she practically knows the film by heart, but she is determined to look for small things that might have escaped her notice earlier, the quickly passing details that ultimately give a film its texture. Already in the first scene, when Dana Andrews is at the airport, unsuccessfully trying to book a ticket back to Boone City, she is struck by the businessman with the golf clubs, Mr. Gibbons, who calmly pays his excess-baggage charge while ignoring air force captain Andrews, who has just helped win the war for Mr. Gibbons and his fellow countrymen, and from now on, she decides, she will take note of each act of civilian indifference toward the returning soldiers. She is gratified to see how rapidly they mount up as the film progresses: the desk clerk at the apartment building where Fredric March lives, for example, who is reluctant to let the uniformed sergeant into his own house, or the manager of Midway Drugs, Mr. Thorpe, who snidely dismisses Andrews's war record as he offers him a low-paying job, or even Andrews's wife, Virginia Mayo, who tells him to *snap out of it,* that he won't get anywhere until he stops thinking about the war, as if going to war ranked as a minor inconvenience, equivalent to a painful session at the dentist.

More details, more small things: Virginia Mayo removing her false eyelashes; the rheumy Mr. Thorpe squirting nasal spray into his left nostril; Myrna Loy trying to kiss the sleeping Fredric March, who nearly slugs her in response; the choked sob from Harold Russell's mother when she sees her son's prosthetic hooks for the first time; Dana Andrews reaching into his pocket to look for his bank roll after Teresa Wright wakes him up, suggesting in one quick, instinctive move how many nights he must have spent with low-life women overseas; Myrna Loy putting flowers on her husband's breakfast tray, then deciding to take them off; Dana Andrews picking up the photo from the country club dinner, tearing it in half to preserve the shot of Teresa Wright sitting next to him, and then, after a brief hesitation, tearing up that half as well; Harold Russell stumbling over his marriage vows in the wedding scene at the end; Dana Andrews's father awkwardly trying to conceal his gin bottle on his son's first day home from the war; a sign seen through the window of a passing cab: *Settle for a Hot Dog?*

She is especially interested in Teresa Wright's performance in the role of Peggy, the young woman who falls in love with unhappily married Dana Andrews. She wants to know why she is drawn to this character when everything tells her that Peggy is too perfect to be credible as a human being—too poised, too good, too pretty, too smart, one of the purest incarnations of the ideal American girl she can think of—and yet each time she watches the film, she finds herself more involved with this character than any of the others. The moment Wright makes her first appearance on-screen, then—early in the film, when her father, Fredric March, returns home to Myrna Loy and his two children—she makes up her mind to track every nuance of Wright's behavior, to scrutinize the finest points of her performance in order to understand why this character, who is potentially the weakest link in the film, ends up holding the story together. She is not alone in thinking this. Even Agee, so harsh in his judgment of other aspects of the movie, is effusive in his admiration of Wright's accomplishment. *This new performance of hers, entirely lacking in big scenes, tricks or obstreperousness—one can hardly think of it as acting—seems to be one of the wisest and most beautiful pieces of work I have seen in years.*

Just after the long two-shot of March and Loy embracing at the end of the hall (one of the signature moments in the film), the camera cuts to a close-up of Wright—and just then, during those few seconds when Peggy occupies the screen alone, Alice knows what she has to look for. Wright's performance is concentrated entirely in her eyes and face. Follow the eyes and face, and the riddle of her mastery is solved, for the eyes are unusually expressive eyes, subtly but vividly expressive, and the face registers her emotions with such a highly sensitive, understated authenticity that you can't help but believe in her as a fully embodied character. Because of her eyes and face, Wright as Peggy is able to bring the inside to the outside, and even when she is silent, we know what she is thinking and feeling. Yes, she is without question the healthiest, most earnest character in the film, but how not to respond to her angry declaration to her parents about Andrews and his wife, *I'm going to break that marriage up,* or the irritated brush-off she gives her rich, handsome dinner date when he tries to kiss her, saying *Don't be a bore, Woody,* or the short, complicitous laugh she shares with her mother when they say good night to each other after the two drunken men have been put to bed? That explains why Andrews thinks she should be put in mass production. Because there is only one of her, and how much better off the world would be (how much better off men would be!) if there were more Peggys to go around.

She is doing her best to concentrate, to keep her eyes fixed on the screen, but midway into the film her thoughts begin to wander. Watching Harold Russell, the third male protagonist along with March and Andrews, the nonprofessional actor who lost his hands during the war, she begins to think about her great-uncle Stan, the husband of her grandmother's sister Caroline, the one-armed D-day veteran with the bushy eyebrows, Stan Fitzpatrick, belting back drinks at family parties, telling dirty jokes to her brothers on their grandparents' back porch, one of the many who never managed to pull themselves together after the war, the man with thirty-seven different jobs, old Uncle Stan, dead for a good ten years now, and the stories her grandmother has told her lately about how he used to *knock Caroline around a bit,* the now departed Caroline, knocked around so much she lost a couple of teeth one day, and then there are her two grandfathers, both of them still alive, one fading and the other lucid, who fought in the Pacific and Europe as young men, such young men they were scarcely older than boys, and even though she has tried to get the lucid grandfather to talk to her, Bill Bergstrom, the husband of her one surviving grandmother, he never says much, speaks only in the foggiest generalities, it simply isn't possible for him to talk about those years, they all came home insane, damaged for life, and even the years after the war were still part of the war, the years of bad dreams and night sweats, the years of wanting to punch your fist through walls, so her grandfather humors her by talking about going to college on the G.I. Bill, about meeting her grandmother on a bus one day and falling in love with her at first sight, bullshit, bullshit from start to finish, but he is one of those men who can't talk, a card-carrying member from the generation of men who can't talk, and therefore she has to rely on her grandmother for the stories, but she wasn't a soldier during the war, she doesn't know what happened over there, and all she can talk about are her three sisters and their husbands, the dead Caroline and Stan Fitzpatrick and Annabelle, the one whose husband was killed at Anzio and who later married again, to a man named Jim Farnsworth, another vet from the Pacific, but that marriage didn't last long either, he was unfaithful to her, he forged checks or was involved in a stock swindle, the details are unclear, but Farnsworth vanished long before she was born, and the only husband she ever knew was Mike Meggert, the traveling salesman, who never talked about the war either, and finally there is Gloria, Gloria and Frank Krushniak, the couple with the six children, but Frank's war was different from the others' war, he faked a disability and never had to serve, which means that he has nothing to say either, and when she thinks of that generation of silent men, the boys who lived through the Depression and grew up to become soldiers or not-soldiers in the war, she doesn't blame them for refusing to talk, for not wanting to go back into the past, but how curious it is, she thinks, how sublimely incoherent that her generation, which doesn't have much of anything to talk about yet, has produced men who never stop talking, men like Bing, for example, or men like Jake, who talks about himself at the slightest prompting, who has an opinion on every subject, who spews forth words from morning to night, but just because he talks, that doesn't mean she wants to listen to him, whereas with the silent men, the old men, the ones who are nearly gone now, she would give anything to hear what they have to say.

Ellen Brice

She is standing on the front porch of the house, looking into the fog. It is Sunday morning, and the air outside is almost warm, too warm for the beginning of December, making it feel like a day from another season or another latitude, a damp, balmy sort of weather that reminds her of the tropics. When she looks across the street, the fog is so dense that the cemetery is invisible. A strange morning, she says to herself. The clouds have descended all the way to the ground, and the world has become invisible—which is neither a good thing nor a bad thing, she decides, merely strange.

It is early, early for a Sunday in any case, a few minutes past seven o'clock, and Alice and Bing are still asleep in their beds on the second floor, but she is up at first light again as usual, even if there is little light to speak of on this dull, fog-saturated morning. She can't remember the last time she managed to sleep for six full hours, six uninterrupted hours without waking from a rough dream or discovering her eyes had opened at dawn, and she knows these sleep difficulties are a bad sign, an unmistakable warning of trouble ahead, but in spite of what her mother keeps telling her, she doesn't want to go back on the medication. Taking one of those pills is like swallowing a small dose of death. Once you start with those things, your days are turned into a numbing regimen of forgetfulness and confusion, and there isn't a moment when you don't feel your head is stuffed with cotton balls and wadded-up shreds of paper. She doesn't want to shut down her life in order to survive her life. She wants her senses to be awake, to think thoughts that don't vanish the moment they occur to her, to feel alive in all the ways she once felt alive. Crack-ups are off the agenda now. She can't allow herself to surrender anymore, but in spite of her efforts to hold her ground in the here and now, the pressure has been building up inside her again, and she is beginning to feel twinges of the old panic, the knot in her throat, the blood rushing too quickly through her veins, the clenched heart and frantic rhythms of her pulse. Fear without an object, as Dr. Burnham once described it to her. No, she says to herself now: fear of dying without having lived.

There is no question that coming here was the right move, and she has never regretted leaving behind that small apartment on President Street in Park Slope. She feels emboldened by the risk they have taken together, and Bing and Alice have been so good to her, so generous and protective, so constant in their friendship, but in spite of the fact that she is less lonely now, there have been times, many times in fact, when being with them has only made things worse. When she lived on her own, she never had to compare herself with anyone. Her struggles were her struggles, her failures were her failures, and she could suffer through them within the confines of her small, solitary space. Now she is surrounded by impassioned, energetic people, and next to them she feels like a dim sluggard, a hopeless nonentity. Alice will soon have her Ph.D. and an academic post somewhere, Jake is publishing story after story in little magazines, Bing has his band and his goofy underground business, and even Millie, the sharp-tongued, never-to-be-missed Millie, is thriving as a dancer. As for her, she is getting nowhere fast, faster than it takes for a young dog to become an old dog, faster than it takes for a flower to bloom and wilt. Her work as an artist has crashed into a wall, and the bulk of her time is spent showing empty apartments to prospective tenants—a job for which she is thoroughly ill-suited and which she fears she could be fired from any day. All that has been hard enough, but then there is the business of sex, the fucking she has had to listen to through the thin walls upstairs, the fact of being the only single person in a house of two couples. It has been a long time since anyone made love to her, eighteen months by her latest reckoning, and she is so starved for physical contact that she can barely think about anything else now. She masturbates in her bed every night, but masturbation isn't a solution, it offers only temporary relief, it's like an aspirin you take to kill the pain of a throbbing tooth, and she doesn't know how much longer she can go on without being kissed, without being loved. Bing is available now, it's true, and she can feel that he is interested in her, but somehow she can't imagine herself with Bing, can't see herself putting her arms around his broad, hairy back or trying to find his lips through the bramble of that thick beard. Again and again since Millie's departure, she has thought about making an advance on him, but then she sees Bing at breakfast in the morning and knows it isn't possible.

Her thoughts have begun to disturb her, the little games she plays in her mind without wanting to, the sudden, uncontrollable fugues into the dark. Sometimes they come to her in brief flashes—an impulse to burn down the house, to seduce Alice, to steal money from the safe at her real estate firm—and then, just as quickly as they arrive, they dwindle off into nothing. Others are more constant, more enduring in their impact. Even going out is fraught with hazards now, for there are days when she can no longer look at the people she passes on the street without undressing them in her imagination, stripping off their clothes with a quick, violent tug and then examining their naked bodies as they walk by. These strangers aren't people to her anymore, they are simply the bodies that belong to them, structures of flesh wrapped around bones and tissue and inner organs, and with the heavy pedestrian traffic that moves along Seventh Avenue, the street where her office is located, hundreds if not thousands of specimens are thrust before her eyes every day. She sees the enormous, unwieldy breasts of fat women, the tiny penises of young boys, the budding pubic hair of thirteen-year-old children, the pink vaginas of mothers pushing their babies in strollers, the assholes of old men, the hairless pudenda of little girls, luxuriant thighs, skinny thighs, vast, quivering buttocks, chest hair, recessed navels, inverted nipples, bellies scarred by appendix operations and cesarean births, turds sliding out of open anuses, piss flowing from long, partly erect penises. She is revolted by these images, appalled that her mind is capable of manufacturing such filth, but once they start coming to her, she is powerless to make them go away. Sometimes she even goes so far as to imagine herself pausing to slip her tongue into the mouth of each passerby, each and every person who falls within her sight, whether old or young, whether beautiful or deformed, pausing to lick the entire length of each naked body, pushing her tongue into moistened vaginas, putting her mouth around thick, hardened penises, giving herself with equal fervor to every man, woman, and child in an orgy of indiscriminate, democratic love. She doesn't know how to stop these visions. They leave her feeling wretched and exhausted, but the wild thoughts enter her head as if they were planted there by someone else, and even though she battles to suppress them, it is a battle she never wins.

Transient detours, mental conniptions, ordure rising from the inner depths, but out in the external world of solid things she has allowed her desires to run away from her only once, only once with any lasting consequences. The ballad of Benjamin Samuels dates back to the summer of 2000, eight years ago, eight and a half years ago to be exact, which means that close to one-third of her life has been lived since then, and still it remains with her, she has never stopped listening to the song in her mind, and as she stands on the porch this foggy Sunday morning, she wonders if anything as momentous will ever happen to her again. She was twenty years old and had just finished her sophomore year at Smith. Alice was going back to Wisconsin to work as head counselor at a summer camp near Lake Oconomowoc, and she asked her if she wanted a job there as well, which was something she could easily arrange. No, she wasn't interested in summer camps, she said, she'd had an unhappy experience at camp when she was eleven, and so she wound up taking another job closer to home, for Professor Samuels and his wife, who had rented a place in southern Vermont for two and a half months and needed someone to look after their kids—Bea, Cora, and Ben, girls of five and seven and a boy of sixteen. The boy was too old to require looking after, but he had messed up in school that year, barely passing several of his courses, and she was supposed to tutor him in English, American history, and algebra. He was in a foul temper when the summer began—barred from attending his beloved soccer camp in Northampton and faced with the prospect of eleven weeks of excruciating exile with his parents and sisters in the middle of nowhere. But she was beautiful then, never more beautiful than she was that summer, so much rounder and softer than the scrawny creature she has turned into now, and why would a sixteen-year-old boy complain about having to take lessons from an enticing young woman in sleeveless tank tops and black spandex shorts? By the beginning of the second week they were friends, and by the beginning of the third week they were spending most of their evenings together in the pavilion, a small outbuilding about fifty yards from the main house, where they watched the films she would pick up from Al's Video Store on her shopping excursions to Brattleboro. The girls and their parents were always asleep by then. Professor Samuels and his wife were both writing books that summer, and they kept to a rigid schedule, up at five-thirty every morning and lights out by nine-thirty or ten. They weren't the least bit concerned that she and their son were spending so much time together in the pavilion. She was Ellen Brice, after all, the soft-spoken, dependable girl who had done so well in Professor Samuels's art history class, and they could count on her to behave responsibly in all situations.

Having sex with Ben wasn't her idea—at least not at first. She loved looking at him, the strength and leanness of his soccer player's body often aroused her, but he was still just a boy, less than six months ago he had been fifteen, and however attractive she might have found him, she had no intention of doing anything about it. But one month into the two and a half months she stayed there, on a warm July night filled with the sounds of tree frogs and a million cicadas, the boy made the first move. They were sitting in their usual positions at opposite ends of the small sofa, the moths were banging against the screen windows as usual, the night air smelled of pines and damp earth as usual, a dumb comedy or western was playing as usual (the selection at Al's was limited), and she was beginning to feel drowsy, drowsy enough to lean back her head and close her eyes for a few seconds, perhaps ten seconds, perhaps twenty seconds, and before she was able to open them again, young Mr. Samuels had moved over to her side of the sofa and was kissing her on the mouth. She should have pushed him away, or turned her head away, or stood up and walked away, but she couldn't think fast enough to do any of those things, and so she remained where she was, sitting on the sofa with her eyes closed, and allowed him to go on kissing her.

They were never caught. For a month and a half they carried on with their little sex affair (she could never bring herself to think of it as a love affair), and then the summer came to an end. She might not have fallen in love with Ben, but she was in love with his body, and even now, eight and a half years later, she still thinks about the uncanny smoothness of his skin, the feel of his long arms wrapped around her, the sweetness of his mouth, the taste of him. She would have continued seeing Ben in Northampton after the summer, but his miserable academic performance the previous year had alarmed his parents so much that they shipped him off to a boarding school in New Hampshire, and suddenly he was gone from her life. She missed him a good deal more than she was expecting to, but before she understood how long it would take to get over him, how many weeks or months or years, she found herself in a new kind of fix. Her period was late. She told Alice about it, and her friend promptly dragged her off to the nearest pharmacy to buy a home-pregnancy-test kit. The results were positive, which is to say, negative, disastrously and irrevocably negative. She thought they had been so prudent, so careful to avoid just this thing from happening, but clearly they had slipped up somewhere along the way, and now what was she going to do? She couldn't tell anyone who the father was. Not even Alice, who pressed her about it again and again, and not even the father himself, who was just a sixteen-year-old boy, and why punish him with this news when there was nothing he could do to help her, when she was the one to blame for the whole sordid business? She couldn't talk to Alice, she couldn't talk to Ben, and she couldn't talk to her parents—not just about who the father was, but about who she was as well. A pregnant girl, an idiot college girl with a baby growing inside her. Her mother and father could never know what had happened. The mere thought of trying to tell them about it was enough to make her want to die.

If she had been a braver person, she would have had the child. In spite of the upheavals a full-term pregnancy would have caused, she wanted to go ahead with it and let the baby be born, but she was too scared of the questions she would be asked, too ashamed to confront her family, too weak to assert herself and drop out of school to join the ranks of *unwed mothers.* Alice drove her to the clinic. It was supposed to be a quick, uncomplicated procedure, and in medical terms everything came off as advertised, but she found it gruesome and humiliating, and she hated herself for having gone against her deepest impulses, her deepest convictions. Four days later, she downed half a bottle of vodka and twenty sleeping pills. Alice was supposed to be gone for the weekend, and if she hadn't changed her plans at the last minute and returned to their dormitory suite at four o'clock that afternoon, her sleeping roommate would still be sleeping now. They took her to Cooley Dickinson Hospital and pumped her stomach, and that was the end of Smith, the end of Ellen Brice as a so-called normal person. She was transferred to the psych ward of the hospital and kept there for twenty days, and then she returned to New York, where she spent a long, infinitely depressing period living with her parents, sleeping in her old childhood bedroom, seeing Dr. Burnham three times a week, attending group therapy sessions, and ingesting her daily quantum of the pills that were supposed to make her feel better but didn't. Eventually, she took it upon herself to enroll in some drawing classes at the School of Visual Arts, which turned into painting classes the following year, and little by little she began to feel that she was almost living in the world again, that there might be something that resembled a future for her, after all. When her sister's husband's brother-in-law offered her a job with his real estate firm in Brooklyn, she finally moved out of her parents' apartment and started living on her own. She knew that it was the wrong job for her, that having to talk to so many people every day could become an unrelenting trial on her nerves, but she accepted the job anyway. She needed to get out, needed to be free of the ever-worried eyes of her mother and father, and this was her only chance.

That was five years ago. Now, as she stands on the front porch of the house wrapped in her overcoat and drinking her morning coffee, she realizes that she must begin again. Painful as it was to listen to Millie's words two months ago, the brutal and dismissive condemnation of her drawings and canvases was fully deserved. Her work doesn't speak to anyone. She knows she is not without skill, not without talent even, but she has boxed herself into a corner by pursuing a single idea, and that idea isn't strong enough to bear the weight of what she has been trying to accomplish. She thought the delicacy of her touch could lead her to the sublime and austere realm that Morandi had once inhabited. She wanted to make pictures that would evoke the mute wonder of pure thingness, the holy ether breathing in the spaces between things, a translation of human existence into a minute rendering of all that is *out there* beyond us, around us, in the same way she knows the invisible graveyard is standing there in front of her, even if she cannot see it. But she was wrong to put her trust in things, to trust in things only, to have squandered her time on the innumerable buildings she has drawn and painted, the empty streets devoid of people, the garages and gas stations and factories, the bridges and elevated highways, the red bricks of old warehouses glinting in the dusky New York light. It comes across as timid evasion, an empty exercise in style, whereas all she has ever wanted is to draw and paint representations of her own feelings. There will be no hope for her unless she starts again from the beginning. No more inanimate objects, she tells herself, no more still lifes. She will return to the human figure and force her strokes to become bolder and more expressive, more gestural, more wild if need be, as wild as the wildest thought within her.

She will ask Alice to pose for her. It is Sunday, a quiet Sunday without much of anything going on, and even if Alice will be working on her dissertation today, she might be able to spare her a couple of hours between now and bed. She goes back into the house and walks up the stairs to her room. Bing and Alice are still asleep, and she moves cautiously so as not to wake them, pulling off her overcoat and the flannel nightgown under it and then climbing into a pair of old jeans and a thick cotton sweater, not bothering with panties or a bra, just her bare skin under the soft fabrics, wanting to feel as loose and mobile as she can this morning, unencumbered for the day ahead. She takes her drawing pad and a Faber-Castell pencil off the top of the bureau, then sits down on the bed and opens the pad to the first empty page. Holding the pencil in her right hand, she raises her left hand in the air, tilts it at a forty-five-degree angle, and keeps it suspended about twelve inches from her face, studying it until it no longer seems attached to her body. It is an alien hand now, a hand that belongs to someone else, to no one, a woman's hand with its slender fingers and rounded nails, the half-moons above the cuticles, the narrow wrist with its small bump of bone sticking out on the left side, the ivory-shaded knuckles and joints, the nearly translucent white skin sheathed over rivulets of veins, blue veins bearing the red blood that meanders through her system as her heart beats and the air moves in and out of her lungs. Digits, carpus, metacarpus, phalanges, dermis. She presses the point of the pencil against the blank page and begins to draw the hand.

At nine-thirty, she knocks on Alice's door. Diligent Bergstrom is already at work, a swarm of fingers darting across the keyboard of her laptop, eyes fixed on the screen in front of her, and Ellen apologizes for interrupting her. No, no, Alice says, it's perfectly all right, and then she stops typing and turns to her friend with one of those warm Alice smiles on her face, no, more than just a warm smile, a maternal smile somehow, not the way Ellen's mother smiles at her, perhaps, but the kind of smile all mothers should give their children, a smile that is not a greeting so much as an offering, a benediction. She thinks: Alice will make a terrific mother when the time comes . . . a superior mother, she says to herself, and then, because of the juxtaposition of those two words, she transforms Alice into a Mother Superior, suddenly seeing her in a nun's habit, and because of this momentary digression she loses her train of thought and doesn't have time to ask Alice if she would be willing to pose for her before Alice is asking a question of her own:

Have you ever seen *The Best Years of Our Lives*?

Of course, Ellen says. Everyone knows that film.

Do you like it?

Very much. It's one of my favorite Hollywood movies.

Why do you like it?

I don't know. It touches me. I always cry when I see it.

You don't find it a little too pat?

Of course it's pat. It's a Hollywood movie, isn't it? All Hollywood movies are a bit contrived, don't you think?

Good point. But this one is a little less contrived than most—is that what you're saying?

Think of the scene when the father helps prepare his son for bed.

Harold Russell, the soldier who lost his hands in the war.

The boy can't take off the hooks by himself, he can't button up his own pajamas, he can't put out his cigarette. His father has to do everything for him. As I remember it, there's no music in that scene, hardly a word of dialogue, but it's a great moment in the film. Completely honest. Incredibly moving.

Does everyone live happily ever after?

Maybe yes, maybe no. Dana Andrews tells the girl—

Teresa Wright—

He tells Teresa Wright that they're going to get kicked

around a lot. Maybe they will, maybe they won't. And the Fredric March character is a drunk, a serious, nonstop, raving alcoholic, so his life isn't going to be much fun a few years down the road.

What about Harold Russell?

He marries his sweetheart at the end, but what kind of marriage is it going to be? He's a simple, good-hearted boy, but so damned inarticulate, so bottled up emotionally, I don't see how he's going to make his wife very happy.

I hadn't realized you knew the film so well.

My grandmother was crazy about it. She was about sixteen when the war broke out, and she always said *The Best Years of Our Lives* was *her* movie. We must have watched it together five or six times.

They go on talking about the film for a few more minutes, and then she finally remembers to ask Alice the question that prompted her to knock on the door in the first place. Alice is busy now, but she will be glad to break for an hour after lunch and pose for her then. What Alice doesn't understand is that Ellen isn't interested in doing a portrait of her face, she wants to make a drawing of her whole body, and not that body hidden by clothes but a full nude sketch, perhaps several sketches, similar to the ones she did in her life classes at art school. It is therefore an awkward moment for both of them when they go upstairs to Ellen's room after lunch and Ellen asks Alice to take off her clothes. Alice has never worked as a model, she is not accustomed to having her naked body scrutinized by anyone, and although she and Ellen occasionally catch glimpses of each other going in and out of the bathroom, that has nothing to do with the torture of having to sit stock-still for an hour as your closest friend looks you over from top to bottom, especially now, when she is feeling so miserable about her weight, and even though Ellen tells Alice that she is beautiful, that she has nothing to worry about, it is merely an art exercise, artists are used to looking at other people's bodies, Alice is too embarrassed to give in to her friend's request, she is sorry, terribly sorry, but she can't go through with it and must say no. Ellen is stung by Alice's refusal to do this simple thing for her, which is in fact the first step in reinventing herself as an artist, which is no less than reinventing herself as a woman, a human being, and while she understands that Alice has no intention of hurting her, she can't help feeling hurt, and when she asks Alice to leave the room, she closes the door, sits down on the bed, and starts to cry.

Miles Heller

He thinks of it as a six-month prison sentence with no time off for good behavior. The Christmas and Easter holidays will give Pilar temporary visiting rights, but he will be confined to his cell for the full six months. He mustn't dream of escape. No digging of tunnels in the middle of the night, no confrontations with the guards, no hacking through barbed wire, no mad dashes into the woods pursued by dogs. If he can last through his term without running into trouble or going to pieces, he will be on a bus heading back to Florida on May twenty-second, and on the twenty-third he will be with Pilar to celebrate her birthday. Until then, he will go on holding his breath.

Going to pieces. That was the phrase he kept using during the course of his trip, during the seven conversations he had with her over the thirty-four hours he spent on the road. *You mustn't go to pieces.* When she wasn't sobbing into the phone or ranting against her maniac bitch of a sister, she seemed to understand what he was trying to tell her. He heard himself uttering platitudes that just two days earlier he couldn't have imagined would ever cross his lips, and yet a part of him believed in what he was saying. They had to be strong. This was a test, and their love would only deepen because of it. And then there was the practical advice, the injunctions to go on doing well at school, to remember to eat enough, to go to bed early every night, to change the oil in the car at regular intervals, to read the books he left for her. Was it a man talking to his future wife or a father talking to his child? A little of both, perhaps. It was Miles talking to Pilar. Miles doing his best to hold the girl together, to hold himself together.

He walks into the Hospital for Broken Things at three o'clock on Monday afternoon. That was the arrangement. If he came in after six o'clock, he was to head straight for the house in Sunset Park. If he arrived during the day, he was to meet Bing at his store on Fifth Avenue in Brooklyn. A bell tinkles as he opens and shuts the door, and when he steps inside he is struck by how small the place is, surely it is the smallest hospital in the world, he thinks, a dingy, cluttered shrine with ancient typewriters on display, a cigar-store Indian standing in the far corner to his left, model biplanes and Piper Cubs hanging from the ceiling, and the walls covered with signs and posters advertising products that left the American scene decades ago: Black Jack gum, O'Dell's Hair Trainer, Geritol, Carter's Little Liver Pills, Old Gold cigarettes. At the sound of the bell, Bing emerges from a back room behind the counter, looking larger and bushier than he remembers, a great big grinning oaf rushing toward him with open arms. Bing is all smiles and laughs, all bear hugs and kisses on the cheek, and Miles, caught off guard by this slobbering welcome, bursts out laughing himself as he wriggles free of his friend's crushing embrace.

Bing closes up the Hospital early, and because he suspects Miles is hungry after the long trip, he leads him a few blocks down Fifth Avenue to what he calls his favorite lunch place, a scruffy beanery that serves fish and chips, shepherd's pies, bangers and mash, a full menu of authentic Limey grub. No wonder Bing has broadened so much, Miles thinks, lunching on this greasy slop several times a week, but the truth is that he is famished just now, and what could be better than a hot shepherd's pie to fill you up on a cold day? Meanwhile, Bing is talking to him about the house, about his band, about his failed love affair with Millie, punctuating his remarks every so often with a brief word about how well he thinks Miles is looking and how glad he is to see him again. Miles doesn't say much in response, he is busy with his food, but he is impressed by

Bing's high spirits and lunging goodwill, and the more Bing talks, the more he feels that his pen pal of the past seven years is the same person he was when they last saw each other, a little older, of course, a little more in possession of himself, perhaps, but essentially the same person, whereas he, Miles, is altogether different now, a black sheep who bears no resemblance to the lamb he was seven years ago.

Toward the end of the meal, a look of discomfort comes over Bing's face. He pauses for a few moments, fidgeting with his fork, casting his eyes down at the table, apparently at a loss for words, and when he finally speaks again, his voice is far more subdued than it was earlier, almost hushed.

I don't mean to pry, he says, but I was wondering if you have any plans.

Plans to do what? Miles asks.

To see your parents, for one thing.

Is that any of your business?

Yes, unfortunately it is. I've been your source for a long time now, and I think I want to retire.

You already have. The moment I stepped off the bus today, you were given your gold watch. For years of devoted service. You know how grateful I am to you, don't you?

I don't want your gratitude, Miles. I just don't want to see you fuck up your life anymore. It hasn't been easy on them, you know.

I know. Don't think I don't know.

Well? Are you going to see them or not?

I want to, I'm hoping to . . .

That's no kind of answer. Yes or no?

Yes. Of course I will, he says, not knowing if he will or not, not knowing that Bing has talked to his parents fifty-two times in the past seven years, not knowing that his father and mother and Willa have all been told he will be landing in New York today. Of course I will, he says again. Just give me a chance to settle in first.

The house is like no house he has ever seen in New York. He is aware that the city is filled with anomalous structures that have no apparent connection to urban life—the brick houses and garden apartments in certain sections of Queens, for example, with their timid, suburban aspirations, or the few remaining wooden houses in the northernmost parts of Brooklyn Heights, historical remnants from the 1840s—but this house in Sunset Park is neither suburban nor historic, it is merely a shack, a forlorn piece of architectural stupidity that would not fit in anywhere, neither in New York nor out of it. Bing didn't send any photographs with his letter, didn't describe what it looked like in any detail, and therefore he had no idea what to expect, but if he did expect anything, it certainly wasn't this.

Cracked gray shingles, red trim around the three sash windows on the second floor, a flimsy balustrade on the porch with diamond-shaped openings painted white, the four posts propping up the roof on the porch painted red, the same brick red as the trim around the windows, but no paint on the front steps or handrails, which are too splintered for a paint job and have been left as bare, weathered wood. Alice and Ellen are both still at work when he and Bing walk up the six steps to the front porch and go inside. Bing gives him the grand tour, clearly proud of all they have accomplished, and while the house seems cramped to him (not just because of the size of the rooms or the number of rooms but because of the many things that have been jammed into them—Bing's drums, Ellen's canvases, Alice's books), the interior is remarkably clean, with a patched-up, freshly painted brightness, and therefore perhaps even livable. The kitchen, the bathroom, and the back bedroom downstairs; the three bedrooms upstairs. But no living room or parlor, which means that the kitchen is the only communal space—along with the porch in times of good weather. He will be inheriting Millie's old bedroom on the ground floor, which is something of a relief, since that room affords the most privacy, if living in a room off the kitchen can be considered privacy. He puts his bag down on the bed, and as he looks out the windows on either side of him, the one with a view of the vacant lot with the junked car in it, the other with a view of the abandoned construction site, Bing is telling him about the various routines and protocols that have been established since they moved in. Each person has a job to perform, but beyond the responsibilities of that job, everyone is free to come and go at will. He is the handyman-janitor, Ellen is the cleaning woman, and Alice does the shopping and most of the cooking. Perhaps Miles would like to share Alice's job with her, taking turns with the shopping and cooking. Miles has no objection. He enjoys cooking, he says, he's developed a knack for it over the years, and that won't be a problem. Bing goes on to say they generally eat breakfast and dinner together because they are all low on money and are trying to spend as little as they can. Pooling their resources has helped them get by, and now that Miles has joined the household, everyone's expenses will go down accordingly. They will all benefit because he is here, and by that he isn't talking only about money, it's about everything Miles will add to the spirit of the house, and Bing wants him to understand how happy it makes him to know that he is finally back where he belongs. Miles shrugs, saying he hopes he can manage to fit in, but secretly he is wondering if he is cut out for this sort of group living, if he wouldn't be better off looking for a place of his own. The only problem is cash, the same problem all the others are facing. He no longer has a job, and the three thousand dollars he brought with him amount to little more than pennies. Like it or not, then, for the time being he is stuck, and unless something comes along that dramatically alters his circumstances, he will just have to make the best of it. So his prison sentence begins. Pilar's sister has turned him into the newest member of the Sunset Park Four.

That night, they throw a dinner in his honor. It is a gesture of welcome, and although he would prefer not to have been made the center of attention, he tries to get through it without showing how uncomfortable he feels. What are his first impressions of them? He finds Alice to be the most likable, the most grounded, and he is rather taken by her blunt, boyish, midwestern approach to things. A well-read person with a good mind, he discovers, but unaffected, self-deprecating, with a talent for tossing off subtle wisecracks at unexpected moments. Ellen is more of a puzzle to him. She is both attractive and not attractive, both open and closed off, and from one minute to the next her personality seems to change. Long, awkward silences, and then, when she finally speaks, she rarely fails to deliver some astute remark. He senses inner turbulence, disarray, and yet deep kindness as well. If only she wouldn't stare at him so much, he might be able to warm up to her a little, but her eyes have been on him ever since they sat down at the table, and he feels discomfited by her blatant, overly intrusive interest in him. Then there is Jake, the sometime visitor to Sunset Park, a thin, balding person with a sharp nose and big ears, Jake Baum the writer, Alice's boyfriend. For the first few minutes he seems pleasant enough, but then Miles begins to change his opinion of him, noticing that he barely takes the trouble to listen to anyone but himself, especially Alice, whom he interrupts again and again, often cutting her off in midsentence to pursue some thought of his own, and before long Miles concludes that Jake Baum is a bore, even if he can recite Pound from memory and reel off the opponents from every World Series since 1932. Thankfully, Bing seems to be in top fettle, exuberantly playing his role as master of ceremonies, and in spite of the invisible tensions in the air, he has deftly maintained the frivolous tone of the evening. Each time another bottle of wine is opened, he stands up to pronounce a toast, celebrating Miles's homecoming, celebrating the imminent four-month anniversary of their little revolution, celebrating the rights of squatters all over the world. The only negative in all this conviviality is the fact that Miles doesn't drink, and he knows that when people meet someone who abstains from alcohol, they automatically assume he is a recovering drunk. Miles was never an alcoholic, but there was a time when he felt he was drinking too much, and when he cut himself off three years ago, it was as much about saving money as it was about his health. They can think whatever they like, he tells himself, it's of no importance to him, but each time Bing lifts his glass for another toast, Jake turns to Miles and urges him to join in. An honest mistake the first time, perhaps, but there have been two more toasts since then, and Jake has kept on doing it. If he knew what

Miles was capable of when he is angry, the needling would stop at once, but Jake doesn't know, and if he does it again the next time, he could end up with a bloody nose or a broken jaw. All the years of battling to keep his temper under control, and now, on his first day back in New York, Miles is seething again, ready to tear someone apart.

It gets worse. Before the dinner, he asked Bing not to let anyone know who his parents were, to keep the names Morris Heller and Mary-Lee Swann out of the discussion, and Bing said of course, that went without saying, but now, just when the dinner is finally coming to an end, Jake starts talking about Renzo Michaelson's most recent novel, *The Mountain Dialogues,* which was published by his father's company in September. Perhaps there is nothing unusual about that, the book is doing extremely well, no doubt many people are talking about it, and Baum is a writer himself, which means that he is bound to be acquainted with Renzo's work, but Miles doesn't want to listen to him blather on about it, not about this book in any case, which he read down in Florida when it was first published, read only when Pilar wasn't around the apartment because it was too much for him, he understood on the first page that the two sixty-year-old men sitting and talking on that mountaintop in the Berkshires were in fact based on Renzo and his father, and it was impossible for him to read that book without breaking down in tears, knowing that he himself was implicated in the sorrows of that story, the two men talking back and forth about the things they had lived through, old friends, the best of old friends, his father and his godfather, and here is pompous Jake Baum making his declarations about that book, and with all his heart Miles wishes he would stop. Baum says he would love to interview Michaelson. He knows he rarely talks to journalists, but there are so many questions he would like to ask him, and wouldn't it be *a feather in his cap* if he could persuade Michaelson to give him a couple of hours? Baum is thinking only about his own petty ambitions, trying to aggrandize himself by feeding off someone who is ten thousand times greater than he will ever be, and then stupid Bing pipes in with the news that he is the person who cleans and repairs Renzo's typewriter, good old Michaelson, one of the last of a dying breed, a novelist who still hasn't switched over to a computer, and yes, he knows him a little bit, and maybe he could put in a word for Jake the next time Renzo comes into the shop. By now, Miles is ready to jump on Bing and strangle him, but just then, fortunately, the conversation is deflected onto another subject when Alice lets out a loud, booming sneeze, and suddenly Bing is talking about flus and winter colds, and no more mention is made of interviewing Renzo Michaelson.

After that dinner, he resolves to make himself scarce whenever Jake is around, to avoid having any more meals with him. He doesn't want to do anything he will later regret, and Jake is the kind of man who inevitably brings out the worst in him. As it happens, the problem is not as grave as he supposes it will be. Baum comes by only once in the next two weeks, and although Alice spends a couple of nights with him in Manhattan, Miles senses there is trouble between them, that they are facing a rugged patch or perhaps even the end. It shouldn't concern him, but now that he has come to know Alice, he hopes it is the end, for Baum doesn't deserve a woman like Alice, and she herself deserves far better.

Three days after his arrival, he calls his father's office. The receptionist tells him that Mr. Heller is out of the country and won't be returning to work until January fifth. Would he like to leave a message? No, he says, he'll call back next month, thank you.

He reads in the paper that previews of his mother's play will begin on January thirteenth.

He doesn't know what to do with himself. Besides his daily conversations with Pilar, which tend to last between one and two hours, there is no structure to his life anymore. He wanders around the streets, trying to familiarize himself with the neighborhood, but he quickly loses interest in Sunset Park. There is something dead about the place, he finds, the mournful emptiness of poverty and immigrant struggle, an area without banks or bookstores, only check-cashing operations and a decrepit public library, a small world apart from the world where time moves so slowly that few people bother to wear a watch.

He spends an afternoon taking photographs of some of the factories near the waterfront, the old buildings that house the last surviving companies in the neighborhood, manufacturers of windows and doors, swimming pools, ladies' clothes and nurses' uniforms, but the pictures are nondescript somehow, lacking in urgency, uninspired. The next day, he ventures up to the Chinatown on Eighth Avenue, with its dense grouping of shops and businesses, its crowded sidewalks, the ducks hanging in the butchers' windows, a hundred potential scenes to capture, vivid colors all around him, but still he feels flattened out, unengaged, and he leaves without taking a single picture. He will need time to adjust, he tells himself. His body might be here now, but his mind is still with Pilar in Florida, and even if he is home again, this New York is not his New York, not the New York of his memory. For all the distance he has traveled, he might just as well have come to a foreign city, a city anywhere else in America.

Little by little, he has been acclimating himself to Ellen's eyes. He no longer feels threatened by her curiosity in him, and if she talks less than anyone else at their shared breakfasts and dinners around the kitchen table, she can be quite voluble when he is alone with her. She communicates largely by asking questions, not personal questions about his life or past history, but questions about his opinions on topics ranging from the weather to the state of the world. Does he like winter? Who does he think is a better artist, Picasso or Matisse? Is he worried about global warming? Was he happy when Obama was elected last month? Why do men like sports so much? Who is his favorite photographer? No doubt there is something infantile about her directness, but at the same time her questions often provoke spirited exchanges, and following the path of Alice and Bing before him, he feels an ever-growing responsibility to protect her. He understands that Ellen is lonely and would like nothing better than to spend every night in his bed, but he has already told her enough about Pilar for her to know that this won't be possible. On one of her days off, she invites him to go walking with her in Green-Wood Cemetery, a visit to the City of the Dead, as she calls it, and for the first time since coming to Sunset Park, he feels something stir inside him. There were the abandoned things down in Florida, and now he has stumbled upon the abandoned people of Brooklyn. He suspects it is a terrain well worth exploring.

With Alice, he has been given the chance to talk to someone about books, a thing that has happened to him only rarely in the years between college and Pilar. Early on, he discovers that she is mostly ignorant of European and South American literature, which comes as a small disappointment, but she is one of those specialized academics steeped in her narrow Anglo-American world, far more familiar with *Beowulf* and Dreiser than with Dante and Borges, but that hardly qualifies as a problem, there is still much they can talk about, and before many days have passed they have already developed a private shorthand to express their likes and dislikes, a language consisting of grunts, frowns, raised eyebrows, nods of the head, and sudden slaps to the knee. She doesn't talk to him about Jake, and therefore he doesn't ask her any questions. He has told her about Pilar, however, but not much, not much of anything beyond her name and the fact that she will be coming up from Florida to visit over Christmas break. He uses the word *break* instead of *vacation,* since *break* suggests college and *vacation* always means school, and he doesn't want anyone in the house to know how young Pilar is until she is already here—at which point, he hopes, no one will bother to ask her age. But even if it happens, he isn't worried. The only person to worry about is Angela, and Angela won't know that Pilar is gone. He has discussed this detail with Pilar again and again. She mustn't let any of her sisters know that she is leaving, not just Angela, but Teresa and Maria as well, for the minute one of them knows, they will all know, and even if the odds are against it, Angela might just be crazy enough to follow Pilar to New York.

He has bought a small illustrated book about Green-Wood Cemetery, and he goes in there every day with his camera now, roaming among the graves and monuments and mausoleums, nearly always alone in the frigid December air, carefully studying the lavish, often bombastic architecture of certain plots, the marble pillars and obelisks, the Greek temples and Egyptian pyramids, the enormous statues of supine, weeping women. The cemetery is more than half the size of Central Park, ample enough space for a person to get lost in there, to forget that he is a prisoner serving out his time in a dreary part of Brooklyn, and to walk among the thousands of trees and plantings, to climb the hillocks and traverse the sweeping paths of this vast necropolis is to leave the city behind you and enclose yourself in the absolute quiet of the dead. He takes pictures of the tombs of gangsters and poets, generals and industrialists, murder victims and newspaper publishers, children dead before their time, a woman who lived seventeen years beyond her hundredth birthday, and Theodore Roosevelt's wife and mother, who were buried next to each other on the same day. There is Elias Howe, inventor of the sewing machine, the Kampfe brothers, inventors of the safety razor, Henry Steinway, founder of the Steinway Piano Company, John Underwood, founder of the Underwood Typewriter Company, Henry Chadwick, inventor of the baseball scoring system, Elmer Sperry, inventor of the gyroscope. The crematory built in the mid-twentieth century has incinerated the bodies of John Steinbeck, Woody Guthrie, Edward R. Murrow, Eubie Blake, and how many more, both known and unknown, how many more souls have been transformed into smoke in this eerie, beautiful place? He has embarked on another useless project, employing his camera as an instrument to record his stray, useless thoughts, but at least it is something to do, a way to pass the time until his life starts again, and where else but in Green-Wood Cemetery could he have learned that the real name of Frank Morgan, the actor who played the Wizard of Oz, was Wuppermann?

MORRIS HELLER

1

It is the last day of the year, and he has come home from England a week early to attend the funeral of Martin Rothstein's twenty-three-year-old daughter, who committed suicide in Venice the night before Christmas Eve. He has been publishing Rothstein's work since the founding of Heller Books. Marty and Renzo were the only Americans on the first list, two Americans along with Per Carlsen from Denmark and Annette Louverain from France, and thirty-five years later he is still publishing them all, they are the core writers of the house, and he knows he would be nothing without them. The news came on the evening of the twenty-fourth, a mass e-mail sent to hundreds of friends and acquaintances, which he read on Willa's computer in their room at the Charlotte Street Hotel in London, the grim, naked message from Marty and Nina that Suki had taken her own life, with further information to follow about the date of the funeral. Willa didn't want him to go. She thought the funeral would be too hard on him, there had been too many funerals in the past year, too many of their friends were dying now, and she knew how ravaged he was by the losses, that was the word she used, *ravaged,* but he said he had to be there for them, it wouldn't be possible not to go, the duties of friendship demanded it, and four days later he was on a plane back to New York.

Now it is December thirty-first, late morning on the final day of 2008, and as he steps off the No. 1 train and climbs the stairs to Broadway and Seventy-ninth Street, the air is clogged with snow, a wet, heavy snow is falling from the white-gray sky, thick flakes tumbling through the blustery dimness, muting the colors of the traffic lights, whitening the hoods of passing cars, and by the time he reaches the community center on Amsterdam Avenue, he looks as if he is wearing a hat of snow. Suki Rothstein, birth name Susanna, the baby girl he first glimpsed sleeping in the crook of her father's right arm twenty-three years ago, the young woman who graduated summa cum laude from the University of Chicago, the budding artist, the precociously gifted thinker, writer, photographer who went to Venice this past fall to work as an intern at the Peggy Guggenheim Collection, and it was there, in the women's room of that museum, just days after conducting a seminar about her own work, that she hanged herself. Willa was right, he knows that, but how not to feel ravaged by Suki's death, how not to put himself inside her father's skin and suffer the ravages of this pointless death?

He remembers running into her some years back on Houston Street in the brightness of a late afternoon at the end of spring, the beginning of summer. She was on her way to her high school prom, decked out in a flamboyant red dress, as red as the reddest Jersey tomato, and Suki was all lit up with smiles when he chanced upon her that afternoon, surrounded by her friends, happy, affectionately kissing him hello and good-bye, and from that day forward he held that picture of her in his mind as the quintessential embodiment of youthful exuberance and promise, a singular example of *youth on fire.* Now he thinks about the dank chill of Venice in the dead of winter, the canals overflowing onto streets knee-deep in water, the shivering loneliness of unheated rooms, a head splitting open from the sheer force of the darkness within it, a life broken apart by the too-much and too-little of this world.

He shuffles into the building with the other people, a slowly gathering crowd that builds to two or three hundred, and he sees any number of familiar faces in the throng, Renzo's among them, but also Sally Fuchs, Don Willingham, Gordon Field, any number of old friends, writers, poets, artists, editors, and many young people as well, dozens and dozens of young men and women, Suki's friends from childhood, from high school, from college, and everyone is speaking in low voices, as if speaking above a whisper would be an offense, an insult against the silence of the dead, and as he looks at the faces around him, everyone seems numb and depleted, not quite fully there, *ravaged.* He makes his way to a small room at the end of the corridor where Marty and Nina are welcoming the visitors, the guests, the mourners, whatever word is used to describe people who come to a funeral, and as he steps forward to put his arms around his old friend, tears are pouring down Marty's face, and then Marty throws his arms around him and presses his head against his shoulder, saying Morris, Morris, Morris as his body convulses against him in a spasm of breathless sobs.

Martin Rothstein is not a man built for tragedies of this magnitude. He is a person of wit and effervescent charm, a comic writer of baroque, hilariously constructed sentences and spot-on satirical flair, an intellectual agitator with grand appetites and countless friends and a sense of humor equal to the best of the Borscht Belt wise guys. Now he is weeping his heart out, overcome by grief, by the cruelest, most lacerating form of grief, and Morris wonders how anyone can expect a man in this condition to stand up and talk in front of all these people when the service begins. And yet, sometime later, when the mourners have taken their seats in the auditorium and Marty climbs onto the stage to deliver his eulogy, he is calm, dry-eyed, completely recovered from his breakdown in the reception room. He reads from a text he has written, a text no doubt made possible by the length of time it took for Suki's body to be shipped from Venice to New York, making the gap between death and burial longer than usual, and in those empty, unsettled days of waiting for his daughter's corpse to arrive, Marty sat down and wrote this text. With Bobby, there had been no words. Willa hadn't been capable of writing or saying anything, he hadn't been capable of writing or saying anything, the accident had crushed them into a state of mute incomprehension, a dumb, bleeding sorrow that had lasted for months, but Marty is a writer, his whole life has been spent putting words and sentences together, paragraphs together, books together, and the only way he could respond to Suki's death was to write about her.

The coffin is on the stage, a white coffin surrounded by red flowers, but it is not a religious service. No rabbi has come to officiate, no prayers are recited, and no one who appears onstage tries to draw any meaning or consolation from Suki's death—there is nothing more than the fact of it, the horror of it. Someone plays a solo piece for saxophone, someone else plays a Bach chorale on the piano, and at one point Suki's younger brother, Anton, wearing red nail polish in honor of his sister, performs an unaccompanied, dirgelike rendition of a Cole Porter song (Ev'ry time we say good-bye / I die a little) that is so drastically slowed down, so drenched in melancholy, so painful to listen to that most of the gathering is in tears by the time he comes to the end. Writers walk up to the lectern and read poems by Shakespeare and Yeats. Friends and classmates tell stories about Suki, reminisce, evoke the *burning intensity of her spirit.* The director of the gallery where she had her one and only exhibition talks about her work. Morris follows every word spoken, listens to every note played and sung, on the verge of disintegration throughout the entire one-and-a-half-hour service, but it is Marty's speech that comes closest to destroying him, a brave and stunning piece of eloquence that shocks him with its candor, the brutal precision of its thinking, the rage and sorrow and guilt and love that permeate each of its articulations. All during Marty's twenty-minute talk, Morris imagines himself trying to talk about Bobby, about Miles, about the long-dead Bobby and the absent Miles, but he knows he would never have the courage to stand up in public and express his feelings with such naked honesty.

Afterward, there is a pause. Only the Rothsteins and their closest relatives will be going to the cemetery in Queens. Everyone is invited to Marty and Nina's apartment at four o'clock, but for now the mourners must disperse. He is glad to have been spared the ordeal of watching the coffin being lowered into the ground, the bulldozer pushing the dirt back into the hole, the sight of Marty and Nina collapsing into tears again. Renzo tracks him down in the entrance hall, and the two of them go back out into the snow together to look for a place to have lunch. Renzo is intelligent enough to have brought along an umbrella, and as Morris squeezes in beside him, Renzo puts his arm around his shoulder. Neither one of them says a word. They have been friends for fifty years, and each knows what the other is thinking.

They wind up in a Jewish delicatessen on Broadway in the low Eighties, a throwback to their New York childhoods, the all but vanished cuisine of chopped liver, matzo-ball soup, corned beef and pastrami sandwiches, pot roasts, cheese blintzes, sour pickles. Renzo has been traveling, they haven't seen each other since the publication of *The Mountain Dialogues* in September, and Morris feels that Renzo is looking tired, more haggard than usual. How did they get to be so old? he wonders. They are both sixty-two now, and while neither of them is in bad health, neither one of them fat or bald or ready for the glue factory, their heads have turned gray, their hairlines are receding, and they have reached that point in their lives when women under thirty, perhaps even forty, look right through them. He remembers Renzo as a young, young writer just out of college, living in a forty-nine-dollar-a-month apartment on the Lower East Side, one of those tenement railroad flats with a tub in the kitchen and six thousand cockroaches holding political conventions in every cupboard, so poor that he had to limit himself to one meal a day, working for three years on his first novel, which he destroyed because he felt it wasn't good enough, destroyed in the face of Morris's protests, his girlfriend's protests, who both felt it was very good indeed, and now look at him, Morris thinks, after how many books since that burned manuscript (seventeen? twenty?), published in every country of the world, even Iran, for God's sake, with how many literary prizes, how many medals, keys to cities, honorary doctorates, how many books and dissertations written about his work, and none of it matters to him, he is glad to have some money now, glad to be free of the suffocating hardships of the early years, but his fame leaves him cold, he has lost all interest in himself as a so-called public figure. I just want to disappear, he once told Morris, muttering in the lowest of low voices, staring off with a pained look in his eyes, as if he were talking to himself. I just want to disappear.

They order their soups and sandwiches, and when the Latino waiter walks off with their menus (a Latino waiter in a Jewish restaurant, they both like that), Morris and Renzo start talking about the funeral, sharing their impressions of what they have just witnessed in the community center auditorium. Renzo didn't know Suki, he met her only once when she was a small child, but he agrees with Morris that Rothstein's talk was a powerful piece of work, almost unimaginable when you consider that it was written under the most appalling duress, at a time when few people would have the strength to pull themselves together and write a single word, let alone the passionate, complex, and clear-sighted eulogy they heard this morning. Renzo has no children, two ex-wives but no children, and given what Marty and Nina are going through now, given what he and Willa have already gone through, first with Bobby and then with Miles, Morris feels something close to envy, thinking that Renzo made the right decision all those years ago to steer clear of the kid business, to avoid the unavoidable mess and potential devastation of fatherhood. He is half-expecting Renzo to start talking about Bobby now, the parallel is so evident, and surely he understands how difficult this funeral has been for him, but precisely because Renzo does understand, he does not talk about it. He is too discreet for that, too aware of what Morris is thinking to barge in on his pain, and just seconds afterward Morris himself understands his friend's reluctance to intrude on him when Renzo changes the subject, skirting past Bobby and the gloomy realm of dead children, and asks him how he is weathering the crisis, meaning the economic crisis, and whither Heller Books in this storm of trouble?

Morris tells him that the ship is still afloat, but listing somewhat to the starboard side now, and for the past few months they have been throwing excess equipment overboard. His primary concern is to keep the staff intact, and so far he hasn't had to let anyone go, but the list has been reduced, cut down by twenty or twenty-five percent. Last year, they published forty-seven books, this year thirty-eight, but their profits have gone down by only eleven percent, in large part thanks to *The Mountain Dialogues,* which is in its third printing, with forty-five thousand hardcovers sold. The Christmas sales figures won't be in for a while, but even if they turn out to be lower than expected, he isn't predicting out-and-out disaster. Louverain, Wyatt, and Tomesetti all published strong books this fall, and the paperback crime series seems to be off to a good start, but it's a rough time for first novels, very rough, and he's been forced to reject some good young writers, books he would have taken a chance on a year or two ago, and he finds that troubling, since the whole point of Heller Books is to encourage new talent. They're planning only thirty-three books for 2009, but Carlsen is on the list, Davenport is on the list, and then, needless to say, there is Renzo's novella, the little book he wrote just after *The Mountain Dialogues,* the unanticipated bonus book he has such high hopes for, and who knows, if every independent bookstore in America doesn't go bankrupt in the next twelve months, they might be in for a decent year. Listening to himself talk, he almost begins to feel optimistic, but he is telling Renzo only part of the story, leaving out the fact that when the returns start coming in on *The Mountain Dialogues* sales will fall by seven to ten thousand, leaving out the fact that 2008 will be the worst year for the house in three decades, leaving out the fact that he needs a new investor to put additional capital into the company or the ship will go down within two years. But there is no need for Renzo to know any of this. Renzo writes books, and he publishes them, and Renzo will go on writing and publishing books even if he is no longer in business.

After the soup comes, Renzo asks: What's the latest on the boy?

He's here, Morris says. As of two or three weeks ago.

Here in New York?

In Brooklyn. Living in an abandoned house in Sunset Park with some other people.

Our drummer friend told you this?

Our drummer friend is one of the people living there. He invited Miles to come up from Florida, and the boy accepted. Don't ask me why.

It sounds like good news to me.

Maybe. Time will tell. Bing says he's planning to call me, but no messages yet.

And what if he doesn't call?

Then nothing changes.

Think about it, Morris. All you have to do is jump in a cab, drive out to Brooklyn, and knock on the door. Aren't you tempted?

Of course I'm tempted. But I can't do it. He's the one who left, and he's the one who has to come back.

Renzo doesn't insist, and Morris is thankful to him for letting the matter drop there. As godfather to the boy and longtime friend of the father, Renzo has been participating in this grim saga for seven years, and by now there is little of anything left to say. Morris asks him about his recent travels, the trips to Prague, Copenhagen, and Paris, his reading at the Max Reinhardt Theater in Berlin, the prize he was given in Spain, and Renzo says it was a welcome diversion, he has been in a slump lately, and it felt good to be somewhere else for a few weeks, someplace other than inside his own head. Morris has been listening to this kind of talk from Renzo for as long as he can remember. Renzo is always in a slump, each book he finishes is always the last book he will ever write, and then, somehow, the slump mysteriously ends, and he is back in his room writing another book. Yes, Renzo says, he knows he's talked this way in the past, but this time it feels different, he doesn't know why, this time the paralysis is beginning to feel permanent. *Night Walk* was finished at the end of June, he says, more than six months ago, and since then he's done nothing of any account. It was such a short book, just a hundred and fifty-something pages, but it seemed to take everything out of him, he wrote it in a kind of frenzy, less than three months from beginning to end, working harder and with more concentration than at any time in all the years he has been writing, pushing, pushing, like a runner sprinting at full tilt for seven miles, and exhilarating as it was to work at that pace, something in him collapsed when he crossed the finish line. For six months he has had no plans, no ideas, no project to occupy his days. When he hasn't been traveling, he has felt listless and without motivation, with no desire to return to his desk and start writing again. He has experienced similar lulls in the past, yes, but never anything as stubborn and protracted as this one, and although he hasn't reached a state of alarm yet, he is beginning to wonder if this isn't the end, if the old fire hasn't been extinguished at last. Meanwhile, he spends his days doing next to nothing—reading books, thinking, going out for walks, watching films, following the news of the world. In other words, he is resting, but for all that it is a strange kind of rest, he says, *an anxious repose.*

The waiter brings them their sandwiches, and before Morris can say anything about this half-serious, half-mocking account of mental exhaustion, Renzo, in an abrupt about-face, contradicting everything he has just said, tells Morris that a small notion occurred to him while he was flying home from Europe the other day, the tiniest germ of an idea—for an essay, a piece of nonfiction, something. Morris smiles. I thought you had run out of ideas, he says. Well, Renzo answers, shrugging defensively, but with a glint of humor in his eye, one does have an occasional *flicker.*

He was on the plane, he says, a first-class ticket paid for by the people who gave him the prize, the dread of flying dulled somewhat by soft leather seats, caviar and champagne, imbecilic luxe among the clouds, with an abundant choice of films at his disposal, not just new films from Europe and America but old ones as well, venerated classics, ancient fluff from the dream factories on both sides of the Atlantic. He wound up watching *The Best Years of Our Lives,* something he had seen once a long time ago and therefore had utterly forgotten, a nice movie, he felt, well played by the actors, a charming piece of propaganda designed to persuade Americans that the soldiers returning from World War II will eventually adjust to civilian life, not without a few bumps along the way, of course, but in the end everything will work out, because this is America, and in America everything always works out. Be that as it may, he enjoyed the film, it helped pass the time, but what interested him most about the film was not the film itself but a minor role played by one of the actors in it, Steve Cochran. He has only one bit of any importance, a short, smirking confrontation with the hero, whose wife has been running around with Cochran on the sly, but that finally isn't what interested him either, Cochran's performance is a matter of complete indifference to him, what counts is the story his mother once told him about having known Cochran during the war, yes, his mother, Anita Michaelson, née Cannobio, who died four years ago at the age of eighty. His mother was an elusive woman, not given to opening up about the past, but when Cochran died at forty-eight in 1965, just after Renzo had turned nineteen, she must have been thrown sufficiently off guard to feel a need to unburden herself, and so she told him about her brief infatuation with the theater in the early forties, a girl of fifteen, sixteen, seventeen, and how she crossed paths with Cochran in some New York theater group and *fell for him.* He was such a handsome man, she said, one of those rugged black-Irish heartthrobs, but what *falling* meant was never quite clear to Renzo. Did his mother lose her virginity to Steve Cochran in 1942 when she was seventeen years old? Did they have an actual fling—or was it only a thing, an adolescent crush on an up-and-coming twenty-five-year-old actor? Impossible to say, but what his mother did report was that Cochran wanted her to go to California with him, and she was prepared to go, but when her parents got wind of what was brewing, they put an immediate stop to it. No daughter of theirs, no scandals in this family, forget it, Anita. So Cochran left, his mother stayed and married his father, and that was how he came to be born—because his mother hadn't run off with Steve Cochran. That is the idea he is toying with, Renzo says, to write an essay about the things that don't happen, the lives not lived, the wars not fought, the shadow worlds that run parallel to the world we take to be the real world, the not-said and the not-done, the not-remembered. Chancy territory, perhaps, but it could be worth exploring.

After he came home, Renzo says, he felt curious enough to do a little digging into Cochran's life and career. Gangster roles for the most part, a couple of plays on Broadway with Mae West, of all people, *White Heat* with James Cagney, the lead in Antonioni's *Il Grido,* and appearances on various television shows in the fifties: *Bonanza, The Untouchables, Route 66, The Twilight Zone.* He formed his own production company, which produced little or nothing (information is scant, and although Renzo is curious, he is not curious enough to explore this point further), but Cochran seems to have acquired a reputation as one of the most active skirt chasers of his time. This probably explains why his mother fell for him, Renzo continues, sadly contemplating how easy it must have been for a practiced seducer to soften the heart of an inexperienced seventeen-year-old girl. How could she have resisted the man who later went on to have affairs with Joan Crawford, Merle Oberon, Kay Kendall, Ida Lupino, and Jayne Mansfield? There was also Mamie Van Doren, who apparently wrote at great length about her sex life with Cochran in an autobiography published twenty years ago, but Renzo has no plans to read the book. In the end, what fascinates him most is how thoroughly he suppressed the facts about Cochran's death, which he must have heard about when he was nineteen, but even after the conversation with his mother (which theoretically should have made the story impossible to forget), he forgot everything. In 1965, hoping to rejuvenate his moribund production company, Cochran developed a project for a film to be set in Central or South America. With three young women between the ages of fourteen and twenty-five, supposedly hired as assistants, he set out for Costa Rica on his forty-foot yacht to begin scouting locations. Some weeks later, the boat washed ashore along the coast of Guatemala. Cochran had died on board from a severe lung infection, and the three panic-stricken young women, who knew nothing about sailing, nothing about navigating forty-foot yachts, had been drifting through the ocean for the past ten days, alone with Cochran's putrefying corpse. Renzo says he cannot efface the image from his mind. The three frightened women lost at sea with the decomposing body of the dead movie star below deck, convinced they will never touch land again.

So much, he says, for the best years of our lives.

2

He has been invited to four New Year's Eve parties in four different parts of Manhattan, East Side and West Side, uptown and downtown, but after the funeral, after the lunch with Renzo, after the two hours spent at Marty and Nina's place, he has no desire to see anyone. He goes home to the apartment on Downing Street, unable to stop thinking about Suki, unable to free himself of the story Renzo told about the dead actor on the drifting boat. How many corpses has he seen in his life? he wonders. Not the embalmed dead lying in their open coffins, the wax-museum figures drained of blood who no longer appear to have been human, but actual dead bodies, the vivid dead, as it were, before they could be touched by the mortician's scalpel? His father, thirty years ago. Bobby, twelve years ago. His mother, five years ago. Three. Just three in more than sixty years.

He goes into the kitchen and pours himself a scotch. He already knocked off two of them at Marty and Nina's place, but he doesn't feel the least bit wobbly or disabled, his head is clear, and after the enormous lunch he consumed at the delicatessen, which is still sitting in his stomach like a stone, he has no appetite for dinner. He tells himself that he will end the year by catching up on the manuscripts he should have read in England, but he understands that this is merely a ruse, a trick to propel him into the comfortable armchair in the living room, and once he sits down in that chair, he will not return to Samantha Jewett's novel, which he has already decided not to publish.

It is seven-thirty, four and a half hours before another year begins, the tired ritual of noisemakers and fireworks, the blast of drunken voices that will echo across the neighborhood at midnight, always the same eruption on this particular midnight, but he is far from that now, alone with his scotch and his thoughts, and if he can go deeply enough into those thoughts, he won't even hear the voices and the clamor when the time comes. Five years ago this past May, the call from his mother's cleaning woman, who had just let herself into the apartment with her duplicate key. He was at the office, he remembers, a Tuesday morning around ten o'clock, talking with Jill Hertzberg about Renzo's latest manuscript and whether to use an illustration on the cover or go with pure graphics. Why remember a detail like that? No reason, no reason that he can think of, except that reason and memory are nearly always at odds, and then he was in a cab heading up Broadway to West Eighty-fourth Street, trying to get his mind around the fact that his mother, who had been wisecracking with him over the phone on Saturday, was now dead.

The body. That is what he is thinking about now, the corpse of his mother lying on the bed five years ago, and the terror he felt when he looked down at her face, the blue-gray skin, the half-open-half-closed eyes, the terrifying *immobility* of what had once been a living person. She had been lying there for roughly forty-eight hours before she was discovered by the cleaning woman. Still dressed in her nightgown, his mother had been reading the Sunday edition of the *New York Times* when she died—no doubt of a sudden, cataclysmic heart attack. One bare leg was hanging over the edge of the bed, and he wondered if she had tried to get up when the attack began (to search for a pill? to call for help?), and if so, given that she had moved only a few inches, it struck him that she must have died within seconds.

He looked at her for a brief moment, for several moments, and then he turned away and walked into the living room. It was too much for him; to see her in that state of frozen vulnerability was more than he could bear. He can't remember if he looked at her again when the police arrived, if it was necessary for him to make a formal identification of the body or not, but he is certain that when the paramedics came to pack up the corpse in a black rubber body bag, he couldn't look. He remained in the living room staring down at the rug, studying the clouds through the window, listening to himself breathe. It was simply too much for him, and he couldn't bring himself to look anymore.

The revelation of that morning, the blunt, incontestable minim of knowledge he finally grasped when the paramedics were wheeling her out of the apartment, the idea that has continued to haunt him ever since: there can be no memories of the womb, not for him or anyone else, but he accepts it as an article of faith, or else wills himself to understand it through a leap of the imagination, that his own life as a sentient being began as part of the now dead body they were pushing through the opened door, that his life began *within her.*

She was a child of the war, just as Renzo's mother was, just as all their parents were, whether their fathers had fought in the war or not, whether their mothers had been fifteen or seventeen or twenty-two when the war began. A strangely optimistic generation, he thinks now, tough, dependable, hardworking, and a little stupid as well, perhaps, but they all bought into the myth of American greatness, and they lived with fewer doubts than their children did, the boys and girls of Vietnam, the angry postwar children who saw their country turn into a sick, destructive monster. Spunky. That is the word that comes to him whenever he thinks about his mother. Spunky and outspoken, strong-willed and loving, impossible. She remarried twice after his father's death in seventy-eight, lost both of the new husbands to cancer, one in ninety-two, the other in oh-three, and even then, in the last year of her life, at age seventy-nine, eighty, she was still hoping to catch another man. I was born married, she said to him once. She had turned into the Wife of Bath, and fitting as that role might have been for her, playing the son of the Wife of Bath had not been entirely pleasant. His sisters had shared the burden with him, of course, but Cathy lives in Millburn, New Jersey, and Ann is in Scarsdale, just out of reach, on the fringes of the combat zone, and because he was the oldest, and because his mother trusted men more than women, he was the one she came to with her troubles, which were never classified as troubles (all negative words had been expunged from her vocabulary) but as *little somethings*, as in, I have a little something to discuss with you. Willful blindness is what he called it, an obdurate insistence on looking for silver linings, moral victories, a darkest-before-the-dawn attitude in the face of the most wrenching facts—burying three husbands, the disappearance of her grandson, the accidental death of her stepgrandson—but that was the world she came from, an ethical universe patched together from the righteous platitudes of Hollywood films—pluck, spunk, and never say die. Admirable in its way, yes, but also maddening, and as the years moved forward he understood that much of it was a sham, that inside her supposedly indomitable spirit there was also fear and panic and crushing sadness. Who could blame her? Having lived through the various maladies of her three husbands, how could she not have turned into a world-class hypochondriac? If your experience has taught you that all bodies must and will betray the person they belong to, why wouldn't you think that a small pain in the stomach is a prelude to stomach cancer, that a headache signifies brain tumor, that a forgotten word or name is an augury of dementia? Her last years were spent visiting doctors, dozens of specialists for this condition or that syndrome, and it's true that she was having problems with her heart (two angioplasties), but no one thought she was in any real danger. He figured she would go on complaining about her imaginary illnesses until she was ninety, that she would outlive him, that she would outlive them all, and then, without warning, less than twenty-four hours after cracking jokes to him on the phone, she was dead. And once he had come to terms with it, the frightening thing about her death was that he felt relieved, or at least some part of him felt relieved, and he hates himself for being callous enough to admit it, but he knows he is lucky to have been spared the rigors of seeing her through a long old age. She left the world at the right time. No prolonged suffering, no descent into decrepitude or senility, no broken hips or adult diapers, no blank stares into empty space. A light goes on, a light goes off. He misses her, but he can live with the fact that she is gone.

He misses his father more. He is callous enough to admit that, too, but his father has been dead for thirty years now, and he has spent half his life walking beside that ghost. Sixty-three, just one year older than he is now, in good condition, still playing tennis four times a week, still strong enough to trounce his thirty-two-year-old son in three sets of singles, probably still strong enough to beat him at arm wrestling, a strict nonsmoker, alcohol consumption close to zero, never ill with anything, not even colds or flus, a broad-shouldered six-one, without flab or gut or stoop, a man who looked ten years younger than his age, and then a minor problem, an attack of bursitis in his left elbow, the proverbial tennis elbow, extremely painful, yes, but hardly life-threatening, and so he went to a doctor for the first time in how many years, a quack who prescribed cortisone pills instead of some mild painkiller, and his father, unaccustomed to taking pills, carried around the cortisone in his pocket as if it were a bottle of aspirin, tossing another pill down his throat every time the elbow acted up, thus tampering with the functioning of his heart, putting undue strain on his cardiovascular system without even knowing it, and one night, as he was making love to his wife (a consoling thought: to know that his parents were still active in the sex department at that point in their marriage), the night of November 26, 1978, as Alvin Heller was approaching an orgasm in the arms of his wife, Constance, better known as Connie, his heart gave out on him, rupturing inside his chest, exploding inside his chest, and that was the end.

There were never any of the conflicts he witnessed so often with his friends and their fathers, the boys with the slapping fathers, the shouting fathers, the aggressive fathers who pushed their frightened six-year-old sons into swimming pools, the contemptuous fathers who sneered at their adolescent sons for liking the wrong music, wearing the wrong clothes, looking at them in the wrong way, the war-veteran fathers who punched out their twenty-year-old sons for resisting the draft, the weak fathers who were afraid of their grown-up sons, the shut-down fathers who couldn't remember the names of their sons' children. From beginning to end, there had been none of those antagonisms or dramas between them, no more than some sharp differences of opinion, small punishments doled out mechanically for small infractions of the rules, a harsh word or two when he was unkind to his sisters or forgot his mother's birthday, but nothing of any significance, no slaps or shouts or angry insults, and unlike most of his friends, he never felt embarrassed by his father or turned against him. At the same time, it would be wrong to presume that they were especially close. His father wasn't one of those warmhearted buddy fathers who thought his son should be his best pal, he was simply a man who felt responsible for his wife and children, a quiet, even-tempered man with a talent for making money, a skill his son failed to appreciate until the last years of his father's life, when his father became the principal backer and founding partner of Heller Books, but even if they weren't close in the way some fathers and sons are, even if the one thing they ever talked about with any passion together was sports, he knew that his father respected him, and to have that unflagging respect from beginning to end was more important than any open declaration of love.

When he was very young, five years old, six years old, he felt disappointed that his father had not fought in the war, unlike the fathers of most of his friends, and that while they had been off in far-flung parts of the world killing Japs and Nazis and turning themselves into heroes, his father had been in New York, immersed in the petty details of his real estate business, buying buildings, managing buildings, endlessly repairing buildings, and it puzzled him that his father, who seemed so strong and fit, had been rejected by the army when he tried to join up. But he was still too young at that point to understand how badly his father's eye was injured, to have been told that his father had been legally blind in his left eye since the age of seventeen, and because his father had so thoroughly mastered the art of living with and compensating for his handicap, he failed to understand that his powerhouse of a father was impaired. Later on, when he was eight or nine and his mother finally told him the story of the injury (his father never talked about it), he realized that his father's wound was no different from a war wound, that a part of his life had been shot down on that Bronx ball field in 1932 in the same way a soldier's arm can be shot off on a battlefield in Europe. He was the top pitcher for his high school baseball team, a hard-throwing left-hander who was already beginning to attract attention from major league scouts, and when he took the mound for Monroe that day in early June, he had an undefeated record and what appeared to be an unhittable arm. On the first pitch of the game, just as the fielders were settling into their positions behind him, he threw a low fastball to the Clinton shortstop, Tommy DeLucca, and the line drive that came flying back at him was struck so hard, with such ferocious power and speed, that he had no time to lift his glove and protect his face. It was the same injury that destroyed Herb Score's career in 1957, the same bone-breaking shot that changes the course of a life. And if that ball hadn't slammed his father in the eye, who is to say he wouldn't have been killed in the war—before his marriage, before the birth of his children? Now Herb Score is dead, too, Morris thinks, dead as of six or seven weeks ago, Herb Score, with the prophetic middle name of Jude, and he remembers how badly shaken his father was when he read about Score's injury in the morning paper, and how, for years after, right up to the end of his life, he would periodically refer to Score, saying that injury was one of the saddest things that ever happened in the history of the game. Never a word about himself, never the slightest hint of any personal connection. Only Score, poor Herb Score.

Without his father's help, the publishing house never would have been born. He knew he didn't have the stuff to become a writer, not when he had the example of young

Renzo to compare himself to, his dormitory roommate for four years at Amherst, the immense, grinding struggle of it, the long solitary hours, the everlasting uncertainty and compulsive need, and so he opted for the next best thing, teaching literature instead of making it, but after one year of graduate school at Columbia, he withdrew from the Ph.D. program, understanding that he wasn't cut out for an academic life either. He wandered into publishing instead, spent four years rising through the ranks of two different companies, at last finding a place for himself, a mission, a calling, whatever word best applies to a sense of commitment and purpose, but there were too many frustrations and compromises at the top levels of commercial publishing, and when, in the space of two short months, his senior editor quashed his recommendation that they publish Renzo's first novel (the one following the burned manuscript) and similarly rejected his proposal to publish Marty's first novel, he went to his father and told him he wanted to quit the august company he was working for and start a little house of his own. His father knew nothing about books or publishing, but he must have seen something in his son's eyes that persuaded him to throw a losable fraction of his money into a venture that was all but certain to fail. Or perhaps he felt this certain failure would teach the boy a lesson, help him work the bug out of his system, and before long he would return to the security of a normal job. But they didn't fail, or at least the losses were not egregious enough to make them want to stop, and after that inaugural list of just four books, his father opened his pockets again, staking him to a new investment worth ten times the amount of his initial outlay, and suddenly Heller Books was off the ground, a small but viable entity, a real publishing house with an office on lower West Broadway (dirt-cheap rents back then in a Tribeca that was not yet Tribeca), a staff of four, a distributor, well-designed catalogues, and a growing stable of authors. His father never interfered. He called himself *the silent partner,* and for the last four years of his life he used those words to announce himself whenever they talked on the phone. No more *This is your father* or *This is your old man* but, without fail, one hundred percent of the time, *Hello there, Morris, this is your silent partner.* How not to miss him? How not to feel that every book he has published in the past thirty-five years is a product of his father's invisible hand?

It is nine-thirty. He meant to call Willa to say happy new year, but it is two-thirty in England now, and no doubt she has been asleep for hours. He returns to the kitchen to pour himself another scotch, his third since coming back to the apartment, and it is only now, for the first time all evening, that he remembers to check the answering machine, suddenly thinking that Willa might have called while he was at Marty and Nina's or on his way home from the Upper West Side. There are twelve new messages. One by one, he listens to them all—but no word from Willa.

He is being punished. That is why she accepted the job at Exeter for the year, and that is why she never calls—because she is punishing him for the meaningless indiscretion he committed eighteen months ago, a stupid act of sexual weakness that he regretted even as he was crawling into bed with his partner in crime. Under normal circumstances (but when is anything ever normal?) Willa never would have found out, but not long after he did what he did, she went to her gynecologist for her semi-annual checkup and was told she had something called chlamydia, a mild but unpleasant condition that can be contracted only through sexual intercourse. The doctor asked her if she had slept with anyone besides her husband lately, and because the answer was no, the culprit could have been none other than said husband, and when Willa confronted him with the news that evening, he had no choice but to confess. He didn't provide any names or details, but he admitted that when she was in Chicago delivering her paper on George Eliot, he had gone to bed with someone. No, he wasn't having an affair, it had happened only that one time, and he had no intention of ever doing it again. He was sorry, he said, deeply and truly sorry, he had been drinking too much, it was a terrible mistake, but even though she believed him, how could he blame her for feeling angry, not just because he had been unfaithful to her for the first time in their marriage, no, that was bad enough, but because he had infected her as well. A venereal disease! she shouted. It's disgusting! You stick your dumb-ass penis into another woman's vagina, and you wind up infecting me! Aren't you ashamed of yourself, Morris? Yes, he said, he was horribly ashamed, more ashamed than he had ever been in his life.

It torments him to think about that evening now, the idiocy of it all, the frantic little coupling that led to such enduring havoc. A dinner invitation from Nancy Greenwald, a literary agent in her early forties, someone he had been doing business with for six or seven years, divorced, not unattractive, but until that night he had never given her much thought. A dinner for six at Nancy's apartment in Chelsea, and the only reason he accepted was because Willa was out of town, a fairly tedious dinner as it turned out, and when the four other guests gathered up their things and left, he agreed to stay on for a last drink before walking home to the Village. That was when it happened, about twenty minutes after the others disappeared, a quick crazy fuck of no earthly importance to anyone. After Willa's announcement about chlamydia, he wondered how many other dumb-ass penises had found comfort in Nancy's vagina, although the truth was that there hadn't been much comfort for him, and even as they went at it together, he had felt too wretched about betraying Willa to lose himself in the supposed pleasure of the moment.

After his confession, after the round of antibiotics that purged the venereal microbes from Willa's system, he thought that would be the end of it. He knew she believed him when he told her it had happened only once, but this tiny lapse of attention, this breach of solidarity after close to twenty-four years of marriage, had shaken Willa's confidence in him. She doesn't trust him anymore. She believes he is on the prowl, searching for younger and more beautiful women, and even if he isn't up to anything at this particular moment, she has convinced herself that sooner or later it is bound to happen again. He has done everything he can to reassure her, but his arguments seem to have no effect. He is too old for adventures now, he says, he wants to live out the rest of his days with her and die in her arms. And she says: A sixty-two-year-old man is still young, a sixty-year-old woman is old. He says: After all they've been through together, all the nightmares and sorrows, all the poundings they've taken, all the miseries they've survived, how can a little thing like this make any difference? And she answers: Maybe it's been too much for you, Morris. Maybe you want a fresh start with someone else.

The trip to England didn't help. They had been apart for three and a half months when he finally went over there for the Christmas break, and he understood that she was using this enforced separation as a test, to see whether it would be possible for her to live without him over the long haul. So far, the experiment seems to be working rather well. Her anger toward him has changed into a kind of willed detachment, an aloofness that made him feel awkward around her for much of the visit, never quite sure what he should say or how he should act. The first night, she was reluctant to have sex with him, but then, just as he was drifting off, she reached out for him in bed and started kissing him in the old way, giving herself up to the old intimacies as if there were no trouble between them. That was the thing that so confounded him—their silent companionship in bed at night followed by moody, disjointed days, tenderness and irritability alternating in wholly unpredictable patterns, a feeling that she was both pushing him away from her and trying to hold on to him at the same time. There was only one vicious outburst, one full-blown argument. It occurred on the third or fourth day, when they were still in her Exeter flat, taking out their bags to prepare for their trip to London, and the quarrel began as many others had in the past few years, with Willa attacking him for not wanting to have children of their own, for being content with her son and his son as their only family, but no family of their own, just the two of them and their own boy or girl, without the specters of Karl and Mary-Lee hovering in the background, and now that Bobby was dead and Miles had gone missing, just look at them, she said, they were nothing, they had nothing, and it was his fault for talking her out of another child all those years ago, and she was a goddamned fool for listening to him. In principle, he didn't disagree with her, had never disagreed with her, but how could they have known what would happen, and by the time Miles took off, they were too old to think about having babies. He didn't resent her for bringing up the subject again, it was altogether natural for her to feel this grief, this loss, the history of the past twelve years could have produced no other outcome, but then she said something that shocked him, that hurt him so badly he still hasn't recovered from it. But Miles is back in New York, he said. He'll be contacting them any day now, any week, and before long the whole miserable chapter will come to an end. Instead of answering him, Willa picked up her suitcase and threw it angrily on the floor—a furious gesture, more violent than any response he had ever seen from her. It's too late, she shouted. Miles is sick. Miles is no good. Miles has wrecked them, and from this day forward she cuts him out of her heart. She doesn't want to see him. Even if he calls, she doesn't want to see him. Never again. It's finished, she said, it's finished, and every night she will get down on her knees and pray he doesn't call.

It was somewhat better in London. The hotel was neutral ground, a no-man's-land devoid of any associations with the past, and there were some good days of walking through museums and sitting in pubs, seeing old friends for dinner, browsing in bookstores, not to mention the sublime indulgence of doing nothing at all, which seemed to have a restorative effect on Willa. One afternoon, she read aloud to him from the most recent chapter of the book she is writing on the late novels of Dickens. The next morning, over breakfast, she asked him about his search for a new investor, and he told her about his meeting with the German at the Frankfurt Book Fair in October, his conversation with the Israeli in New York last month, the steps he has taken to find the needed cash. Several good days, or at least not bad days, and then came the e-mail from Marty and the news of Suki's death. Willa didn't want him to go back to New York, she argued fiercely and persuasively why she thought the funeral would be too much for him, but when he asked her to make the trip with him, her face tensed up, she seemed thrown by the suggestion, which was an entirely reasonable suggestion to his mind, and then she said no, she couldn't. He asked her why. Because she couldn't, she said, repeating her answer as she searched for the right words, clearly at war with herself, unprepared to make any crucial decisions at that moment, because she wasn't ready to go back, she said, because she needed more time. Again, she asked him to stay, to remain in London until January third as originally planned, and he understood that she was testing him, forcing him to make a choice between her and his friends, and if he didn't choose her, she would feel betrayed. But he had to go back, he said, it was out of the question not to go back.

One week later, as he sits in his New York apartment on New Year's Eve, sipping scotch in the darkened living room and thinking about his wife, he tells himself that a marriage can't stand or fall on a simple matter of leaving London a few days early to attend a funeral. And if it does stand or fall on that matter, perhaps it was destined to fall in the first place.

He is in danger of losing his wife. He is in danger of losing his business. As long as there is breath in him, he says to himself, remembering that homely, worn-out phrase, which he has always been fond of, as long as there is breath in him he will not allow either one of those things to happen.

Where is he now? Straddling the border between inevitable extinction and the possibility of continued life. Overall, the situation is bleak, but there are some encouraging signs that have given him cause for hope—or, if not quite hope, a sense that it is still too early to succumb to resignation and despair. How much he reminds himself of his mother whenever he starts thinking like this, how obstinately she goes on living inside him. Let the house come crashing down around him, let his marriage burst into flames, and Connie Heller's son will find a way to rebuild the house and put out the fire. Lucky Lohrke walking calmly through a barrage of bullets. Or else the ghost dance of the Oglala Sioux—and the conviction that the white man's bullets would evaporate into thin air before they ever touched them.

He drinks another scotch and then staggers off to bed. Exhausted, so exhausted that he is already asleep before the shouting and the fireworks begin.

3

He knows why Miles left. Even before the letter came, he was all but certain the boy had spent the night in the apartment, the night preceding the morning when he and Willa had talked so brutally about him in the kitchen. After breakfast, he had cracked open the door of Miles's room to find out if the boy had come home for the weekend, and when he saw that the bed was empty, he went in to discover an ashtray filled with cigarette butts, a forgotten paperback anthology of Jacobean drama lying on the floor, and a flattened, unplumped pillow on the hastily made bed—sure signs that the boy had spent the night there, and if he had stolen off early that morning without bothering to greet them, without a hello or a good-bye, it could only mean that he had overheard the cruel things that had been said about him and was too upset to face his parents. Morris didn't mention his discovery to Willa, but at that point there was no reason to suspect the conversation would lead to such a drastic response from Miles. He felt terrible about having said those things, angry with himself for not having defended the boy more vociferously against Willa's harsh attacks, but he figured he would have a chance to apologize the next time they saw each other, to clear the air somehow and put the matter behind them. Then came the letter, the mad, falsely cheerful letter with the disturbing news that Miles had quit college. *Burned out on school.* The boy wasn't burned out. He loved being in school, he was sailing through with top honors, and just two weeks before, when they met for Sunday breakfast at Joe Junior's, Miles had been talking about the courses he was planning to take in his senior year. No, quitting had been a hostile act of revenge and self-sabotage, a symbolic suicide, and there was no doubt in Morris's mind that it was a direct result of that conversation overheard in the apartment a few days earlier.

Still, there was no reason to panic. Miles was going to L.A. to spend a couple of weeks with his mother, and all Morris had to do was pick up the telephone and call him. He would do what he could to talk some sense into the boy, and if that didn't work, he would fly to California and have it out with him face to face. But not only was Miles not at Mary-Lee's, Mary-Lee was not at home either. She was in San Francisco, filming the pilot of a new television series, and the person he spoke to was Korngold, who told him that Miles hadn't been heard from in more than a month and that as far as he knew there were no plans for him to visit California anytime that summer.

From that moment on, they were in it together, all four of them, the two parents and the two stepparents, and when they hired a private detective to look for the missing boy, each couple bore half the cost, living through eight dismal months of progress reports that reported no progress, no leads, no signs of hope, not a single microdot of information. Morris held fast to the theory that Miles had vanished on purpose, but after three or four months both Willa and Korngold began to waver, gradually coming to the conclusion that Miles was dead. An accident of some kind, they thought, perhaps murdered, perhaps killed by his own hand, it was impossible to say. Mary-Lee took an agnostic position on the matter—she simply didn't know. He could have been dead, yes, but on the other hand, the kid had *issues,* the thing with Bobby had been an absolute devastation, Miles had closed in on himself since then, and it was clear that he had *a lot of stuff to work out.* Running away was a stupid thing to do, of course, but maybe some good would come of it in the end, maybe being on his own for a while would give him a chance to straighten himself out. Morris didn't disagree with this analysis. In fact, he found Mary-Lee's attitude rather impressive—calm, compassionate, and thoughtful, not judging Miles so much as trying to understand him—and now that they were locked in this crisis together, he realized that the indifferent, irresponsible mother was far more attached to her son than he had imagined. If anything positive emerged from Miles's disappearance, it was this shift in his perception of Mary-Lee. They were no longer enemies. They had become allies now, perhaps even friends.

Then Bing Nathan called, and everything turned upside down again. Miles was working as a short-order cook in Chicago, and Morris's first impulse was to go out there and talk to him—not to make any demands, merely to find out what was going on—but Willa was against it, and after he called California to share the good news with Mary-Lee and Korngold, they took Willa's side. Their argument was this: the boy was twenty-one now and capable of making his own decisions; as long as his health was sound, as long as he wasn't in trouble with the law, as long as he wasn't in a mental hospital, as long as he wasn't asking them for money, they had no right to force him to do anything against his will—not even to make him talk to them, which he obviously had no wish to do. Give him time, they said. He'll figure it out.

But Morris didn't listen to them. He took a plane to Chicago the next morning, and by three o'clock he had parked his rented car across the street from Duke's, a shabby, heavily frequented diner in a rough neighborhood on the South Side. Two hours later, Miles walked out of the restaurant wearing his leather jacket (the one Morris had bought for him on his nineteenth birthday) and looking well, very well in fact, a bit taller and more filled out than he'd been at that Sunday breakfast eight and a half months ago, and at his side there was a tall, attractive black woman who appeared to be in her mid-twenties, and the moment the two of them walked out the door, Miles put his arm around the woman's shoulder, drew her toward him, and planted a kiss on her mouth. It was a joyful kiss, somehow, the kiss of a man who has just put in eight hours of work and is back with the woman he loves, and the woman laughed at this sudden outburst of affection, threw her arms around him, and returned his kiss with one of her own. A moment after that, they were walking down the street together, holding hands and talking in that intense, intimate way that is possible only in the closest friendships, the closest loves, and Morris just sat there, frozen in the seat of his rented car, not daring to roll down the window and call out to Miles, not daring to jump out and run after him, and ten seconds later Miles and the woman turned left at the first corner they came to and vanished from sight.

He has done it three more times since then, once in Arizona, once in New Hampshire, and once in Florida, always watching from a place where he couldn't be seen, the warehouse parking lot where Miles was loading crates onto the back of a truck, the hotel lobby where the boy rushed past him in a bellhop's uniform, the little park he sat in one day as his son read *The Great Gatsby* and then talked to the cute high school girl who happened to be reading the same book, always tempted to step forward and say something, always tempted to pick a fight with him, to punch him, to take him in his arms, to take the boy in his arms and kiss him, but never doing anything, never saying anything, keeping himself hidden, watching Miles grow older, watching his son turn into a man as his own life dwindles into something small, too small to care about anymore, listening to Willa's tirade in Exeter, all the damage that has been done to her, his brave, battered Willa, Bobby on the road, Miles gone, and yet he grimly perseveres, never quite able to let go of it, still thinking the story hasn't come to an end, and when thinking about the story becomes unbearable, he sometimes diverts himself with childish reveries about dressing up in costumes, disguising himself so thoroughly that not even his own son would recognize him, a demon of disguise in the spirit of Sherlock Holmes, not just the clothes and the shoes but an entirely different face, entirely different hair, an entirely different voice, an utter transformation from one being into another, and how many different old men has he invented since the idea occurred to him, wrinkled pensioners hobbling along with their canes and aluminum walkers, old men with flowing white hair, flowing white beards, Walt Whitman in his dotage, a friendly old fellow who has lost his way and stops thc young man to ask for directions, and then they would begin to talk, the old man would invite the young man for a drink, and little by little the two of them would become friends, and now that Miles is living in Brooklyn, out there in Sunset Park next to Green-Wood Cemetery, he has come up with another character, a New York character he calls the Can Man, one of those old, broken-down men who forage among dumpsters and recycling bins for bottles and cans, five cents a bottle, five cents a can, a tough way to make a living, but times are tough and one mustn't complain, and in his mind the Can Man is a Mohawk Indian, a descendent of the Mohawks who settled in Brooklyn in the early part of the last century, the community of Mohawks who came here to become construction workers on the tall buildings going up in Manhattan, Mohawks because for some reason Mohawks have no fear of heights, they feel at home in the air and were able to dance along the beams and girders without the slightest dread or vertiginous wobble, and the Can Man is a descendent of those fearless people who built the towers of Manhattan, a crazy customer, alas, not quite right in the head, a daft old loon who spends his days pushing his shopping cart through the neighborhood, collecting the bottles and cans that will fetch him five cents apiece, and when the Can Man speaks, more often than not he will punctuate his remarks with absurd, outlandishly inappropriate advertising slogans, such as, *I'd walk a mile for a Camel*, or: *Don't leave home without it*, or: *Reach out and touch someone,* and perhaps Miles will be amused by a man who would walk a mile for a Camel, and when the Can Man wearies of his advertising slogans, he will start quoting from the Bible, saying things like: *The wind goeth toward the south, and turneth about unto the north, it whirleth about continually* or *And that which is done is that which shall be done,* and just when Miles is about to turn around and walk away, the Can Man will push his face up against his and shout:

Remember, boy! Bankruptcy is not the end! It's just a new beginning!

It is ten o'clock in the morning, the first morning of the new year, and he is sitting in a booth at Joe Junior's, the diner on the corner of Sixth Avenue and Twelfth Street where he last spoke to Miles more than two thousand seven hundred days ago, sitting, as it happens, in the same booth the two of them sat in that morning, eating his scrambled eggs and buttered toast as he toys with the notion of turning himself into the Can Man. Joe Junior's is a small place, a simple, down-at-the-heels neighborhood joint featuring a curved Formica counter with chrome trim, eight swivel stools, three tables by the window in front, and four booths along the northern wall. The food is ordinary at best, the standard greasy-spoon fare of two dozen breakfast combinations, grilled ham-and-cheese sandwiches, tuna fish salads, hamburgers, hot open turkey sandwiches, and fried onion rings. He has never sampled the onion rings, but legend has it that one of the old regulars, Carlton Rabb, now deceased, was so enamored of them that he added a clause to his will stipulating that an order of Joe Junior's fried onion rings be smuggled into his coffin before his body was laid to rest. Morris is fully aware of Joe Junior's shortcomings as a dining establishment, but among its advantages are the total absence of music, the chance to eavesdrop on stimulating, often hilarious conversations, the broad spectrum of its clientele (from homeless beggars to wealthy home owners), and, most important, the role it plays in his memory. Joe Junior's was the site of the ritual Saturday breakfast, the place where he brought the boys every week throughout their childhoods, the quiet Saturday mornings when the three of them would tiptoe out of the apartment as Willa caught an extra hour or two of sleep, and to sit in this place now, this drab little restaurant on the corner of Sixth Avenue and Twelfth Street, is to return to those countless Saturdays of long ago and remember the Eden he once lived in.

Bobby lost interest in coming here when he was thirteen (the boy liked his sleep), but Miles carried on the tradition all the way to the end of high school. Not every Saturday morning, of course, at least not after he turned seven and started playing in the local kids' baseball league, but often enough to feel that the room is still saturated with his presence. Such a bright young thing, such an earnest young thing, so little laughter in that somber face of his, but just below the surface a frolicking sort of inner mirth, and the pleasure he took in the various teams they made up together with the names of real players, the all-body-parts team, for example, with a lineup of Bill Hands, Barry Foote, Rollie Fingers, Elroy Face, Ed Head, and Walt "No-Neck" Williams, along with substitutes such as Tony Armas (Arm) and Jerry Hairston (Hair), or the all-finance team, consisting of Dave Cash, Don Money, Bobby Bonds, Barry Bonds, Ernie Banks, Elmer Pence, Bill Pounds, and Wes Stock. Yes, Miles loved that nonsense when he was a boy, and when laughter did come out of him, it was propulsive and unstoppable, red-faced, breathless, as if an unseen phantom were tickling him all over his body. But most often the breakfasts were subdued affairs, quiet conversations about his classmates, his aversion to his piano lessons (he eventually quit), his disagreements with Bobby, his homework, the books he was reading, the fortunes of the Mets and football Giants, the finer points of pitching. Of all the regrets Morris has accumulated over the course of his life, there is the lingering sadness that his father did not live long enough to know his grandson, but if he had, and if by some miracle he had lasted into the boy's teens, there would have been the happiness of seeing Miles pitch, the right-handed version of his young self, living proof that all the hours he had spent teaching his son how to throw properly had not been wasted, that even if Morris never developed much of an arm himself, he had passed on his father's lessons to his own son, and until Miles quit in his junior year, the results had been promising—no, more than promising—excellent. Pitching was the ideal position for him. Solitude and strength, concentration and will, the lone wolf standing in the middle of the infield, carrying the entire game on his back. It was all fastballs and changeups back then, two pitches and endless work on his delivery, the fluid motion, the arm whipping forward at the same angle every time, the coiled right leg pushing off the rubber until the moment of release, but no curveballs or sliders, at sixteen he was still growing, and young arms can be ruined by the unnatural torque required to snap off a good breaking ball. He was disappointed, yes, but he never blamed Miles for quitting when he did. The self-flagellating grief of surviving Bobby had demanded a sacrifice of some kind, and so he gave up the thing he loved doing most at that point in his life. But willing yourself out of something is not the same as renouncing it in your heart. Four years ago, when Bing called to report the arrival of another letter—from Albany, California, just outside Berkeley—he mentioned that Miles was pitching for a team in a Bay Area amateur league, competing against ex–college players who hadn't been good enough or interested enough to turn pro, but serious competition for all that, and he was holding his own, Miles said, winning twice as many games as he lost, and he had finally taught himself how to throw a curveball. He went on to say that the San Francisco Giants were sponsoring an open tryout later that month, and his teammates were urging him to go, recommending that he lie about his age and tell them he was nineteen, not twenty-four, but he wasn't going to do it. Imagine him signing a contract to play in the low minor leagues, he said. Preposterous.

The Can Man is thinking, remembering, sifting through the countless Saturday mornings he ate breakfast here with the boy, and now, as he lifts his arm and asks for the check, just a minute or two before he will be stepping out into the cold air again, he stumbles across something that hasn't occurred to him in years, an unearthed shard, a shining piece of glass to put in his pocket and take home with him. Miles was ten or eleven. It was one of the first times they came here without Bobby, just the two of them sitting across from each other in one of the booths, perhaps this booth, perhaps another, he can't recall which one now, and the boy had brought along a book report he had written for his fifth- or sixth-grade class, no, not a report exactly, a short paper of six or seven hundred words, an analysis of the book the teacher had assigned to the pupils, the book they had been reading and discussing for the past several weeks, and now each child had to produce a paper, an interpretation of the novel they had all finished, *To Kill a Mockingbird,* a sweet book, Morris felt, a good book for children of that age, and the boy wanted his father to read over what he had done. The Can Man remembers how tense the boy looked as he removed the three sheets of paper, the four sheets of paper from his backpack, awaiting his father's judgment on what he had written, his first attempt at literary criticism, his first grown-up assignment, and from the look in the boy's eyes, his father understood how much work and thought had gone into this little piece of writing. The paper was about wounds. The father of the two children, the lawyer, is blind in one eye, the boy wrote, and the black man he defends against the false charge of rape has a withered arm, and late in the book, when the lawyer's son falls out of the tree, he breaks his arm, the same arm as the withered arm of the innocent black man, left or right, the Can Man no longer remembers, and the point of all this, the young Miles wrote, is that wounds are an essential part of life, and until you are wounded in some way, you cannot become a man. His father wondered how it was possible for a ten- or eleven-year-old child to read a book so carefully, to pull together such disparate, unemphasized elements of a story and see a pattern develop over the course of hundreds of pages, to hear the repeated notes, notes so easily lost in the whirl of fugues and cadenzas that form the totality of a book, and not only was he impressed by the mind that had paid such close attention to the smallest details of the novel, he was impressed by the heart that had come up with such a profound conclusion. Until you are wounded, you cannot become a man. He told the boy he had done a superior job, that most readers twice or three times his age could never have written anything half as good as this, and only a person with a great soul could have thought about the book in this way. He was very moved, he said to his son that morning seventeen or eighteen years ago, and the fact is that he is still moved by the thoughts expressed in that short paper, and as he collects his change from the cashier and walks out into the cold, he goes on thinking about these thoughts, and just before he reaches his house, the Can Man stops and says to himself: When?

4

She has come to New York to act in Samuel Beckett's *Happy Days*. She will be Winnie, the woman buried up to her waist in Act I and then buried up to her neck in Act II, and the challenge in front of her, the formidable challenge will be to hold forth within these constricted emplacements for an hour and a half, delivering what amounts to a sixty-page monologue, with occasional interruptions from the hapless, mostly invisible Willie, and she can think of no theatrical role she has played in the past, neither Nora nor Miss Julie, neither Blanche nor Desdemona, that is more demanding than this one. But she loves Winnie, she responds deeply to the combination of pathos, comedy, and terror in the play, and even if Beckett is inordinately difficult, cerebral, at times obscure, the language is so clean and precise, so gorgeous in its simplicity, that it gives her physical pleasure to feel the words coming out of her mouth. Tongue, palate, lips, and throat are all in harmony as she pronounces Winnie's long, halting rambles, and now that she has finally mastered and memorized the text, the rehearsals have been steadily improving, and when the previews begin ten days from now, she hopes she will be ready to give the performance she hopes to give. Tony Gilbert has been hard on her, and every time the young director cuts her off for making the wrong gesture or not pausing long enough between phrases, she consoles herself with the thought that he begged her to come to New York to play Winnie, that again and again he has told her that no actress alive could do a better job in this role.

He has been hard on her, yes, but the play is hard, and she has worked hard because of it, even letting her body go to hell in order to put on the twenty extra pounds she felt she needed to become Winnie, to inhabit Winnie (*About fifty, well preserved, blond for preference, plump, arms and shoulders bare, low bodice, big bosom . . .*), and she has done much homework in preparation, reading up on Beckett, studying his correspondence with Alan Schneider, the original director of the play, and she now knows that a *bumper* is a brimming glass, that *bast* is a fibrous twine used by gardeners, that the words Winnie speaks at the beginning of Act II, *Hail, holy light,* are a quotation from Book III of *Paradise Lost,* that *beechen green* comes from *Ode to a Nightingale,* and that *bird of dawning* comes from *Hamlet.* What world the play is set in has never been clear to her, a world without darkness, a world of hot, unending light, a sort of purgatory, perhaps, a post-human wilderness of ever-diminishing possibilities, ever-diminishing movement, but she also suspects that this world might be none other than the stage she will be performing on, and even if Winnie is essentially alone, talking to herself and Willie, she is also aware that she is in the presence of others, that the audience is out there in the dark. *Someone is looking at me still. Caring for me still. That is what I find so wonderful. Eyes on my eyes.* She can understand this. Her entire life has been about this, only this.

It is the third day of the year, the evening of Saturday, January third, and Morris is having dinner with Mary-Lee and Korngold at the Odeon, not far from the Tribeca loft they have rented for their four-month stay in New York. They arrived in the city just as he was preparing to leave for England, and although they have talked on the telephone several times in the past few months, they have not seen each other in a long while, not since 2007, he thinks, perhaps even 2006. Mary-Lee has just turned fifty-four, and their brief, disputatious marriage is no more than a dim memory now. He bears her no grudge or ill will, is in fact quite fond of her, but she is still a conundrum to him, a puzzling mixture of warmth and distance, keen intelligence hidden behind brash, rough-and-tumble manners, by turns good-hearted and selfish, droll and boring (she tends to go on at times), vain and utterly indifferent to herself. Witness the increased poundage for her new role. She has always taken pride in her slim, well-maintained figure, has fretted over the fat content of every morsel of food that enters her mouth, has made a religion of eating *properly,* but now, for the sake of her work, she has calmly tossed her diet to the four winds. Morris is intrigued by this fuller, more ample version of his ex-wife, and he tells her that she is looking beautiful, to which she responds, laughing and then puffing out her cheeks: A big, beautiful hippo. But she *is* beautiful, he thinks, still beautiful even now, and unlike most actresses of her generation, she has not marred her face with cosmetic surgery or wrinkle-removing injections, for the simple reason that she intends to go on working as long as she can, deep into her old age if possible, and, as she once jokingly put it to him, If all the sixty-year-old broads come across as bizarre-looking thirty-year-olds, who's going to be left to play the mothers and grandmothers?

She has been acting steadily for a long time now, ever since she was in her early twenties, and there is not a person in the crowded restaurant who does not know who she is, glance after glance is directed toward their table, *eyes are on her eyes,* but she pretends to pay no attention, she is used to this kind of thing, but Morris senses that she is secretly enjoying it, that silent adulation of this sort is a boon that never grows old. Not many actors manage to keep it going for thirty years, especially women, especially women who act in films, but Mary-Lee has been smart and flexible, willing to reinvent herself at each step along the way. Even during the early run of successful films that got her started, she would take time off to work in plays, always good plays, the best plays, the Bard and his modern heirs, Ibsen, Chekhov, Williams, Albee, and then, when she was in her mid-thirties and the big studios stopped making films for grown-ups, she didn't hesitate to accept parts in small, low-budget independent films (many of them produced by Korngold), and then, more years down the road, when she reached the point at which she was beginning to play mothers, she jumped into television, starring in a weekly series called *Martha Kane, Attorney-at-Law,* something Morris and Willa actually watched from time to time, and during the five-year span of that show she attracted an audience in the millions and grew ever more popular, which is very popular indeed. Drama and comedy, good girls and bad girls, feisty secretaries and drug-addicted hookers, wives, lovers, and mistresses, a singer and a painter, an undercover cop and the mayor of a large city, she has played all kinds of roles in all kinds of films, many of them quite decent, a few clumsy stinkers, but no mediocre performances that Morris can recall, with a number of memorable turns that have touched him in the same way he was touched when he first saw her as Cordelia in 1978. He is glad she is doing the Beckett, he thinks she is wise to have accepted such a daunting role, and as he looks at her across the table now, he wonders how this attractive but wholly ordinary woman, this woman with her fluctuating moods and vulgar passion for dirty jokes, has it in her to transform herself into so many distinct and totally different characters, to make one feel she carries all humanity inside her. Does it require an act of courage to stand up and turn your guts inside out before an audience of strangers, or is it a compulsion, a need to be looked at, a reckless lack of inhibition that drives a person to do what she does? He has never been able to put his finger on the line that separates life from art. Renzo is the same as Mary-Lee, they are both prisoners of what they do, for years both have been plunging forward from one project to the next, both have produced lasting works of art, and yet their lives have been a bollix, both divorced twice, both with a tremendous talent for self-pity, both ultimately inaccessible to others—not failed human beings, exactly, but not successful ones either. Damaged souls. The walking wounded, opening their veins and bleeding in public.

He finds it odd to be with her now, sitting across from his ex-wife and her husband, sitting in yet another booth in yet another New York restaurant, odd because the love he once felt for her is entirely gone, and he knows that Korngold is a far better husband for her than he ever could have been, and she is lucky to have a man like this to take care of her, to prop her up whenever she begins to stagger, to give her the advice she has been listening to and following for years, to love her in a way that has tamped down her anxieties and frantic distempers, whereas he, Morris, was never up to the task of loving her in the way she needed to be loved, could never give her advice about her career, could never prop her up or understand what was whirling about in that beautiful head of hers. She is so much better than she was thirty years ago, and he gives Korngold all the credit, he admires him for having rescued her after two bad marriages, for throwing out the vodka bottles and the pill bottles she began collecting after the second divorce, for sticking by her through what must have been some harrowing moments, and beyond what Korngold has done for Mary-Lee, Morris admires him pure and simple, in and of himself, not just because he was good to his son during the years when the boy was still visible, not just because he has anguished over Miles's disappearance as a true member of the family, but because he discovered many years ago that Simon Korngold is a thoroughly likable person, and what Morris likes most about him is the fact that he never complains. Everyone is suffering because of the crash, the slump, whatever word people are using to talk about the new depression, book publishers not excepted, of course, but Simon is in much worse shape than he is, the independent film business has been destroyed, production companies and distributors are folding up like collapsible chairs every day of the week, and it has been two years now since he last put a movie together, which means that he unofficially retired this fall, accepting a job to teach film courses at UCLA instead of making films, but he isn't bitter about it, or at least he shows no bitterness, and the only thing he says to account for what has happened to him is to mention that he is fifty-eight years old and that independent film producing is a young person's job. The grinding search for money can crush the spirit out of you unless you're made of steel, he says, and the tall and short of it is that he isn't made of steel anymore.

But that comes later. The talk about Winnie and *Hail, holy light* and men of steel does not begin until after they have talked about why Mary-Lee called Morris three hours ago and asked him to dinner on such short notice. There is news. That is the first article on the agenda, and moments after they enter the restaurant and take their seats at the table, Mary-Lee tells him about the message she found on her answering machine at four o'clock this afternoon.

It was Miles, she says. I recognized his voice.

His voice, Morris says. You mean he didn't give his name?

No. Only the message—a short, confusing message. As follows, in its entirety. *Um.* Long pause. *Sorry.* Long pause. *I'll call back.*

Are you sure it was Miles?

Positive.

Korngold says: I'm still trying to figure out what *sorry* means. Sorry for calling? Sorry because he was too flustered to leave a proper message? Sorry for everything he's done?

Impossible to say, Morris replies, but I would tend to go with flustered.

Something's going to happen, Mary-Lee says. Very soon. Any day now.

I talked to Bing this morning, Morris says, just to check in and see if everything is all right. He told me Miles has a girlfriend, a young Cuban girl from Florida, and that she's been in New York for the past week or so visiting him. I think she went back today. According to Bing, Miles was planning to get in touch with us as soon as she left. That would explain the message.

But why call me and not you? Mary-Lee asks.

Because Miles thinks I'm still in England and won't be reachable until Monday.

And how does he know that? Korngold says.

Apparently, he called my office two or three weeks ago and was told I'd be back at work on the fifth. That's what Bing reported, in any case, and I don't see why the boy would lie to him.

We owe Bing Nathan a lot, Korngold says.

We owe him everything, Morris says. Try to imagine these past seven years without him.

We should do something for him, Mary-Lee says. Write him a check, send him on a world cruise, something.

I've tried, Morris says, but he won't take any money from me. He was very insulted the first time I offered, and even more insulted the second time. He says: You don't accept money for acting like a human being. A young man with principles. I can respect that.

What else? Mary-Lee asks. Any word on how Miles is doing?

Not much, Morris answers. Bing says he mostly keeps to himself, but the other people in the house like him and he gets on well with them. Quiet, as usual. A bit low, as usual, but then he perked up when the girl came.

And now she's gone, Mary-Lee says, and he's left a message on my machine saying he'll call me back. I don't know what I'm going to do when I see him. Slap him across the face—or throw my arms around him and kiss him?

Do both, Morris says. The slap first, and then the kiss.

They stop talking about Miles after that and move on to *Happy Days,* the future of independent films, the strange death of Steve Cochran, the advantages and disadvantages of living in New York, Mary-Lee's new rotundity (which inspires the puffed-out cheeks and the beautiful-hippo comment), the forthcoming novels from Heller Books, and Willa, needless to say Willa, it is the polite question that must be asked, but Morris has no desire to tell them the truth, no desire to unburden himself and talk about his fear that he might be losing her, that he has already lost her, and so he says that Willa is flourishing, in top form, that his trip to England was like a second honeymoon, and he is hard-pressed to recall a time when he ever felt happier. His answer comes and goes in just a few seconds, and then they move on to other things, other digressions, other chatter about any number of relevant and irrelevant subjects, but Willa is on his mind now, he can't shake free of her, and watching Korngold and his ex-wife across the table, the comfort and amiability of their interactions, the furtive, unspoken complicity that exists between them, he understands how lonely he is, how lonely he has become, and now that the dinner is nearing its conclusion, he dreads returning to the empty apartment on Downing Street. Mary-Lee has drunk enough wine to be in one of those expansive, bountiful moods of hers, and when the three of them go outside to part company, she opens her arms and says to him, Give us a hug, Morris. A nice long squeeze for the fat old woman. He embraces the bulky winter overcoat hard enough to feel the flesh inside it, the body of the mother of his son, and as he does so, she holds on to him just as tightly, and then, with her left hand, she begins patting the back of his head, as if to tell him not to worry anymore, the dark time will soon be over, and all will be forgiven.

He walks back to Downing Street in the cold, his red scarf wrapped around his neck, hands thrust deep into the pockets of his coat, and the wind shooting off the Hudson is especially strong tonight as he heads up Varick toward the West Village, but he doesn't stop to flag down a taxi, he wants to walk this evening, the rhythm of his steps calms him in the way that music sometimes calms him, in the way children can be calmed when their parents rock them to sleep. It is ten o'clock, not late, several hours to go before he will be ready for sleep himself, and as he unlocks the door of the apartment, he imagines he will settle into the comfortable chair in the living room and spend the last hours of the day reading a book, but which book, he asks himself, which book from all the thousands crammed onto the shelves of the two floors of the duplex, perhaps the Beckett play if he can find it, he thinks, the one Mary-Lee is doing now, the one they talked about tonight, or if not that play perhaps another play by Shakespeare, the little project he has taken on in Willa's absence, rereading all of Shakespeare, the words that have filled the hours between work and sleep these past months, and he is up to *The Tempest* now, he believes, or perhaps *The Winter's Tale,* and if reading is too much for him tonight, if his thoughts are too jumbled with Miles and Mary-Lee and Willa for him to concentrate on the words, he will watch a film on television, the one sedative that can always be counted on, the tranquilizing flicker of images, voices, music, the pull of the stories, always the stories, the thousands of stories, the millions of stories, and yet one never tires of them, there is always room in the brain for another story, another book, another film, and after pouring himself a scotch in the kitchen, he walks into the living room thinking film, he will opt for a film if anything watchable is playing tonight.

Before he can sit down in the comfortable chair and switch on the TV, however, the telephone starts ringing in the kitchen, and so he turns around and walks back into the kitchen to answer it, puzzled by the lateness of the call, wondering who could possibly want to talk to him at ten-thirty on a Saturday night. His first thought is Miles, Miles following up his call to his mother with a call to his father, but no, that couldn't be it, Miles won't be calling him until Monday at the earliest, unless he supposes, perhaps, that his father has already returned from England and is spending the weekend at home, or, if not that, perhaps he simply wants to leave a message on the machine, in the same way he left a message on his mother's machine this afternoon.

It is Willa, calling from Exeter at three-thirty in the morning, Willa sobbing and in distress, saying that she is cracking apart, that her world is in ruins, that she no longer wants to be alive. Her tears are relentless, and the voice talking through those tears is barely audible, high-pitched, the voice of a child, and it is a true collapse, he tells himself, a person beyond anger, beyond hope, a person entirely spent, miserable, miserable, pulverized by the weight of the world, a sadness as heavy as the weight of the world. He doesn't know what to do except talk to her in the most comforting voice he can manage, to tell her he loves her, that he will be on the early plane to London tomorrow morning, that she must hold on until he gets there, less than twenty-four hours, just one more day, and he reminds her of the breakdown about a year after Bobby's death, the same tears, the same weakened voice, the same words, and she pulled through that crisis then and will pull through this crisis now, trust him, he knows what he is talking about, he will take care of her, he will always take care of her, and she mustn't blame herself for things that aren't her fault. They talk for an hour, for two hours, and eventually the tears subside, eventually she begins to calm down, but just when he is beginning to feel it will be safe to hang up the phone, the tears begin again. She needs him so much, she says, she can't survive without him, she has been so horrible to him, so mean and vindictive and cruel, she has become a horrible person, a monster, and she hates herself now, she can never forgive herself, and again he tries to soothe her, telling her that she must go to sleep now, that she is exhausted and must go to sleep, that he will be there with her tomorrow, and finally, finally, she promises that she will go to bed, and even if she can't sleep, she promises not to do anything stupid, she will behave herself, she promises. They hang up at last, and before another night falls in New York City, Morris Heller is back in England, traveling between London and Exeter to see his wife.

ALL

Miles Heller

It was the best thing that could have happened to him, it was the worst thing that could have happened to him. Eleven days with Pilar in New York, and then the agony of putting her on the bus and sending her back to Florida.

One thing is certain, however. He loves her more than any other person on this earth, and he will go on loving her until the day he stops breathing.

The joy of looking at her face again, the joy of holding her again, the joy of listening to her laugh again, the joy of hearing her voice again, the joy of watching her eat again, the joy of looking at her hands again, the joy of looking at her naked body again, the joy of touching her naked body again, the joy of kissing her naked body again, the joy of watching her frown again, the joy of watching her brush her hair again, the joy of watching her paint her nails again, the joy of standing in the shower with her again, the joy of talking to her about books again, the joy of watching her eyes fill up with tears again, the joy of watching her walk again, the joy of listening to her insult Angela again, the joy of reading out loud to her again, the joy of listening to her burp again, the joy of watching her brush her teeth again, the joy of undressing her again, the joy of putting his mouth against her mouth again, the joy of looking at her neck again, the joy of walking down the street with her again, the joy of putting his arm around her shoulders again, the joy of licking her breasts again, the joy of entering her body again, the joy of waking up beside her again, the joy of discussing math with her again, the joy of buying clothes for her again, the joy of giving and receiving back rubs again, the joy of talking about the future again, the joy of living in the present with her again, the joy of being told she loves him again, the joy of telling her he loves her again, the joy of living under the gaze of her fierce dark eyes again, and then the agony of watching her board the bus at the Port Authority terminal on the afternoon of January third with the certain knowledge that it will not be until April, more than three months from now, that he will have a chance to be with her again.

It was her first trip to New York, the only time she has ever set foot outside the state of Florida, her maiden voyage to the land of winter. Miami is the one large city she is familiar with, but Miami is not large when compared to New York, and he hoped she wouldn't feel intimidated by the jangle and immensity of the place, that she wouldn't be put off by the noise and the dirt, the crowded subway cars, the bad weather. He imagined he would have to lead her into it cautiously, like someone walking into a cold lake with a young swimmer, giving her time to adjust to the frigid water, letting her tell him when she was ready to go in up to her waist, up to her neck, and if and when she wanted to put her head under. Now that she is gone, he cannot fathom why he felt so timid on her behalf, why or how he could have underestimated her resolve. Pilar ran into the lake with flapping arms, whooping excitedly as the cold water hit her bare skin, and seconds after that she was taking the plunge, dunking her head below the surface and gliding along as smoothly as a practiced veteran. The little one had done her homework. During the long trek up the Atlantic coast, she digested the contents of three guidebooks and a history of New York, and by the time the bus pulled into the terminal, she had already drawn up a list of the places she wanted to see, the things she wanted to do. Nor had she neglected his advice to prepare herself for the low temperatures and possible storms. She had gone out and bought a pair of snow boots, a couple of warm sweaters, a scarf, woolen gloves, and a snappy green down parka with a fur-fringed hood. She was Nanook of the North, he said, his intrepid Eskimo girl armed to beat back the assaults of the harshest climes, and yes, she looked adorable in that thing, and again and again he told her the Cuban-American-Eskimo look was destined to stay in fashion for years to come.

They went to the top of the Empire State Building, they walked through the marble halls of the Public Library at Fifth Avenue and Forty-second Street, they visited Ground Zero, they spent one day going from the Metropolitan Museum to the Frick Collection to MoMA, he bought her a dress and a pair of shoes at Macy's, they walked across the Brooklyn Bridge, they ate oysters at the Oyster Bar in Grand Central Station, they watched the ice skaters at Rockefeller Center, and then, on the seventh day of her visit, they rode the subway uptown to 116th Street and Broadway and checked out the Barnard College campus, the Columbia campus across the street, the various seminaries and music academies spread across Morningside Heights, and he said to her, Look, all this is possible for you now, you're as good as any of the people studying here, and when they send you your letter of acceptance this spring, which I'm sure they will, there's a better than eighty percent chance they're going to want you, think long and hard before you decide to stay in Florida, all right? He wasn't telling her what to do, he was merely asking her to consider the matter carefully, to weigh the consequences of accepting or turning down what in all likelihood would be offered to her, and for once Pilar was silent, not willing to share her thoughts with him, and he didn't press her to say anything, for it was clear from the look in her eyes that she was already pondering this very question, trying to project herself into the future, trying to imagine what going to college in New York would mean to her or not mean to her, and as they walked among the deserted grounds and studied the façades of the buildings, he felt as if she were changing in front of him, growing older in front of him, and he suddenly understood what she would be like ten years from now, twenty years from now, Pilar in the full vigor of her evolving womanhood, Pilar all grown into herself and yet still walking with the shadow of the pensive girl walking beside him now, the young woman walking beside him now.

He wishes they could have been alone for the full eleven days, living and sleeping in a room or an apartment not shared with anyone else, but the only option available to them was the house in Sunset Park. A hotel would have been perfect, but he didn't have the money for a hotel, and besides, there was the question of Pilar's age, and even if he could have afforded to put them up in style, there was the same risk in New York as there was in Florida, and he wasn't willing to take it. About a week before Christmas, he and Ellen discussed the possibility of borrowing the keys to one of the empty apartments on her firm's rental list, but little by little they talked themselves out of that absurd idea. Not only could Ellen have found herself in serious trouble, with instant dismissal from her job just one of the many gruesome things that could happen to her, but when they pictured what it would be like to hole up in a place without furniture, without blinds or curtains, without electricity, without a bed to sleep in, they both realized that staying in the shabby little house across from Green-Wood Cemetery would be far better.

Pilar knows they are squatting there illegally, and she doesn't approve. Not only is it wrong to break the law, she says, but she is frightened that something will happen to him, something bad, something irreversible, and how ironic it would be, she says (they have had this conversation on the phone more than once), if he left Florida to avoid going to jail only to land in another jail up north. But he won't go to jail for squatting, he tells her, the worst that can happen is an untimely eviction, and she mustn't forget that living there is only a stopgap arrangement for him, and once he heads back to Florida on May twenty-second, his little adventure in trespassing will be over. At this point in the conversation, Pilar invariably starts talking about Angela, cursing her greedy, no-good sister for having done this to them, the injustice of it all, the sickness of it all, and now she lives in constant fear that something will happen to him, and Angela is entirely to blame for it.

Because the house frightened her, she wanted to spend as little time there as possible. For very different reasons, he felt the same way, which meant they were out and about for the better part of her visit, mostly in Manhattan, mostly eating dinner in restaurants, cheap restaurants so as not to waste their money, diners and pizzerias and Chinese dumpling houses, and ninety percent of the time they spent in the house they were in his room, either making love or sleeping. Still, there were the unavoidable encounters with the others, the breakfasts in the morning, the accidental meetings in front of the bathroom door, the night when they returned to the house around ten o'clock and Alice asked them up to her room to watch a movie, which she described as her *obsession of the moment,* a film called *The Best Years of Our Lives,* since she wanted to know what they thought of it (he gave it a B-plus overall and an A for photography, Pilar gave it an A for everything), but his objective was to keep her contacts with the rest of the household to a minimum. It wasn't that they weren't friendly to her, but he had watched their faces when he introduced her to them on the first evening, and one by one he had noted the brief instant of shock when they understood how young she was, and he felt reluctant to expose her to situations in which she could be patronized by them, talked down to, hurt. It might have been different if she were taller than five feet four, if her breasts were larger, if her hips were wider, but Pilar must have struck them as a tiny, childlike thing, just as she had struck him the first time he saw her, and there was no point in trying to undo their initial impressions of her. The visit was going to be too short for that, and he wanted her to himself anyway. To be fair to them, however, nothing unpleasant happened. Alice had agreed to cook all the dinners while Pilar was in town, and therefore it was up to him to do the grocery shopping, which he took care of first thing every morning, and while he was out at the store, Alice and Pilar had a number of one-on-one talks at the kitchen table. It didn't take Alice long to figure out how intelligent Pilar was, and later on, after they had left the house, Pilar would tell him how impressed she was by Alice, how she admired the work she was doing, how much she liked her. But Alice was the only one who actively reached out to Pilar. Bing seemed nonplussed, a bit bowled over, befuddled by her presence, and by the second day he had adopted a jocular persona to communicate with her (Bing trying to be funny), talking in the voice of a movie cowboy, addressing her as Miss Pilar and coming out with such original remarks as Howdy there, Miss Pilar, and how's the purdy lady this mornin'? Ellen was polite but distant, and the one time Jake was there, he ignored her.

She is coping with her altered circumstances in Florida, but this is the first time she has lived alone, and there have been some difficult days, dark days when she has had to struggle against the urge to let go and cry for hours on end. She is still on good terms with Teresa and Maria, but the rift with Angela is absolute and forever, and she avoids going to the house when her oldest sister will be there. Maria continues to date Eddie Martinez, and Teresa's husband, Carlos, is coming to the end of his tour of duty and is scheduled to be rotated out of Iraq in March. She is bored with school, she hates going there every morning, and it requires an enormous effort of will not to cut classes, not to skip whole days, but she forges on because she doesn't want to disappoint him. She finds the other students to be idiots, especially the boys, and she has only two or three friends, just two or three girls in her A.P. English class who seem worth talking to. She has been careful with the money, spending as little as she can, and the only unforeseen expense came just before her trip to New York, when she had to replace the carburetor and spark plugs in the Toyota. She is still a pathetic cook, but a little less pathetic than before, and she hasn't lost or gained any weight, which must mean she is on top of things in spite of her shortcomings. Lots of fruits and vegetables, rice and beans, an occasional chicken cutlet or hamburger (both are easy to cook), and a real breakfast every morning—melon, plain yogurt and berries, Special K. It's been a strange time, she said to him on her last morning in

New York, the strangest time she has ever known, and she wishes the days would pass more quickly down there, that they wouldn't drag so much, but each turn of the clock creeps along like a tired fat man walking up a hundred flights of stairs, and now that she has to go back, it's bound to be even worse, because at least there was New York to look forward to after he left, for three weeks that was the thing that kept her going, but now they are looking at three months, she can barely wrap her mind around that thought, three months before she gets to see him again, and it will be like living in limbo, like going on a vacation in hell, and all because of a stupid date on her birth certificate, an arbitrary number, an irrational number that means nothing to anyone.

All during her visit, he was tempted to tell her the truth about himself, to open up to her and give the full story about everything—his parents and Bobby, his childhood in New York, the three years at Brown, the seven and a half years of crazed, self-inflicted exile, everything. On the morning they walked around the Village, they went past Saint Vincent's, the hospital where he was born, went past P.S. 41, the school he attended as a boy, went past the house on Downing Street, the place where his father and stepmother still live, and then they ate lunch at Joe Junior's, the family canteen for the first twenty years of his life, a whole morning and part of an afternoon in the very heart of his old stomping grounds, and that was the day when he came closest to doing it, but desperate as he was to tell her these things about himself, he held back and told her nothing. It wasn't a question of fear. He could have told her then, but he didn't want to spoil the good time they were having together. Pilar was struggling down in Florida, the trip to New York had reanimated her and brought her back to her hopeful, spirited self, and it simply wasn't the moment to confess his lies to her, to pull her down into the bleakness of the Heller family chronicle. He will do it when the time is right, and that time will come only after he has talked to his father and mother, only after he has seen his father and mother, only after he has asked them to take him back into their lives. He is ready to face them now, ready to confront the terrible thing he did to them, and Pilar is solely responsible for giving him the courage to do this—because in order to be worthy of Pilar, he must have this courage.

She left for Florida on the third, two days ago. Wretched farewells, the agony of looking at her face through the window, and then the bus drove down the ramp and disappeared. He took the subway back to Sunset Park, and the moment he walked into his room, he sat down on the bed, took out his cell phone, and called his mother. He wouldn't be able to talk to his father until Monday, but he had to do something now, watching the bus drive down the ramp had made it impossible not to do something, and if his father wasn't available, then he would begin with his mother. He was about to call the theater first, thinking that would be the best way to get hold of her, but then it occurred to him that perhaps her cell phone number was the same one she had seven years ago. He called to find out, and there was her voice telling the world that she would be in New York for the next four months, and if you wanted to get in touch with her there, this was the number. It was a Saturday afternoon, a cold Saturday afternoon in early January, and he assumed she would be at home on a crummy day like this, keeping her toes warm and doing crossword puzzles on the sofa, and when he called the New York number, he was fully confident she would pick up on the second or third ring. But she didn't. The telephone rang four times, and then a message came on, another message with her voice, telling the caller that she was out and please wait for the beep. He was so flummoxed by this unexpected turn that he suddenly went blank, and all he could think to say was: *Um.* Long pause. *Sorry.* Long pause. *I'll call back.*

He decided to reverse course, return to his original plan, and talk to his father first.

It is Monday morning now, January fifth, and he has just called his father's office, only to be told that his father flew back to England yesterday on urgent business. He asks when Mr. Heller will be coming back to New York. It isn't clear, the voice tells him. Call at the end of the week. There might be some news then.

Nine hours later, he calls his mother's New York number again. This time she is in. This time she picks up the phone and answers it.

Ellen Brice

Two trumps one. One is better than four. Three can be too many or just enough. Five is taking it too far. Six is delirium.

She is advancing now, traveling deeper and deeper into the netherworld of her own nothingness, the place in her that coincides with everything she is not. The sky above her is gray or blue or white, sometimes yellow or red, at times purple. The earth below her is green or brown. Her body stands at the juncture of earth and sky, and it belongs to her and no one else. Her thoughts belong to her. Her desires belong to her. Stranded in the realm of the one, she conjures up the two and three and four and five. Sometimes the six. Sometimes even the sixty.

After the unfortunate scene with Alice last month, she understood that she would have to carry on alone. Because of her job, she is too busy to enroll in a class, to waste precious hours riding on subways to and from Pratt or Cooper Union or SVA. The work is what counts, and if she intends to make any progress, she must work continually, with or without a teacher, with or without live models, for the essence of the work resides in her hand, and whenever she manages to lift herself out of herself and put her mind in abeyance, she can will that hand to see. Experiment has taught her that wine helps. A couple of glasses of wine to make her forget who she is, and then she can keep on going for hours, often far into the night.

The human body is strange and flawed and unpredictable. The human body has many secrets, and it does not divulge them to anyone, except those who have learned to wait. The human body has ears. The human body has hands. The human body is created inside another human body, and the human being who emerges from that other human body is necessarily small and weak and helpless. The human body is created in the image of God. The human body has feet. The human body has eyes. The human body is multitudinous in its forms, its manifestations, its degrees of size and shape and color, and to look at one human body is to apprehend only that human body and no other. The human body can be apprehended, but it cannot be comprehended. The human body has shoulders. The human body has knees. The human body is an object and a subject, the outside of an inside that cannot be seen. The human body grows from the small of infancy to the large of adulthood, and then it begins to die. The human body has hips. The human body has elbows. The human body lives in the mind of one who possesses a human body, and to live inside the human body possessed of the mind that perceives another human body is to live in a world of others. The human body has hair. The human body has a mouth. The human body has genitals. The human body is created out of dust, and when that human body is no more, it returns to the dust from whence it came.

She works from several different sources now: reproductions of paintings and drawings by other artists, black-and-white photographs of male and female nudes, medical photographs of babies, children, and old people, the body-length mirror she attached to the wall opposite her bed in order to have a full view of herself, porn magazines aimed at various appetites and proclivities (from cheesecake shots of women to two-sex copulations to male-male copulations to female-female copulations to threesome, foursome, and five-some copulations in all their mathematical permutations), and the small hand mirror she uses to study her own vagina. A door has opened inside her, and she has crossed the threshold into a new way of thinking. The human body is an instrument of knowledge.

There is no time for painting now. Drawing is faster and

more tactile, better suited to the urgency of her project, and she has filled sketchbook after sketchbook this past month with her attempts to break free of her old methods. For the first hour after setting to work, she warms up by concentrating on details, isolated areas of a body culled from her collection of images or found in one of the two mirrors. A page of hands. A page of eyes. A page of buttocks. A page of arms. Then she moves on to whole bodies, portraits of single figures in various poses: a naked woman standing with her back to the viewer, a naked man sitting on the floor, a naked man stretched out on a bed, a naked girl squatting on the ground and urinating, a naked woman sitting in a chair with her head thrown back as she cups her right breast in her right hand and squeezes the nipple of her left breast with her left hand. These are intimate portraits, she tells herself, not erotic drawings, human bodies doing what human bodies do when no one is watching them, and if many of the men in these single portraits have erections, that is because the average man has fifty erections and semi-erections per day—or so she has been told. Then, in the last part of the exercise, she brings these figures together. A naked woman holding a naked infant in her arms. A naked man kissing the neck of a naked woman. An old naked man and an old naked woman sitting on a bed with their arms around each other. A naked woman kissing a naked man's penis. Two trumps one, followed by the mystery of three: three naked women; two naked women and one naked man; one naked woman and two naked men; three naked men. The porn magazines are quite explicit about what goes on in these situations, and their frankness inspires her to work without fear or inhibition. Fingers have entered vaginas. Mouths have encircled erect penises. Penises have entered vaginas. Anuses have been breached. It is important to note the difference between photography and drawing, however. If one leaves nothing to the imagination, the other dwells exclusively in the realm of the imagination, and therefore her entire being is ablaze when she works on these drawings, since she never simply copies the photograph she is looking at but uses it to imagine a new scene of her own invention. She is sometimes aroused by what her pencil does to the page in front of her, aroused because of the pictures bubbling in her head as she draws, which are similar to the pictures that bubble in her head when she masturbates at night, but arousal is only a minor by-product of the effort, and mostly what she feels are the demands of the work itself, the constant, ever-pressing desire to get it right. The drawings are rough and usually left unfinished. She wants her human bodies to convey the miraculous strangeness of being alive—no more than that, as much as all that. She doesn't concern herself with the idea of beauty. Beauty can take care of itself.

Two weeks ago, there was a heartening development, something unexpected that is still in the process of playing itself out. Several days before the girl from Florida came to Brooklyn and destroyed her hopes of ever conquering Miles, Bing asked to see her new work. She took him upstairs to her bedroom after dinner, trepidation mounting in her with each step they climbed, certain he would laugh at her as he casually flipped through the sketchbooks and then dismiss her with a polite smile and a pat on the shoulder, but she felt she had to risk this potential humiliation, she was burning up inside, the drawings were consuming her now, and someone had to look at them besides herself. Normally, she would have asked Alice, but Alice had let her down that day in December when the fog had blanked out the cemetery, and even though they had long since forgiven each other for that ludicrous misunderstanding, she was afraid to ask Alice because she thought Alice would be embarrassed by the pictures, shocked by them, repulsed by them even, because good and loyal a friend as Alice has been to her, she has always been something of a stodge. Bing is more open-minded, more direct (if often crude) in discussing sexual matters, and as she walked up the stairs with him and opened the door, she realized there was a lot of sexy stuff in those drawings, pretty dirty stuff if you wanted to look at it that way, and maybe this obsession with human bodies was getting a little out of hand, maybe it showed that she was beginning to fall apart again—the first sign of another crack-up. But Bing loved the pictures, he thought they were *stupendous,* a bold, extraordinary breakthrough, and because he spontaneously jumped off the bed and kissed her after he had looked at the last drawing, she knew he wasn't lying to her.

Bing's opinion means nothing, of course. He has no understanding of visual art, no knowledge of the history of art, no ability to judge what he is seeing. When she showed him a reproduction of Courbet's *The Origin of the World,* his eyes opened wide, but when she showed him a similar image of a woman's private parts in one of her skin magazines, his eyes opened wide then too, and she felt saddened to be with someone who was so handicapped aesthetically, a man unable to tell the difference between a brave and revolutionary work of art and a piece of impoverished, run-of-the-mill smut. Nevertheless, she was encouraged by his enthusiasm, stunned by how happy she felt as she listened to him praise her. Untutored or not, Bing's response to the drawings was visceral and genuine, he was moved by what she had done, he couldn't stop talking about how honest and powerful the work was, and in all the years she had been painting and drawing, no one had ever spoken like that to her, not once.

The goodwill emanating from Bing that night made her feel confident enough to ask a question, *the* question, the one question she had not dared ask anyone since Alice turned her down last month. Would he be willing to pose for her? Working from mirrors and two-dimensional images could take her only so far, she said, but if she meant to accomplish anything with this investigation of the human figure, she would have to begin working with live models at some point, three-dimensional people, living and breathing people. Bing seemed flattered by her request, but also a little pained. We're not talking about the body beautiful here, he said. Nonsense, she replied. You embody you, and because you don't want to be anyone but you, you mustn't be afraid.

They each drank two glasses of wine, which is to say, they finished off a bottle between them, and then Bing removed his clothes and sat down in the chair by the desk as she settled onto the bed, sitting Indian-style with the sketchbook in her lap. Remarkably enough, he didn't seem afraid. Lumpy body and all, with his bulging stomach and thick thighs and hirsute chest and broad, flaccid buttocks, he sat there calmly as she drew him, showing no signs of discomfort or timidity, and ten minutes into the first sketch, when she asked him how he was doing, he said fine, he trusted her, he hadn't known how much he would enjoy being looked at in this way. The room was small, they were no more than four feet apart, and when she began drawing his penis for the first time, it occurred to her that she wasn't looking at a penis anymore but a cock, that penis was the word for the thing in the drawing, but cock was the word for the thing just four feet in front of her, and, objectively speaking, she had to admit that Bing had a handsome cock, no longer or shorter than the majority of those she had seen in her life, but thicker than most, well formed and without peculiarities or blemishes, a first-rate example of male equipment, not what they call a pencil dick (where had she heard that phrase?) but a bulky fountain pen, a substantial plug for any orifice. By the third drawing, she asked him if he would mind playing with himself for a little while so she could see what happened to him when he was hard, and he said no problem, posing for her was actually making him rather hot, and he wouldn't mind at all. By the fourth drawing, she asked him to masturbate for her, and again he willingly obliged, but just to make sure, he asked her if she wouldn't prefer taking her clothes off and letting him join her on the bed, but she said no, she would rather keep her clothes on and continue drawing, but if, at the last moment, he would like to get out of the chair, walk over to the bed, and finish off what he was doing in her mouth, she would have no objection.

There have been five more sessions since then. The same thing has happened all five times, but they are no more than brief interruptions, small gifts they bestow on each other for the space of a few minutes, and then the work goes on as before. It is a perfectly fair arrangement, she feels. Her drawings have already improved because of Bing, and she is certain that the prospect of coming in her mouth will keep him interested in posing for her, at least for now, at least for the foreseeable future, and even if she has no desire to shed her clothes for him, the contact is comforting to her, and she takes pleasure in it as well. She would rather be drawing Miles, of course, and if Miles were the one who posed for her and not Bing, she wouldn't hesitate to shed her clothes for him and let him do whatever he wanted to her, but that will never happen, she knows that now, and she mustn't let her disappointment throw her off course. Miles scares her. The power he has over her scares her as much as anything has scared her in years, and yet she can't stop herself from wanting him. But Miles wants the girl from Florida, he adores the girl from Florida, and when the girl came to Brooklyn and she saw how Miles looked at her, she knew that was the end of it. Poor Ellen, she mutters, speaking to no one in the empty room, poor Ellen Brice who always loses out to someone else, don't feel sorry for yourself, go on with your drawings, go on letting Bing come in your mouth, and sooner or later all of you will be gone from Sunset Park, this ratty little house will be torn down and forgotten, and the life you are living now will fade into oblivion, not one person will remember you were ever here, not even you, Ellen Brice, and Miles Heller will vanish from your heart, in the same way you have already vanished from his heart, have never been in his heart, have never been in anyone's heart, not even your own.

Two is the only number that counts. One defines the real, perhaps, but all the others are pure fantasy, pencil lines on a blank white page.

On Sunday, January fourth, she goes to visit her sister on the Upper West Side, and one by one she holds the naked bodies of her twin nephews, Nicholas and Bruno. Such masculine names for such tiny fellows, she thinks, just two months old and everything still before them in a world coming apart at the seams, and as she holds first the one and then the other in her arms, she is awed by the softness of their skin, the smoothness of their bodies as she presses them against her neck and cheeks, feels the young flesh in the palms of her hands and along her bare forearms, and again she remembers the phrase that has been repeating itself to her ever since it came into her head last month: the strangeness of being alive. Just think, she says to her sister, Larry puts his cock in you one night, and nine months later out come these two little men. It doesn't make any sense, does it? Her sister laughs. That's the deal, honey, she says. A few minutes of pleasure, followed by a lifetime of hard work. Then, after a short pause, she looks at Ellen and says: But no, it doesn't make any sense—no sense at all.

Riding home on the subway that evening, she thinks about her own child, the child who was never born, and wonders if that was her only chance or if a time will come when a child starts growing inside her again. She takes out her notebook and writes:

The human body cannot exist without other human bodies.

The human body needs to be touched—not just small human bodies, but large human bodies as well.

The human body has skin.

Alice Bergstrom

Every Monday, Wednesday, and Thursday she takes the subway into Manhattan and goes to her part-time job at the PEN American Center at 588 Broadway, just south of Houston Street. She started working there last summer, abandoning her post as an adjunct at Queens College because that job ate up too many hours and left her with no time for her dissertation. Remedial English and freshman English, just two classes, but fifty students writing one paper a week, and then the obligatory three private conferences with each student every semester, one hundred and fifty conferences in all, seven hundred papers to read and correct and grade, preparation for class, drawing up reading lists, inventing good assignments, the challenge of holding the students' attention, the need to dress well, the long commute out to Flushing and back, and all for an insultingly low salary with no benefits, a salary that came out to less than the minimum wage (she did the math once and calculated how much she earned by the hour), which meant that the pay she received for doing work that prevented her from doing her own work was less than she would have made as a car-wash attendant or a flipper of hamburgers. PEN doesn't pay much either, but she gives them only fifteen hours a week, her dissertation is advancing again, and she believes in the purpose of the organization, the only human rights group in the world devoted exclusively to defending writers—writers imprisoned by unjust governments, writers living under the threat of death, writers banned from publishing their work, writers in exile. P-E-N. Poets and publishers, essayists and editors, novelists. They can pay her only twelve thousand seven hundred dollars for her part-time position, but whenever she walks into the building at 588 Broadway and takes the elevator to the third floor, at least she knows she isn't wasting her time.

She was ten years old when the fatwa was declared against Salman Rushdie. She was already a committed reader then, a girl who lived in the land of books, at that point immersed in the eight novels of the Anne of Green Gables series, dreaming of becoming a writer herself one day, and then came the news about a man living in England who had published a book that angered so many people in distant parts of the world that the bearded leader of one country actually stood up and declared that the man in England should be killed for what he had written. This was incomprehensible to her. Books weren't dangerous, she said to herself, they brought only pleasure and happiness to the people who read them, they made people feel more alive and more connected to one another, and if the bearded leader of that country on the other side of the world was against the Englishman's book, all he had to do was stop reading it, put it away somewhere, and forget about it. Threatening to kill someone for writing a novel, a make-believe story set in a make-believe world, was the stupidest thing she had ever heard of. Words were harmless, with no power to hurt anyone, and even if some words were offensive to some people, words weren't knives or bullets, they were simply black marks on pieces of paper, and they couldn't kill or wound or cause any real damage. That was her response to the fatwa at ten, her naïve but earnest reaction to the absurd injustice that had been committed, and her outrage was all the more intense because it was tinged with fear, for this was the first time she had been exposed to the ugliness of brute, irrational hatred, the first time her young eyes had looked into the darkness of the world. The affair continued, of course, it went on for many years after that denunciation on Valentine's Day 1989, and she grew up with the story of Salman Rushdie—the bookstore bombings, the knife in the heart of his Japanese translator, the bullets in the back of his Norwegian publisher—the story was embedded inside her as she moved from childhood into adolescence, and the older she grew the more she understood about the danger of words, the threat to power words can represent, and in states ruled by tyrants and policemen, every writer who dares to express himself freely is at risk.

PEN's Freedom to Write Program is run by a man named Paul Fowler, a poet in his spare time, a human rights activist by profession, and when he gave Alice her job last summer, he told her that the underlying philosophy of their work was quite simple: to make a lot of noise, as much noise as possible. Paul has a full-time deputy, Linda Nicholson, a woman born on the same day as Alice, and the three of them make up the staff of the small department dedicated to the production of noise. About half of what they do is focused on international issues, the campaign to reform Article 301 of the Turkish penal code, for example, the insult law that has threatened the lives and safety of scores of writers and journalists for making critical remarks about their country, as well as the attempts to win the release of writers imprisoned in various places around the world, the Burmese writers, the Chinese writers, the Cuban writers, many of them suffering from grave medical problems because of harsh treatment and/or neglect, and by putting pressure on the various governments responsible for these violations of international law, exposing these stories to the world press, circulating petitions signed by hundreds of celebrated writers, PEN has often succeeded in embarrassing these governments into letting prisoners go, not as often as they would like, but often enough to know that these methods can work, often enough to keep on trying, and in many cases to keep on trying for years. The other half of what they do is concerned with domestic issues: the banning of books by schools and libraries, for example, or the ongoing Campaign for Core Freedoms, initiated by PEN in 2004 in response to the Patriot Act passed by the Bush administration, which has given the U.S. government unprecedented authority to monitor the activities of American citizens and collect information about their personal associations, reading habits, and opinions. In the report Alice helped Paul compose not long after starting her job, PEN is now calling for the following actions: expanding safeguards for bookstore and library records weakened by the Patriot Act; reining in the use of the National Security Letters; limiting the scope of secret surveillance programs; closing Guantánamo and all remaining secret prisons; ending torture, arbitrary detentions, and extraordinary rendition; expanding refugee resettlement programs for endangered Iraqi writers. On the day she was hired, Paul and Linda told her not to be alarmed by the clicking sounds she would hear when she used the phone. The lines at PEN were tapped, and both the U.S. and Chinese governments had hacked into their computers.

It is the first Monday of the new year, January fifth, and she has just traveled into Manhattan to begin another five-hour stint at PEN headquarters. She will be working from nine in the morning until two o'clock today, at which point she will return to Sunset Park and put in another few hours on her dissertation, forcing herself to sit at her desk until six-thirty, trying to eke out another paragraph or two on *The Best Years of Our Lives.* Six-thirty is when she and Miles arranged to meet in the kitchen to start preparing dinner. They will be cooking together for the first time since Pilar went back to Florida, and she is looking forward to it, looking forward to being alone with Señor Heller again for a little while, for Señor Heller has proved to be every bit as interesting as Bing advertised, and she takes pleasure in being near him, in talking to him, in watching him move. She has not fallen for him in the way poor Ellen has, has not lost her head or cursed the innocent Pilar Sanchez for robbing his heart, but the soft-spoken, brooding, impenetrable Miles Heller has touched a nerve in her, and she finds it difficult to remember what things were like in the house before he moved in. For the fourth night in a row, Jake will not be coming, and it pains her to realize that she is glad.

She is still thinking about Jake as she steps out of the elevator on the third floor, wondering if the moment has finally come for a showdown with him or if she should put it off a little longer, wait until the four pounds she lost in December have become eight pounds, twelve pounds, however many pounds it will take before she stops counting. Paul is already sitting at his desk, talking to someone on the telephone, and he waves to her from the other side of the glass window that separates his office from the outer room, where her desk is located, her small, cluttered desk, where she now sits down and switches on her computer. Linda comes in a couple of minutes later, cheeks flushed from the cold morning air, and before she removes her coat and gets to work, she walks over to Alice, plants a big kiss on her left cheek, and wishes her a happy new year.

Paul makes a grunting sound from within his office, a sound that could signify surprise or disappointment or dismay, nothing is clear, Paul often emits confusing sounds after he hangs up the phone, and as Alice and Linda turn to look through the glass window, Paul is already on his feet and walking toward them. There has been a new development. On December thirty-first, the Chinese authorities allowed Liu Xiaobo to be visited by his wife.

This is their new case, the most pressing case on the current agenda, and ever since Liu Xiaobo was detained in early December, they have worked on little else. Paul and Linda are both pessimistic about the immediate future, both are certain that the Beijing Public Security Bureau will hold Liu until enough evidence has been gathered against him to make a formal arrest on the charge of *inciting subversion of state power,* which could land him in prison for fifteen years. His offense: cowriting a document called Charter 08, a declaration calling for political reform, greater human rights, and an end to one-party rule in China.

Liu Xiaobo began as a literary critic and professor at Beijing Normal University, an important enough figure to have worked as a visiting scholar at a number of foreign institutions, notably the University of Oslo and Columbia University in New York, Alice's Columbia University, the place where she is pushing toward her doctorate, and Liu's activism dates all the way back to 1989, the year of years, the year the Berlin Wall came down, the year of the fatwa, the year of Tiananmen Square, and it was precisely then, in the spring of 1989, that Liu quit his post at Columbia and went back to Beijing, where he staged a hunger strike in Tiananmen Square in support of the students and advocated nonviolent methods of protest in order to prevent further bloodshed. He spent two years in prison for this, and then, in 1996, was sentenced to three years of *reeducation through labor* for suggesting that the Chinese government open discussions with the Dalai Lama of Tibet. More harassments have followed, and he has been living under police surveillance ever since. His latest arrest occurred on December 8, 2008, coincidentally or not coincidentally just one day before the sixtieth anniversary of the Universal Declaration of Human Rights. He is being held in an undisclosed location, with no access to a lawyer, no writing materials, no way to communicate with anyone. Does his wife's visit on New Year's Eve signify an important turn, or was it simply a small act of mercy that will have no bearing on the outcome of the case?

Alice spends the morning and early afternoon writing e-mails to PEN centers all around the world, enlisting support for the massive protest Paul wants to mount in Liu's defense. She works with a kind of righteous fervor, knowing that men like Liu Xiaobo are the bedrock of humanity, that few men or women are brave enough to stand up and risk their lives for others, and beside him the rest of us are nothing, walking around in the chains of our weakness and indifference and dull conformity, and when a man like this is about to be sacrificed for his belief in others, the others must do everything they can to save him, and yet even if Alice is filled with anger as she works, she works in a kind of despair as well, feeling the hopelessness of the effort they are about to launch, sensing that no amount of indignation will alter the plans of the Chinese authorities, and even if PEN can roust a million people to pound on drums across the entire globe, there is little chance those drums will be heard.

She skips lunch and works straight through until it is time

for her to leave, and when she walks out of the building and heads for the subway, she is still under the spell of the Liu Xiaobo case, still trying to figure out how to interpret the visit from his wife on New Year's Eve, the same New Year's Eve she spent with Jake and a group of their friends on the Upper West Side, everyone kissing everyone else at midnight, a silly custom, but she enjoyed it anyway, she liked being kissed by everyone, and she wonders now, as she descends the stairs into the subway, if the Chinese police allowed Liu's wife to stay with him until midnight, and if they did, whether she and her husband kissed at the stroke of twelve, assuming they were allowed to kiss at all, and if they were, what it would be like to kiss your husband under those circumstances, with policemen watching you and no guarantee that you will ever see your husband again.

Normally, she carries along a book to read on the subway, but she overslept by half an hour this morning, and in the scramble to get out of the house in time for work, she forgot to take one with her, and because the train is nearly empty at two-fifteen in the afternoon, there aren't enough people on board for her to use the forty-minute ride to study her fellow passengers, a cherished New York pastime, especially for a New York transplant who grew up in the Midwest, and with nothing to read and not enough faces to look at, she digs into her purse, pulls out a small notebook, and jots down some remarks about the passage she is planning to write when she gets home. Not only are the returning soldiers estranged from their wives, she will argue, but they no longer know how to talk to their sons. There is a scene early in the movie that sets the tone for this generational split, and that is what she will be tackling today, that one scene, in which Fredric March presents his high-school-age boy with his war trophies, a samurai sword and a Japanese flag, and she finds it unexpected but entirely appropriate that the boy shows no interest in these things, that he would rather talk about Hiroshima and the prospect of nuclear annihilation than the presents his father has given him. His mind is already fixed on the future, the *next* war, as if the war that has just been fought is already in the distant past, and consequently he asks his father no questions, is not curious enough to learn how these souvenirs were obtained, and a scene in which one would have imagined the boy wanting to hear his father talk about his adventures on the battlefield ends with the boy forgetting to take the sword and the flag with him when he walks out of the room. The father is not a hero in the eyes of his son—he is a superannuated figure from a bygone age. A bit later, when March and Myrna Loy are alone in the room, he turns to her and says: It's terrifying. Loy: What is? March: Youth! Loy: Didn't you run across any young people in the army? March: No. They were all old men—like me.

Miles Heller is old. The thought comes to her out of nowhere, but once it settles in her mind, she knows that she has discovered an essential truth, the thing that sets him apart from Jake Baum and Bing Nathan and all the other young men she knows, the generation of talking boys, the logorrhea class of 2009, whereas Señor Heller says next to nothing, is incapable of making small talk, and refuses to share his secrets with anyone. Miles has been in a war, and all soldiers are old men by the time they come home, shut-down men who never talk about the battles they have fought. What war did Miles Heller march off to, she wonders, what action has he seen, how long has he been away? It is impossible to know, but there is no question that he has been wounded, that he walks around with an inner wound that will never heal, and perhaps that is why she respects him so much—because he is in pain, and he never says anything about it. Bing rants and Jake whines, but Miles holds his tongue. It is not even clear to her what he is doing in Sunset Park. One day early last month, just after he moved in, she asked him why he had left Florida, but his answer was so vague—*I have some unfinished business to take care of*—it could have meant anything. What unfinished business? And why move away from Pilar? He is so obviously in love with the girl, why on earth would he have come to Brooklyn?

If not for Pilar, she would actively worry about Miles. Yes, it was a little disconcerting to be introduced to someone so young, a *high school girl* in her funny green parka and red woolen gloves, but that sensation quickly wore off when one understood how bright and pulled together she was, and the best thing about this girl is the simple fact that Miles is devoted to her, and from Alice's observations during Pilar's visit, she believes she was looking at what is probably an exceptional love, and if Miles can love someone in the way he loves this girl, it must mean the damage inside him is not systemic, that his wounds are specific wounds in specific areas of his soul and are not bleeding into other parts of him, and therefore the darkness in Miles does not prey on her mind as it did before Pilar lived among them for those ten or eleven days. It was difficult not to feel some envy, of course, watching Miles as he looked at his beloved, talked to his beloved, touched his beloved, not because she wants him to look at her in that way but because Jake doesn't do it anymore, and foolish as it is to measure Jake against Señor Heller, there are times when she can't stop herself. Jake has brains, talent, and ambition, whereas Miles, for all his mental and physical virtues, is completely lacking in ambition, seems content to drift through his days without passion or purpose, and yet Miles is a man and Jake is still a boy, because Miles has been to war and has grown old. Perhaps that explains why the two of them seem to dislike each other so much. Even at the first dinner, when Jake began talking about interviewing Renzo Michaelson, she felt that Miles was ready to punch him or pour a drink over his head. Who knows why Michaelson provoked that response, but the animosity has continued—to such a degree that Miles is rarely at home when Jake comes for dinner. Jake is continuing to pester Bing about helping him set up a meeting with Michaelson, but Bing keeps putting him off, saying that Michaelson is an ornery, reclusive sort of person, and the best way to handle it is to wait until he comes into the store again to have his typewriter cleaned. Alice could probably arrange it herself if she wanted to. Michaelson is a longtime member of PEN, a past vice president with a special attachment to the Freedom to Write Program, and she talked to him on the phone only last week about the Liu Xiaobo case. She could easily call him tomorrow and ask if he has any time to talk to her boyfriend, but she doesn't want to do it. Jake has stuck a knife in her, and she isn't in the mood to do him any favors.

She returns to the empty house just after three o'clock. By three-thirty, she is sitting at her desk, typing up her notes about the father-son conversation in *The Best Years of Our Lives.* At three-fifty, someone starts knocking on the front door. Alice stands up and goes downstairs to see who it is. When she opens the door, a tall, blubbery man in a strange khaki uniform grins at her and tips his hat. He has a splayed, multifaceted nose, pockmarked cheeks, and a large, full-lipped mouth, a curious assortment of facial characteristics that somehow reminds her of a platter of mashed potatoes. She also notes, with a certain sadness, that he is wearing a gun. When she asks him who he is, he says that he is Nestor Gonzalez, New York City marshal, and then he hands her a folded-up piece of paper, a document of some kind. What is this? Alice asks. A court order, Gonzalez says. For what? Alice asks, pretending that she doesn't know. You're breaking the law, ma'am, the marshal replies. You and your friends have to get out.

Bing Nathan

Miles is worried about money. He didn't have enough to begin with, and now that he has spent the better part of two weeks running around the city with Pilar, eating twice a day in restaurants, buying her clothes and perfume, springing for expensive theater tickets, his reserve has been melting even more quickly than he imagined it would. They talk about it on January third, a few hours after Pilar climbs onto the bus and heads back to Florida, a few minutes after Miles leaves the garbled message on his mother's answering machine, and Bing says there is a simple solution to the problem if Miles is willing to accept his offer. He needs help at the Hospital for Broken Things. Mob Rule has finally found a booking agent, and they will be out of town for two weeks at the end of January and two more weeks in February, playing at colleges in New York State and Pennsylvania, and he can't afford to shut down the business while he is away. He can teach Miles how to frame pictures, clean and repair typewriters, fix anything the customers want fixed, and if Miles agrees to work full-time for so many dollars an hour, they can catch up on the unfinished jobs that have been mounting over the past few months, Bing can cut out early to practice with his band whenever the mood strikes him, and whenever the band is traveling, Miles will be in charge. Bing can cover an extra salary now because of the money he has saved by living rent-free in Sunset Park for the past five months—and then, on top of that, it looks as if Mob Rule will be bringing in more cash than at any time in its history. What does Miles think? Miles looks down at his shoes, turns the proposition around for several moments, and then lifts his head and says he is for it. He thinks it will be better to work at the Hospital than to spend his days walking around the cemetery taking photographs, and before he goes out to shop for dinner, he thanks Bing for having rescued him again.

What Miles doesn't understand is that Charles Bingham Nathan would do anything for him, and even if Miles had turned down the offer to work for so many dollars an hour at the Hospital for Broken Things, his friend would have been happy to advance him as much money as he needed, with no obligation to pay back the loan anytime before the end of the twenty-second century. He knows that Miles is only half a person, that his life has been sundered and will never be fully repaired, but the half of Miles that remains is more compelling to him than two of anyone else. It began when they met twelve years ago, in the fall immediately after the death of Miles's brother, Miles just sixteen and Bing a year older, the one following the smart-kid road at Stuyvesant and the other in the music program at LaGuardia, two angry boys who found common cause in their contempt for the hypocrisies of American life, and it was the younger one who taught the older one the value of resistance, how it was possible to refuse to participate in the meaningless games society was asking them to play, and Bing knows that much of what he has become in the years since then is a direct result of Miles's influence on him. It was more than what Miles said, however, more than any one of the hundreds of cutting observations he made about politics and economics, the clarity with which he broke down *the system,* it was what Miles said in combination with who Miles was, and how he seemed to embody the ideas he believed in, the gravity of his bearing, the grief-stricken boy with no illusions, no false hopes, and even if they never became intimate friends, he doubts there is anyone from his generation he admires more.

He was not the only one who felt that way. As far back as he can remember, Miles seemed different from everyone else, to possess some magnetic, animal force that changed the atmosphere whenever he walked into a room. Was it the power of his silences that made him attract so much attention, the mysterious, closed-in nature of his personality that turned him into a kind of mirror for others to project themselves onto, the eerie sense that he was both there and not there at the same time? He was intelligent and good-looking, yes, but not all intelligent and good-looking people exude that magic, and when you added in the fact that everyone knew he was the son of Mary-Lee Swann, the only child of Mary-Lee Swann, perhaps the aura of her fame helped to enhance the feeling that Miles was one of the anointed. Some people resented him, of course, boys in particular, boys but never girls, but why wouldn't boys resent him for his luck with girls, for being the one the girls wanted? Even now, so many years later, the Heller touch seems to have survived the long odyssey to nowhere and back. Look at Alice and Ellen. Alice finds him *wholly admirable* (a direct quote), and Ellen, dear little Ellen, is besotted with him.

Miles has been living in Sunset Park for a month now, and Bing is glad he is here, glad the Paltry Three has been turned back into the Solid Four, although he is still baffled by Miles's sudden change of heart about coming to Brooklyn. First it was no, and the long letter explaining why he wanted to stay in Florida, and then the urgent phone call to the Hospital late one Friday, just as Bing was about to close up and return to the house in Sunset Park, and Miles telling him that *something had come up* and if a place was still open for him, he would be on a bus to New York that weekend. Miles will never explain himself, of course, and it would be pointless to ask, but now that he is here, Bing is heartened that old Mr. Sullen is finally prepared to make peace with his parents and put a stop to the idiocy that has been going on for so long, much too long, and that his own role as double agent and liar will soon be coming to an end. He feels no guilt about having deceived Miles. If anything, he is proud of what he has done, and when Morris Heller called the Hospital this morning to ask for the latest news, he felt a sense of victory when he was able to report that Miles had called his office while he was in England and would be calling back on Monday, and now that Miles has just told him he has called his mother as well, the victory is almost complete. Miles has come round at last, and it is probably a good thing that he is in love with Pilar, even if that love feels a bit strange, more than a little disturbing in fact, such a young girl, the last person one would expect Miles to get himself entangled with, but without question charming and pretty, old beyond her years perhaps, and therefore let Miles have his Pilar and think no more about it. Good news all around, positive things happening on so many fronts, and yet it has been a difficult month for him, one of the most anguishing months of his life, and when he hasn't been wallowing in mud baths of confusion and disarray, he has been close to despair. It started when Miles returned to New York, the moment when he saw Miles standing in the store and he threw his arms around him and kissed him, and ever since that day he has found it nearly impossible not to touch Miles, not to want to touch Miles. He knows that Miles doesn't like it, that he is put off by his spontaneous hugs, his pats on the back, his neck squeezes and shoulder squeezes, but Bing can't stop himself, he knows he should stop but he can't, and because he is afraid he has fallen in love with Miles, because he is afraid he has always been in love with Miles, he is living in a state of despair.

He remembers a summer outing eleven years ago, the summer after he graduated from high school, three boys and two girls packed into a little car driving north to the Catskills. Someone's parents owned a cottage up there, an isolated spot in the woods with a pond and a tennis court, and Miles was in the car with his love of the moment, a girl named Annie, and there was Geoff Taylor with his newest conquest, someone whose name has been forgotten, and last but not least himself, the one with no girlfriend, the odd man out as usual. They arrived late, sometime between midnight and one o'clock in the morning, and because they were hot and stiff after the long drive, someone suggested they cool off in the pond, and suddenly they were running toward the water, stripping off their clothes, and wading in. He remembers how pleasant it was, splashing around in that remote place with the moon and the stars overhead, the crickets singing in the woods, the warm breeze blowing against his back, along with the pleasure of seeing the bodies of the girls, the long-legged Annie with her flat stomach and delightfully curved rear end, and Geoff's girlfriend, short and round, with large breasts and frizzy strands of dark hair twining over her shoulders. But it wasn't sexual pleasure, there was nothing erotic about what they were doing, it was simple corporeal ease, the pleasure of feeling the water and the air against your skin, of lolling around in the open on a hot summer night, of being with your friends. He was the first one to come out, and as he stood at the edge of the pond, he saw that the others had paired off, that the two couples were standing chest-deep in the water, and each couple was embracing, and as he watched Miles and Annie with their arms around each other and their mouths locked in a prolonged kiss, the strangest thought occurred to him, something that took him completely by surprise. Annie was incontestably a beautiful girl, one of the loveliest girls he had ever met, and the logic of the situation demanded that he feel envious of Miles for having such a beautiful girl in his arms, for being attractive enough to have won the affections of such a desirable creature, but as he watched the two of them kissing in the water, he understood that the envy he felt was directed toward Annie, not Miles, that he wanted to be in Annie's place and to be kissing Miles himself. A moment later, they began walking toward the edge of the pond, walking straight toward him, and as Miles's body emerged from the water, Bing saw that he had an erection, a large, fully formed erection, and the sight of that stiffened penis aroused him, excited him in a way he never would have thought possible, and before Miles had touched dry ground, Bing had an erection of his own, a turn of events that so bewildered him that he ran back into the pond and dove under the water to conceal his embarrassment.

He suppressed the memory of that night for years, never returned to it even in the darkest, most private realms of his imagination, but then Miles came back, and with Miles the memory came back, and for the past month Bing has been replaying that scene in his head five times a day, ten times a day, and by now he no longer knows who or what he is. Does his response to that erect phallus glimpsed in the moonlight eleven years ago mean that he prefers men to women, that he is more attracted to male bodies than female bodies, and if that is the case, could that account for his singular run of failure with the women he has courted over the years? He doesn't know. The only thing he can say with any certainty is that he is drawn to Miles, that he thinks about Miles's body and that erect phallus whenever he is with him, which is often, and that he thinks about touching Miles's body and that erect phallus whenever he is not with him, which is more often, and yet to act on these desires would be a grave error, an error that would lead to the most horrendous consequences, for Miles has no interest in coupling with other men, and if Bing even suggested such a possibility, even whispered a single word about what is on his mind, he would lose Miles's friendship forever, which is something he devoutly does not wish to do.

Miles is off-limits, on permanent loan to the world of women. But the tormenting power of that erect phallus has driven Bing to consider other options, to think about looking elsewhere to satisfy his curiosity, for in spite of the fact that Miles is the only man he craves, he wonders if the time hasn't come to experiment with another man, which is the only way he will ever find out who and what he is—a man made for men, a man made for women, a man made for both men and women, or a man made for no one but himself. The problem is where to look. All the members of his band are married or living with their girlfriends, he has no gay friends he can think of, and the idea of cruising for some pickup in a gay bar leaves him cold. He has thought about Jake Baum a few times, plotting various strategies about how and when he could approach him without tipping his hand and humiliating himself in the event of a rebuff, but he suspects there is something ambiguous about Alice's boyfriend, and even if he is with a woman now, it is possible that he has been with men in the past and is not immune to the charms of phallic love. Bing regrets that he is not more attracted to Jake, but in the interests of scientific self-discovery he would be willing to bed down with him to see if he himself has any taste for phallic love. He has yet to do anything about it, however, for just when he was gearing up to cajole Baum into having sex with him by promising to arrange the interview with Renzo Michaelson (not the strongest idea, perhaps, but ideas have been hard to come by), Ellen asked him to pose for her, and his quest for knowledge was temporarily derailed.

He has no idea what they are up to. Something perverse, he feels, but at the same time altogether innocent and without danger. A silent pact of some sort, a mutual understanding that allows them to share their loneliness and frustrations, but even as they draw closer to each other in that silence, he is still lonely and frustrated, and he senses that Ellen is no better off than he is. She draws and he drums. Drumming has always been a way for him to scream, and Ellen's new drawings have turned into screams as well. He takes off his clothes for her and does everything she asks him to do. He doesn't know why he feels so comfortable with her, so unthreatened by her eyes, but donating his body to the cause of her art is a small thing, finally, and he intends to go on doing it until she asks him to stop.

On Sunday, January fourth, he spends eight hours with Miles at the Hospital for Broken Things, giving him his first lessons in the delicate, exacting work of picture framing, introducing him to the sturdy mechanisms of manual typewriters, familiarizing him with the tools and materials in the back room of the tiny shop. The next morning, Monday, January fifth, they go back for more of the same, but this time Miles seems worried, and when Bing asks him what is wrong, Miles explains that he has just called his father's office and was told his father returned to England yesterday *on urgent business,* and he is concerned that it might have something to do with his stepmother. Bing, too, is both worried and perplexed by this news, but he cannot reveal the full scope of his anxiety to Morris Heller's son, nor can he tell him that he spoke to Morris Heller just forty-eight hours ago and that nothing seemed amiss at the time. They work steadily until five-thirty, at which point Miles informs Bing that he wants to take another stab at calling his mother, and Bing deferentially withdraws to a bar down the street, understanding that such a call demands total privacy. Fifteen minutes later, Miles walks into the bar and tells Bing that he and his mother have arranged to meet for dinner tomorrow night. There are a hundred questions Bing would like to ask, but he confines himself to just one: How did she sound? Very well, Miles says. She called him a no-good shithead, an imbecile, and a rotten coward, but then she cried, then they both cried, and afterward her voice became warm and affectionate, she talked to him with far more kindness than he deserved, and hearing her again after all these years was almost too much for him. He regrets everything, he says. He thinks he is the stupidest person who ever lived. If there were any justice in the world, he should be taken outside and shot.

Bing has never seen Miles look more distressed than he is now. For a few moments, he thinks Miles might actually break down in tears. Forgetting his vow not to touch him anymore, he puts his arms around his friend and holds on to him tightly. Cheer up, asshole, he says. At least you know you're the stupidest person who ever lived. How many people are smart enough to admit that?

They take a bus back to Sunset Park and walk into the house a couple of minutes before six-thirty, a couple of minutes before Miles's scheduled rendezvous with Alice in the kitchen. As expected, Alice is already there, as is Ellen, and both of them are sitting at the table, not preparing food, not doing anything but sitting at the table and looking into each other's eyes. Alice is stroking the back of Ellen's right hand, Ellen's left hand is stroking Alice's face, and both of them look miserable. What is it? Bing asks. This, Alice says, and then she picks up a piece of paper and hands it to him.

Bing has been expecting this piece of paper since the day they moved into the house last August. He knew it would come, and he knew what he was going to do when it came, which is precisely what he does now. Without even bothering to read the full text of the court order to vacate the premises, he tears the sheet once, twice, and then a third time, and then he tosses the eight scraps of paper onto the floor.

Don't worry, he says. This doesn't mean a thing. They've found out we're here, but getting us to move will take more than a dumb piece of paper. I know how this stuff works. They've given us notice, and now they'll forget about us for a while. In a month or so, they'll be back with another piece of paper, which we'll tear up and throw on the floor again. And another time, and another time after that, and maybe even another time after that. The city marshals won't do anything to us. They don't want trouble. Their job is to deliver pieces of paper, and that's it. We don't have to worry until they come with the cops. Then it gets serious, but we won't be seeing any cops around here for a long time—if ever. We're small potatoes, and the cops have better things to think about than four quiet people living in a quiet little house in a quiet little nothing neighborhood. Don't panic. We might have to leave someday, but that day isn't today, and until the cops show up, I'm not giving an inch. And even when they do come, they'll have to beat me over the head and drag me out in handcuffs. This is our house. It belongs to us now, and I'd rather go to jail than give up my right to live here.

That's the spirit, Miles says.

So you're with me? Bing asks.

Of course I am, Miles says, lifting his right hand into the air, as if taking an oath. Chief Miles no budge from tepee.

And what about you, Ellen? Do you want to leave or stay?

Stay, Ellen says.

And you, Alice?

Stay.

Mary-Lee Swann

Simon left last night, back to L.A. to teach his film history class, and so begins the grind of comings and goings, the poor man traveling back and forth across the country every week for the next three months, the diabolical red-eye, jet lag, sticky clothes and swollen feet, the awful air in the cabin, the pumped-in artificial air, three days in L.A., four days in New York, and all for the pittance they are paying him, but he says he enjoys the teaching, and surely it is better for him to stay busy, to be doing something rather than nothing, but the timing couldn't have been worse, how much she needs him to be with her now, how much she hates to sleep alone, and this part, Winnie, so grueling and difficult, she fears she will not be up to it, dreads she will fall on her face and become a laughingstock, jitters, jitters, the old knot in the belly before the curtain rises, and how was she to know an emmet is an ant, an archaic word for ant, she had to look it up in the dictionary, and why would Winnie say emmet instead of ant, is it funnier to say emmet instead of ant, yes, no doubt it is funnier, or at least unexpected and therefore strange, *An emmet!*, which leads to Willie's one-word utterance, *Formication*, very droll that, you think he is mispronouncing fornication, but she had to look that one up in the dictionary too before she got the joke, *a sensation of the body resembling that made by the creeping of ants on the skin,* and Fred delivers the word wonderfully well, he is a fine Willie, a good soul to work with, and how nicely he reads the paper early in the first act,

Opening for smart youth, *Wanted bright boy,* she burst out laughing at the first read-through when he spoke those lines, Fred Derry, the same name as a character in that movie she watched with Simon the other night, the one he will be showing to his class today, *The Best Years of Our Lives,* an excellent old film, she choked up at the end and cried, and when she went to rehearsal the next day and asked Fred if his parents had named him after the character in that movie, her stage husband grinned at her and said, Alas, dear woman, no, I am an aged fart who crept into this world five years before that film was made.

Alas, dear woman. She doubts she has ever been dear. Many other things on the long journey from the first day to this day, but not dear, no, never that. Intermittently kind, intermittently lovable, intermittently loving, intermittently unselfish, but not often enough to qualify as dear.

She misses Simon, the place feels sickeningly empty without him, but perhaps it is just as well that he isn't here tonight, this one night, a Tuesday night in early January, the sixth night of the year, because in one hour Miles will be ringing the bell downstairs, in one hour he will be walking into this third-floor loft on Franklin Street, and after seven and a half years of no contact with her son (*seven and a half years*), it is probably best that she see him alone, talk to him alone. She has no idea what will happen, is entirely in the dark about what to expect from the evening, and because she is too afraid to dwell on these imponderables, she has concentrated her attention on the dinner, the meal itself, what to serve and what not to serve, and because rehearsal was going to run too late for her to cook the meal herself, she has called two different restaurants to deliver food to the loft at eight-thirty sharp, two restaurants because after ordering steak dinners from the first, thinking steak was a good bet, everyone likes steak, especially men with healthy appetites, she began to fret that she had made the wrong choice, that maybe her son has become a vegetarian or has an aversion to steak, and she didn't want things to get off to an awkward start by putting Miles in a position that would force him to eat something he doesn't like or, even worse, to serve him a meal that he couldn't or wouldn't eat, and therefore, just to play it safe, she called a second restaurant and ordered a second pair of dinners—meatless lasagna, salads, and grilled winter vegetables. As with food, so with drink. She remembers that he used to like scotch and red wine, but his preferences might have changed since the last time she saw him, and consequently she has bought one case each of red wine and white wine and filled the liquor cabinet with an abundant range of possibilities: scotch, bourbon, vodka, gin, tequila, rye, and three different brands of cognac.

She assumes that Miles has already seen his father, that he made the call to the office first thing yesterday morning as Bing Nathan said he would, and that the two of them had dinner together last night. She was expecting Morris to call her today and give a full account of what happened, but no word yet, no message on the machine or her cell phone, even though Miles must have told him he would be coming here tonight, since she and Miles spoke before dinner hour yesterday, in other words before Miles saw his father, and it is hard to imagine that the subject would not have come up somewhere in their conversation. Who knows why she hasn't heard from Morris? It could be that things went badly last night and he is still too upset to talk about it. Or else he was simply too busy today, his second day back at work after the trip to England, and maybe he got caught up in problems at the office, the publishing house is going through hard times just now, and it's even possible that he's still at the office at seven o'clock, eating Chinese takeout for dinner and settling in for a long night of work. Then, too, it could be that Miles lost his nerve and didn't make the call. Not likely, since he wasn't too afraid to call her, and if this is the week for burying hatchets, his father is the logical place to begin, the one he would go to first, since Morris had a hell of a lot more to do with raising him than she did, but still, it could be true, and while she mustn't let Miles know what Bing Nathan has been up to all these years, she can ask the question tonight and find out if he has been in touch with his father or not.

That was why she shouted at Miles on the phone yesterday—out of solidarity with Morris. He and Willa have borne the brunt of this long, wretched affair, and when she saw him at dinner on Saturday night, he looked so much older to her, the hair so gray now, the cheeks so thin, the eyes so dull with sadness, and she understood what a toll this story has taken on him, and now that she is older and presumably wiser (although that is a matter of some dispute, she believes), she was moved by the surge of affection she felt for him in the restaurant that night, the aging shadow of the man she married so long ago, the father of her only child, and it was for Morris's sake that she shouted at Miles, pretending to share Morris's anger at him for what he has done, trying to act like a proper parent, the hurt, scolding mother, but most of it was performance, nearly every word was a pretend word, the insults, the name-calling, for the fact is that she resents Miles far less than Morris does, and she has not walked around all these years feeling bitter about what happened—disappointed, yes, confused, yes, but not bitter.

She has no right to blame Miles for anything he has done, she has let him down by being such a fitful, incompetent mother, and she knows she has failed at this more dreadfully than anything else in her life, the two failed marriages included, every one of her lapses and bad deeds included, but she wasn't up to motherhood when Miles was born, twenty-six years old but still not ready, too distracted to concentrate, preoccupied by the jump from theater to film, indignant with Morris for having talked her into it, and struggle as she did to fulfill her duties for those first six months, she found herself bored with the baby, there was so little pleasure in taking care of him, and not even the pleasure of breast-feeding was enough, not even the pleasure of looking into his eyes and watching him smile back at her could compensate for the smothering tedium of it all, the incessant wailing, the wet, yellow shit in the diapers, the puked-up milk, the howls in the middle of the night, the lack of sleep, the mindless repetitions, and then *Innocent Dreamer* came along, and she bolted. Looking back on her actions now, she finds them unpardonable, and even if she did fall for the boy later, after the divorce, after he started growing up, she was no good at it, she kept letting him down, couldn't even remember to go to his bloody high school graduation for God's sake, but that was the turning point, the unpardonable sin of not being there when she should have been there, and from then on she became more conscientious, tried to make amends for all the sins she had committed over the years (the beautiful weekend in Providence with Simon, the three of them together as if they were a family, she was so happy there, so proud of the boy), and then, six months after that, he bolted. Mother bolts, boy bolts. Hence her tears on the phone yesterday. She shouted at him for Morris's sake, but the tears were for herself, and the tears spoke the truth. Miles is twenty-eight now, older than she was when she gave birth to him, but he is still her son, and she wants him back, she wants the story to begin again.

Pity the poor hippo, she thinks. Too fat, dear woman, too many extra pounds on the old bones. Why did it have to be Winnie now and not someone a little more graceful, a little more *svelte*? Svelte Salome, for instance. Because she is too old to play Salome, and Tony Gilbert has asked her to play Winnie. *That is what I find so wonderful. (Pause.) Eyes on my eyes.* She has changed three times since returning to the loft, but she still isn't satisfied with the results. The hour is fast approaching, however, and it is too late to consider a fourth option. Pale blue silk pants, white silk blouse, and a gauzy, loose-flowing, semi-transparent, knee-length jacket to mask the flab. Bracelets on each wrist, but no earrings. Chinese slippers. Winnie's short hair, nothing to be done about that. Too much makeup or too little makeup? The red lipstick a bit harsh, perhaps, remove some of it now. Perfume or no perfume? No perfume. And the hands, the telltale hands with their too plump fingers, nothing to be done about them either. A necklace would probably be too much, and besides, no one could see it under the gauzy wrap. What else? The nail polish. Winnie's nail polish, nothing to be done about that either. Jitters, jitters, the old lump in the gut before the emmet crawls out and formicates. *Your eyes on my eyes.* She goes into the bathroom for a last look in the mirror. Old Mother Hubbard or Alice in Motherland? Somewhere in between, perhaps. *Wanted bright boy.* She goes into the kitchen and pours herself a glass of wine. Time for one sip, time for a second sip, and then the doorbell rings.

So much to absorb all at once, so many particulars bombarding her the instant the door opens, the tall young man with his father's dark hair and eyebrows, his mother's gray-blue eyes and mouth, so complete now, the work of growing finally finished, a sterner face than before, she thinks, but softer, more giving eyes, eyes looking into her eyes, and the fierce hug he gives her before either of them can say a word, feeling the great strength of his arms and shoulders through his leather jacket, and again she goes stupid on him without wanting to, breaking down and crying as she holds on to him for dear life, blubbering how sorry she is for all the misunderstandings and grievances that drove him away, but he says none of it has anything to do with her, she is entirely blameless, everything is his fault, and he is the one who is sorry.

He doesn't drink anymore. That is the first new fact she learns about him after she dries her eyes and leads him into the living room. He doesn't drink, but he isn't particular about food, he will be happy to have the steak or the meatless lasagna, whichever she prefers. Why does she feel so nervous around him, so apologetic? She has already apologized, he has already apologized, it is time to move on to more substantial matters, time to begin talking, but then she does the one thing she promised herself she wouldn't do, she mentions the play, she says that is why she is so large now, he is looking at Winnie, not Mary-Lee, an illusion, an imaginary character, and the boy who is no longer a boy smiles at her and says he thinks she is looking grand, *grand* she says to herself, what a curious word, such an old-fashioned way of putting it, no one says *grand* anymore, unless he is referring to her size, of course, her newly begotten rotundity, but no, he seems to be paying her a compliment, and yes, he adds, he has read about the play and is looking forward to seeing it. She notices that she is fidgeting with her bracelet, her lungs feel tight, she can't sit still. I'll go get the wine, she says, but what will it be for you, Miles? Water, juice, ginger ale? As she walks across the large open space of the loft, Miles stands up and follows her, saying he's changed his mind, he'll have some wine after all, he wants to celebrate, and who knows if he means it or is simply dying for a drink because he is just as nervous as she is?

They clink glasses, and as they do so she tells herself to be careful, to remember that Bing Nathan must be kept out of it, that Miles must not discover how closely they have kept track of him, the different jobs in all the different places for all these years, Chicago, New Hampshire, Arizona, California, Florida, the restaurants, the hotels, the warehouses, pitching for the baseball team, the women who have come and gone, the Cuban girl who was with him in New York just now, all the things they know about him must be suppressed, and she must feign ignorance whenever he divulges something, but she can do that, it is her business to do that, she can do that even when she has drunk too much, and from the way Miles has gulped down the first sip of his Pouilly-Fumé, it looks as if much wine will be consumed tonight.

And what about your father? she asks. Have you been in touch with him?

I've called twice, he says. He was in England the first time. They told me to call back on the fifth, but when I tried to reach him yesterday, they said he'd flown off to England again. Something urgent.

Strange, she says. I had dinner with Morris Saturday night, and he didn't say anything about going back. He must have left on Sunday. Very strange.

I hope everything is okay with Willa.

Willa. What makes you think she's in England?

I know she's in England. People tell me things, I have my sources.

I thought you turned your back on us. Not a peep in all this time, and now you tell me you know what we've been up to?

More or less.

If you still cared, why run away in the first place?

That's the big question, isn't it? (*Pause. Another sip of wine.*) Because I thought you'd be better off without me—all of you.

Or you'd be better off without us.

Maybe.

Then why come back now?

Because circumstances brought me up to New York, and once I was here, I understood that the game was over. I'd had enough.

But why so long? When you first went missing, I thought it would be for a few weeks, a few months. You know: confused young man lights out for the territories, grapples with his demons in the wilderness, and comes back a stronger, better person. But seven years, Miles, one-quarter of your life. You see how crazy that is, don't you?

I did want to become a better person. That was the whole point. Become better, become stronger—all very worthy, I suppose, but also a little vague. How do you know when you've become better? It's not like going to college for four years and being handed a diploma to prove you've passed all your courses. There's no way to measure your progress. So I kept at it, not knowing if I was better or not, not knowing if I was stronger or not, and after a while I stopped thinking about the goal and concentrated on the effort. (*Pause. Another sip of wine.*) Does any of this make sense to you? I became addicted to the struggle. I lost track of myself. I kept on doing it, but I didn't know why I was doing it anymore.

Your father thinks you ran away because of a conversation you overheard.

He figured that out? I'm impressed. But that conversation was only the start, the first push. I'm not going to deny how terrible it felt to hear them talking about me like that, but after I took off, I understood they were right, right to be so worried about me, right in their analysis of my fucked-up psyche, and that's why I stayed away—because I didn't want to be that person anymore, and I knew it would take me a long time to get well.

Are you well now?

(*Laughs.*) I doubt it. (*Pause.*) But not as bad off as I was then. Lots of things have changed, especially in the past six months.

Another glass, Miles?

Yes, please. (*Pause.*) I shouldn't be doing this. Out of practice, you know. But it's awfully good wine, and I'm awfully, awfully nervous.

(*Refilling both their glasses.*) Me too, baby.

It was never about you, I hope you understand that. But once I made the break with my father and Willa, I had to break with you and Simon as well.

It's all about Bobby, isn't it?

(*Nods.*)

You have to let it go.

I can't.

You have to.

(*Shakes his head.*) Too many bad memories.

You didn't run him over. It was an accident.

We were arguing. I pushed him into the road, and then the car came—going too fast, coming out of nowhere.

Let it go, Miles. It was an accident.

(*Eyes welling up with tears. Silence, four seconds. Then the downstairs buzzer rings.*)

It must be the food. (*Stands up, walks over to Miles, kisses him on the forehead, and then goes off to let in the deliveryman from the restaurant. Over her shoulder, addressing Miles.*) Which one do you think it is? The vegetarians or the carnivores?

(*Long pause. Forcing a smile.*) Both!

Morris Heller

The Can Man has been to England and back, and his experiences there have changed the color of the world. Since returning to New York on January twenty-fifth, he has given up his cans and bottles in order to devote himself to a life of pure contemplation. The Can Man nearly died in England. The Can Man contracted pneumonia and spent two weeks in a hospital, and the woman he went there to rescue from mental collapse and potential suicide wound up rescuing him from almost certain death and in so doing rescued herself from mental collapse and possibly saved a marriage as well. The Can Man is glad to be alive. The Can Man knows his days are numbered, and therefore he has put aside his quest for cans and bottles in order to study the days as they slip past him, one after the other, each one more quickly than the day before it. Among the numerous observations he has noted down in his book of observations are the following:

January 25. We do not grow stronger as the years advance. The accumulation of sufferings and sorrows weakens our capacity to endure more sufferings and sorrows, and since sufferings and sorrows are inevitable, even a small setback late in life can resound with the same force as a major tragedy when we are young. *The straw that broke the camel's back.* Your dumb-ass penis in another woman's vagina, for example. Willa was on the verge of collapse before that ignominious adventure ever occurred. She has been through too much in her life, has borne more than her fair share of pains, and tough as she has had to be, she is not half as tough as she thinks she is. A dead husband, a dead son, a runaway stepson, and an unfaithful second husband—a nearly dead second husband. What if you had taken the initiative years ago, when you first saw her in that seminar in Philosophy Hall at Columbia, the bright Barnard girl let into a class for graduate students, the one with the delicate, pretty face and slender hands? There was a strong attraction then, all those years ago, long before Karl and Mary-Lee, and young as you both were at the time, twenty-two and twenty, what if you had pursued her a bit harder, what if your little dalliance had led to marriage? Result: no dead husband, no dead son, no runaway stepson. Other sufferings and sorrows, of course, but not those. Now she has brought you back from the dead, averting the final eclipse of all hope, and your still-breathing body must be counted as her greatest triumph. Hope endures, then, but not certainty. There has been a truce, a declaration of a desire for peace, but whether this has been a genuine meeting of minds is not clear. The boy remains an obstacle. She cannot forgive and forget. Not even after he and his mother called from New York to find out how you were, not even after the boy went on calling every day for two weeks to ask for the latest news on your condition. She will remain in England for the Easter break, and you will not be going there again. Too much time has been lost already, and you are needed at the office, the captain of a sinking ship must not abandon his crew. Perhaps she will change her mind as the months roll on. Perhaps she will bend. But you cannot renounce the boy for her sake. Nor can you renounce her for the boy's sake. You want them both, you must have them both, and one way or another, you will, even if they do not have each other.

January 26. Now that you and the boy have spent an evening together, you find yourself curiously let down. Too many years of anticipation, perhaps, too many years of imagining how the reunion would unfold, and therefore a feeling of anticlimax when it finally happened, for the imagination is a powerful weapon, and the imagined reunions that played out in your head so many times over the years were bound to be richer, fuller, and more emotionally satisfying than the real thing. You are also disturbed by the fact that you can't help resenting him. If there is to be any hope for the future, then you too must learn to forgive and forget. But the boy is already standing between you and your wife, and unless your wife undergoes a change of heart and allows him into her world again, the boy will continue to represent the distance that has grown between you. Still and all, it was a miraculous occasion, and the boy is so earnestly repentant, one would have to be made of stone not to want a new chapter to begin. But it will take some time before the two of you feel comfortable together, before you can trust each other again. Physically, he looks well. Strong and fit, with an encouraging brightness in his eyes. Mary-Lee's eyes, the indelible imprint of his mother. He says he has been to two performances of *Happy Days* and thinks she is a splendid Winnie, and when you suggested that the two of you go to see her together—if he could stand to watch the play a third time—he eagerly accepted. He talked at length about the young woman he has fallen in love with, Pilar, Pilar Hernandez, Sanchez, Gomez, her last name escapes you now, and he is looking forward to introducing her to you when she comes back to New York in April. He has no definite plans for the future. For the time being, he is working in Bing Nathan's store, but if he can put together enough money, he is toying with the idea of returning to college next year and getting his degree. Perhaps, maybe, it all depends. You didn't have the courage to confront him with difficult questions about the past. Why he ran away, for example, or why he kept himself hidden for so long. Not to speak of why he left his girlfriend in Florida and came to New York alone. There will be time for questions later. Last night was simply the first round, two boxers feeling each other out before getting down to business. You love him, of course, you love him with all your heart, but you no longer know what to think of him. Let him prove himself to be a worthy son.

January 27. If the company goes down, you will write a book called *Forty Years in the Desert: Publishing Litera-*

ture in a Country Where People Hate Books. The Christmas sales figures were even worse than you feared they would be, the worst showing ever. In the office, everyone looks worried—the old hands, the young kids, everyone from senior editors to baby-faced interns. Nor can the sight of your weakened, emaciated body inspire much confidence about the future. Nevertheless, you are glad to be back, glad to be in the place where you feel you belong, and even though the German and the Israeli have both turned you down, you feel less desperate about the situation than you did before you became ill. Nothing like a brief chat with Death to put things in perspective, and you figure that if you managed to avoid an untimely exit in that British hospital, you will find a way to steer the company through this nasty typhoon. No storm lasts forever, and now that you are back at the helm, you realize how much you savor your position as boss, how nourishing this little enterprise has been for you all these years. And you must be a good boss, or at least an appreciated boss, for when you returned to work yesterday, Jill Hertzberg threw her arms around you and said, Good God, Morris, don't ever do that again, please, I beg of you, and then, one by one, each member of the staff, all nine of them, men and women alike, came into your office and hugged you, welcoming you back after your long, tumultuous absence. Your own family might be in ruins, but this is your family as well, and your job is to protect them and make them understand that in spite of the idiot culture that surrounds them, books still count, and the work they are doing is important work, essential work. No doubt you are a sentimental old fool, a man out of step with the times, but you enjoy swimming against the current, that was the founding principle of the company thirty-five years ago, and you have no intention of changing your ways now. They are all worried about losing their jobs. That is what you see in their faces when you watch them talking to one another, and so you called a general meeting this afternoon and told them to forget 2008, 2008 is history now, and even if 2009 is no better, there will be no layoffs at Heller Books. Consider the publishers' softball league, you said. Any reductions of staff and it will be impossible to field a team in the spring, and Heller Books' proud record of twenty-seven consecutive losing seasons would come to an end. No softball team this year? Unthinkable.

February 6. Writers should never talk to journalists. The interview is a debased literary form that serves no purpose except to simplify that which should never be simplified. Renzo knows this, and because he is a man who acts on what he knows, he has kept his mouth shut for years, but tonight at dinner, concluded just one hour ago, he informed you that he spent part of the afternoon talking into a tape recorder, answering questions posed to him by a young writer of short stories, who intends to publish the results once the text has been edited and Renzo has given his approval. Special circumstances, he said, when you asked him why he had done it. The request came from Bing Nathan, who happens to be a friend of the young writer of short stories, and because Renzo is aware of the great debt you owe Bing Nathan, he felt it would have been rude to turn him down, unforgivable. In other words, Renzo has broken his silence out of friendship for you, and you told him how touched you were by this, grateful, glad he understood how much it meant to you that he could do something for Bing. An interview for Bing's sake, then, for your sake, but with certain restrictions the young writer had to accept before Renzo would agree to talk to him. No questions about his life or work, no questions about politics, no questions about anything except the work of other writers, dead writers, recently dead writers whom Renzo had known, some well, some casually, and whom he wanted to praise. No attacks, he said, only praise. He provided the interviewer with a list of names in advance and instructed him to choose some of them, just five or six, because the list was far too long to talk about them all. William Gaddis, Joseph Heller, George Plimpton, Leonard Michaels, John Gregory Dunne, Alain Robbe-Grillet, Susan Sontag, Arthur Miller, Robert Creeley, Kenneth Koch, William Styron, Ryszard Kapuściński, Kurt Vonnegut, Grace Paley, Norman Mailer,

Harold Pinter, and John Updike, who died just last week, an entire generation gone in the space of a few years. You knew many of those writers as well, talked to them, rubbed shoulders with them, admired them, and as Renzo reeled off their names, you were astonished by how many there were, and a terrible sadness descended on both of you as you raised a glass to their memory. To brighten the mood, Renzo launched into a story about William Styron, an amusing little anecdote from many years ago concerning a French magazine, *Le Nouvel Observateur,* which was planning an entire issue on the subject of America, and among the features they were hoping to include was a long conversation between an older American novelist and a younger American novelist. The magazine had already contacted Styron, and he proposed Renzo as the younger writer he would like to talk to. An editor called Renzo, who was deep into a novel at the time (as usual), and when he told her he was too busy to accept—tremendously flattered by Styron's offer, but too busy—the woman was so shocked by his refusal that she threatened to kill herself, *Je me suicide!,* but Renzo merely laughed, telling her that no one commits suicide over such a trivial matter and she would feel better in the morning. He didn't know Styron well, had met him only once or twice, but he had his number, and after the conversation with the suicidal editor, he called Styron to thank him for suggesting his name, but he wanted him to know that he was hard at work on a novel and had turned down the invitation. He hoped Styron would understand. Completely, Styron said. In fact, that's why he'd suggested Renzo in the first place. He didn't want to do the conversation either, and he was fairly certain, more or less convinced, that Renzo would say no to them and get him off the hook. Thanks, Renzo, he said, you've done me a great favor. Laughter. You and Renzo both cracked up over Styron's remark, and then Renzo said: "Such a polite man, so well mannered. He simply didn't have the heart to turn the editor down, so he used me to do it for him. On the other hand, what would have happened if I had said yes? I suspect he would have pretended to be thrilled, delighted that the two of us would be given a chance to sit down together and shoot our mouths off about the state of the world. That's the way he was. A good person. The last thing he wanted was to hurt anyone's feelings." From Styron's goodness, the two of you went on to talk about the PEN campaign in support of Liu Xiaobo. A large petition signed by writers from all over the world was published on January 20, and PEN is planning to honor him in absentia at its annual fund-raising dinner in April. You will be there, of course, since you never fail to attend that dinner, but the situation looks bleak, and you have little hope that giving Liu Xiaobo a prize in New York will have any effect on his status in Beijing—detained man, no doubt soon-to-be arrested man. According to Renzo, a young woman who works at PEN lives in the same house where the boy is camped out in Brooklyn. A small world, no? Yes, Renzo, a small world indeed.

February 7. You have met with the boy twice more since your reunion on January twenty-sixth. The first time, you went to *Happy Days* together (courtesy of Mary-Lee, who had two tickets waiting for you at the box office), watched the play in a kind of stunned rapture (Mary-Lee was brilliant), and then went to her dressing room after the performance, where she assaulted you both with wild, ebullient kisses. The ecstasy of acting before a live audience, a superabundance of adrenaline coursing through her body, her eyes on fire. The boy looked inordinately pleased, especially at the moment when you and his mother embraced. Later on, you realized that this was probably the first time in his life he had seen this happen. He understands that the war is over now, that the combatants have long since put down their arms and beaten their swords into plowshares. Afterward, dinner with Korngold and Lady Swann in a small restaurant off Union Square. The boy said little but was extremely attentive. Some astute remarks about the play, parsing the opening line of the second act, *Hail, holy light,* and why Beckett chose to refer to Milton at that point, the irony of those words in the context of a world of everlasting day, since light cannot be holy except as an antidote to darkness. His mother's eyes looking at him while he spoke, glistening with adoration. Mary-Lee, the queen of excess, the

Madonna of naked feelings, and yet you sat there watching her with a twinge of envy—somewhat amused, yes, but also asking yourself why you continue to hold back. You felt more at ease in the boy's presence that second time. Getting used to him again, perhaps, but still not ready to warm up to him. The next encounter was more intimate. Dinner at Joe Junior's tonight for old times' sake, just the two of you, chomping on greasy hamburgers and soggy fries, and mostly you talked about baseball, reminding you of numerous conversations you had with your own father, that passionate but wholly neutral subject, safe ground as it were, but then he brought up Herb Score's death and told you how badly he'd wanted to call you that day and talk about it, the pitcher whose career was ruined by the same kind of injury that knocked down your father, the grandfather he never met, but then he decided that a long-distance call was inappropriate, and how odd that his first contact with you ended up being by telephone anyway, the calls between Brooklyn and Exeter when you were in the hospital, and how afraid he was that he would never see you again. You took him back to Downing Street after dinner, and it was there, in the living room of the old apartment, that he suddenly broke down and wept. He and Bobby were fighting that day, he said, out on the hot road all those years ago, and just before the car came, he pushed Bobby, pushed the smaller Bobby hard enough to make him fall down, and that was why he was run over and killed. You listened in silence. No words were available to you anymore. All the years of not knowing, and now this, the sheer banality of it, an adolescent spat between stepbrothers, and all the damage that ensued from that push. So many things became clearer to you after the boy's confession. His savage withdrawal into himself, the escape from his own life, the punishing blue-collar jobs as a form of penance, more than a decade in hell because of one moment of anger. Can he be forgiven? You couldn't get the words out of your mouth tonight, but at least you had the sense to take him in your arms and hold him. More to the point: is there anything that needs to be forgiven? Probably not. But still, he must be forgiven.

February 8. The Sunday phone conversation with Willa.

She is worried about your health, wonders how you are holding up, asks if it wouldn't be better if she quit her job and came home to take care of you. You laugh at the thought of your diligent, hardworking wife telling the university administrators: "So long, fellas, my man's got a tummy ache, gotta be going, and fuck the students I'm teaching, by the way, they can bloody well teach themselves." Willa giggles as you present that scene to her, and it is the first good laugh you have heard from her in some time, the best laugh in many months. You tell her about seeing the boy for dinner last night, but she is unresponsive, asks no questions, a small grunt to let you know she is listening but nothing more than that, and yet you forge on anyway, remarking that the boy finally seems to be coming into his own. Another grunt. Needless to say, you do not bring up the confession. A little pause, and then she tells you that at last she is feeling strong enough to return to her book, which is another good sign in your opinion, and then you tell her that Renzo sends his love, that you send your love, and you are covering her body with a thousand kisses. The conversation ends. Not a bad conversation, all in all, but after you hang up, you wander around the apartment feeling you have been stranded in the middle of nowhere. The boy has asked many questions about Willa, but you still haven't found the courage to tell him that she has *cut him out of her heart.* The Can Man dresses in a suit and tie now. The Can Man goes to work, pays his bills, and has become a model citizen. But the Can Man is still touched in the head, and on nights when the world closes in on him, he still gets down on his hands and knees and howls at the moon.

March 15. You have seen the boy six more times since the last entry about him on February seventh. A visit to the Hospital for Broken Things one Saturday afternoon, where you watched him framing pictures and asked yourself if this is all he aspires to, if he will be content to knock around from one odd job to another until he becomes an old man. You don't push him into making decisions, however. You leave him alone and wait to see what will happen next, although you are privately hoping he will return to college next fall and finish up his degree, which is something he still mentions from time to time. Another dinner foursome with Korngold and La Swann on a Monday night, when the theater was dark. A night out at the movies together to see Bresson's old masterpiece *A Man Escaped.* A midweek lunch, preceded by a visit to the office, where you showed him around and introduced him to your little band of stalwarts, and the mad thought that rushed through your head that afternoon, wondering if a boy with his intelligence and interest in books might not find a place for himself in publishing, as an employee of Heller Books, for example, where he could be groomed as his father's successor, but one mustn't dream too much, thoughts of that kind can plant poisonous seeds in one's head, and it is best to refrain from writing another person's future, especially if that person is your son. A dinner with Renzo near his house in Park Slope, the godfather in good spirits that night, embarked on yet another novel, and no more talk of slumps and doldrums and extinguished flames. And then the visit out to the house where he is living, a chance to see the Sunset Park Four in action. A sad little run-down place, but you enjoyed seeing his friends, Bing most of all, of course, who appears to be flourishing, as well as the two girls, Alice, the one who works at PEN, who talked with great intensity about the Liu Xiaobo case and then asked you a number of probing questions about your parents' generation, the young men and women of World War II, and Ellen, so meek and pretty, who late in the evening showed you a sketchbook filled with some of the raunchiest erotic drawings you have ever seen, which made you stop and wonder—just for an instant—if you couldn't rescue your company by introducing a new line of pornographic art books. They have already been served with two eviction notices, and you expressed your concern that they were pushing their luck and could wind up in a dangerous spot, but Bing slammed his fist down on the table and said they were holding out to the bitter end, and you didn't press your argument any further, since it is not your business to tell them what to do, they are all grown people (more or less) and are perfectly capable of making their own decisions, even if they are the wrong ones. Six more times, and little by little you and the boy have grown closer. He has been opening up to you now, and on one of the nights when you were alone with him, after the Bresson film most likely, he told you the full story about the girl, Pilar Sanchez, and why he had to run away from Florida. To be perfectly honest, you were appalled when he told you how young she is, but after you had thought about it for a moment, you realized that it made sense for him to be in love with someone that age, for the boy's life has been stunted, cut off from its proper and natural development, and although he looks like a full-grown man, his inner self is stuck somewhere around eighteen or nineteen. There was a moment back in January when he was afraid he was going to lose her, he said, there was a terrible flare-up, their first serious argument, and he claimed it was largely his fault, entirely his fault, since when they first met and he still had no idea how important she would become to him, he had lied to her about his family, telling her that his parents were dead, that he had no brother, had never had a brother, and now that he had come back to his parents, he wanted her to know the truth, and when he did tell her the truth, she was so angry at him for having lied to her, she hung up the phone. A week of battles followed, and she was right to feel burned, he said, he had let her down, she had lost faith in him, and it was only when he asked her to marry him that she began to soften, to understand that he would never let her down again. Marriage! Engaged to a girl not yet out of high school! Wait until you meet her next month, the boy said. And you replied, as calmly as you could, that you were looking forward to it very much.

March 29. The Sunday phone conversation with Willa. You finally tell her about the boy's confession, not knowing if this will help matters or make them worse. It is too much for her to take in all at once, and therefore her reaction evolves through several distinct stages over the minutes that follow. First: total silence, a silence that lasts long enough for you to feel compelled to repeat what you have just told her. Second: a soft voice saying "This is horrible, this is too much to bear, how can it be true?" Third: sobbing, as her mind travels back to the road and she fills in the missing parts of the picture, imagines the fight between the boys, sees Bobby being crushed all over again. Fourth: growing anger. "He lied to us," she says, "he betrayed us with his lies," and you answer her by saying that he didn't lie, he simply didn't speak, he was too traumatized by his guilt to speak, and living with that guilt has nearly destroyed him. "He killed my son," she says, and you answer her by saying that he pushed her son into the road and that her son's death was an accident. The two of you go on talking for more than an hour, and again and again you tell her you love her, that no matter what she decides or how she chooses to deal with the boy, you will always love her. She breaks down again, finally putting herself in the boy's shoes, finally telling you that she understands how much he has suffered, but she doesn't know if understanding is enough, it isn't clear to her what she wants to do, she isn't certain if she will have the strength to face him again. She needs time, she says, more time to think it over, and you tell her there is no rush, you will never force her to do anything she doesn't want to do. The conversation ends, and once again you feel you have been stranded in the middle of nowhere. By late afternoon, you have begun to resign yourself to the fact that nowhere is your home now and that is where you will be spending the last years of your life.

April 12. She reminds you of someone you know, but you can't put your finger on who that person is, and then, five or six minutes after you are introduced to her, she laughs for the first time, and you know beyond a shadow of a doubt that the person is Suki Rothstein. Suki Rothstein in the incandescent sunlight of that late afternoon on Houston Street nearly seven years ago, laughing with her friends, decked out in her bright red dress, the promise of youth in its fullest, most glorious incarnation. Pilar Sanchez is the twin of Suki Rothstein, a small luminescent being who carries the flame of life within her, and may the gods be more gentle with her than they were with the doomed child of your friends. She arrived from Florida early Saturday evening, and the next day, Easter Sunday, she and the boy came to the apartment on Downing

Street. The boy had trouble keeping his hands off her, and even as they sat side by side on the sofa talking to you in your comfortable chair, he was kissing her neck, stroking her bare knee, putting his arm around her shoulder. You had already seen her, of course, almost a year ago in that little park in southern Florida, you were a clandestine witness to their first encounter, their first conversation, but you were too far away from her to look into her eyes and see the power that is in them, the dark steady eyes that absorb everything around her, that emit the light that has made the boy fall in love with her. They came with good news, the boy said, the best news, and a moment later you were told that Pilar had been accepted at Barnard with a full scholarship and will be coming to live in New York immediately after her high school graduation in June. You told her that your wife went to Barnard as well, that you saw her for the first time when she was a Barnard student, and the torch has now been passed from the boy's stepmother to her. And then (you almost fell out of your chair when you heard this) the boy announced that he has enrolled in the School of General Studies at Columbia and will start the final leg toward his B.A. in the fall. You asked him how he was going to pay for it, and he said he has some money in the bank and will cover the rest by applying for a student loan. You were impressed that he didn't ask for your help, even though you would be willing to give it, but you know it is better for his morale to take on this burden himself. As the talk continued, you realized that you were becoming more and more happy, that you were happier today than you have been at any time in the past thirteen years, and you wanted to drink in this happiness, to become drunk on this happiness, and it occurred to you that no matter what Willa decides concerning the boy, you will be able to tolerate a split life with the two people you care about most in the world, that you will take your pleasures wherever and whenever you can find them. You booked a table for dinner at the Waverly Inn, that venerable establishment from the old New York, the New York that no longer exists, thinking Pilar would enjoy going to such a place, and she did enjoy it, she actually said she felt she was in heaven, and as the three of you packed away your Easter dinner, the girl was full of questions, she wanted to know everything about running a publishing house, how you met Renzo Michaelson, how you decide whether to accept a book or not, and as you answered her questions, you understood that she was listening to you with intense concentration, that she would not forget a word you had said. At one point, the talk drifted onto math and science, and you found yourself listening to a discussion about quantum physics, a subject that you freely admitted escapes you entirely, and then Pilar turned to you and said: "Think of it this way, Mr. Heller. In the old physics, three times two equals six and two times three equals six are reversible propositions. Not in quantum physics. Three times two and two times three are two different matters, distinct and separate propositions." There are many things in this world for you to worry about, but the boy's love for this girl is not one of them.

April 13. You wake up this morning to the news that Mark Fidrych is dead. Just fifty-four years old, killed on his farm in Northborough, Massachusetts, when the dump truck he was repairing collapsed on top of him. First Herb Score, and now Mark Fidrych, the two cursed geniuses who dazzled the country for a few days, a few months, and then vanished from sight. You remember your father's old refrain: Poor Herb Score. Now you add another casualty to the roster of the fallen: Mark Fidrych. May the Bird rest in peace.

Alice Bergstrom and Ellen Brice

It is Thursday, April thirtieth, and Alice has just completed another five-hour stint at the PEN American Center. Breaking from her established routine of the past several months, she will not be rushing home to Sunset Park to work on her dissertation. Instead, she is on her way to meet Ellen, who has Thursdays off, and the two of them will be splurging on a late lunch at Balthazar, the French brasserie on Spring Street in SoHo, less than a two-minute walk from the PEN offices at 588 Broadway. Yesterday, another court order was delivered to the house by yet another New York City marshal, bringing the total number of eviction notices they have received to four, and earlier in the month, when the third notice arrived, she and Ellen agreed that the next warning would be the last one, that they would turn in their squatters' badges at that point and move on, reluctantly move on. That is why they have arranged to meet in Manhattan this afternoon—to talk things over and figure out what to do next, calmly and thoughtfully, in an environment far from Bing and his aggressive, hotheaded pronouncements, and what better place for a calm and thoughtful discussion than this pricey, elegant restaurant during the quiet interlude between lunch and dinner?

Jake is out of the picture now. The showdown she was preparing herself for when last seen on January fifth finally took place in mid-February, and the hurtful thing about that last conversation was how quickly he assented to her reading of their present circumstances, how little resistance he mounted to the idea of going their separate ways, calling it quits. Something was wrong with him, he said, but it was true that he no longer felt excited when he was with her, that he no longer looked forward to seeing her, and he blamed himself for this shift in his feelings and frankly could not understand what had happened to him. He told her that she was a remarkable person, with numerous outstanding qualities—intelligence, compassion, wisdom—and that he was a damaged soul incapable of loving her in the way she deserved to be loved. He did not explore the problem more deeply than that, did not, for example, delve into the reasons why he had lost interest in her sexually, but that would have been too much to hope for, she realized, since he openly admitted that these changes confused him just as much as they confused her. She asked him if he had ever thought about psychotherapy, and he said yes, he was considering it, his life was in a shambles and there was no question that he needed help. Alice sensed that he was telling her the truth, but she wasn't entirely certain of it, and whenever she replays that conversation in her mind now, she wonders if his passive, self-accusatory position was not simply the easiest way out for him, a lie to mask the fact that he had fallen for someone else. But which someone else? She doesn't know, and in the two and a half months since she last saw him, none of their mutual friends has talked to her about a new person in connection with Jake. It could be that there is no one—or else his love life has become a well-guarded secret. One way or the other, she misses him. Now that he is gone, she tends to recall the good moments they had together and ignore the difficult ones, and oddly enough, what she finds herself missing most about him are the occasional jags of humor that would pour out of him at unpredictable moments, the moments when the distinctly unhumorous Jake Baum would drop his defenses and begin impersonating various comical figures, mostly ones who spoke with heavy foreign accents, Russians, Indians, Koreans, and he was surprisingly good at this, he always got the voices just right, but that was the old Jake, of course, the Jake of a year ago, and the truth is that it had been a long time since he had made her laugh by turning himself into one of those funny characters. *Meese Aleece. Keese mee, Meese Aleece.* She doubts that another man will come along anytime soon, and this worries her, since she is thirty years old now, and the prospect of a childless future fills her with dread.

Her weight is down, however, more from lack of appetite than from scrupulous dieting, but one fifty-four is a decent number for her, and she has stopped thinking of herself as a repulsive cow—that is, whenever she thinks about her body, which seems to happen less often now that Jake is gone and there is no one to touch her anymore. Her dissertation stalled for about two weeks after his departure, but then she pulled herself together and has been working hard ever since, so hard, in fact, that she is well into the concluding chapter now and feels she can finish off the first draft in approximately ten days. For the past three years, the dissertation has been an end in itself, the mountain she set out to climb, but she has rarely thought about what would happen to her after she reached the top. If and when she did think about it, she complacently assumed the next step would be to apply for a teaching position somewhere. That's why you spend all those years struggling to get your Ph.D., isn't it? They give you your doctorate, and then you go out and teach. But now that the end is in sight, she has been reexamining the question, and it is by no means certain anymore that teaching is the answer. She is still inclined to give it a shot, but after her less than happy experience as an adjunct last year, she wonders if toiling in some English department for the next four decades will be fulfilling enough to sustain her. Other possibilities have occurred to her in the past month or so. A bigger, more demanding job at PEN, for example. That work has engaged her far more than she thought it would, and she doesn't want to give it up, which she would be forced to do if she landed a post in an English department—which, by the by, would most likely be at a college eight hundred miles to the south or west of New York. That's the problem, she says to herself, as she pulls open the door of the restaurant and walks in, not the job but the place. She doesn't want to leave New York. She wants to go on living in this immense, unlivable city for as long as she can, and after all these years, the thought of living anywhere else strikes her as insane.

Ellen is already there, sitting at one of the tables along the eastern wall of the restaurant, nursing a glass of white wine as she waits for her friend to show up. Ellen knows more about what Alice's ex-lover has been up to for the past few months than Alice does, but Ellen hasn't said anything to Alice about these goings-on because she promised Bing to keep them a secret, and Ellen is not someone who breaks her word. Bing has continued posing for her once or twice a week throughout the first four months of the year, and many walls have come down between them in that time, all walls in fact, and they have shared confidences with each other that neither one of them would have been willing to share with anyone else. Ellen knows about Bing's infatuation with Miles, for example, and she knows about his anxieties concerning the man-woman problem, the man-man problem, and his doubts about who and what he is. She knows that sometime in late January Bing ventured up to Jake's small apartment in Manhattan and, with the aid of abundant quantities of alcohol and a guarantee to contact Renzo Michaelson about the interview Jake so earnestly wished to conduct with him, managed to seduce Alice's ex-amour into a sexual encounter. That was Bing's first and last experiment in self-discovery, since he found little or no pleasure in Jake Baum's arms, mouth, or private parts, and grudgingly had to admit that while he was still deeply attracted to Miles, he had no interest in making love to men, not even to Miles. Jake, on the other hand, much as Bing had suspected, had been through a number of male-male experiences as an adolescent, and on the strength of his encounter with Bing, which brought him much pleasure, he realized that his interest in men had not waned with the years as he supposed it had. Two weeks later, when Alice forced him into the showdown, he quietly bowed out of their affair to pursue that other interest. Ellen knows about this because Jake and Bing are still in touch. Jake has told Bing about what he has been doing, Bing has passed along this information to Ellen, and

Ellen has kept silent. Alice doesn't know it, but she is much better off without Jake, and if Ellen has any knowledge or understanding of the world, it won't be long before Alice finds herself another man.

This is the new Ellen, the Ellen Brice who last month overhauled the outward trappings of her person in order to express the new relation she has developed with her body, which is a product of the new relation she has developed with her heart, which in turn is a product of the new relation she has developed with her innermost self. In one bold, decisive week in the middle of March, she had her long, stringy hair cut into a short 1920s bob, threw out every article of clothing in her bureau and closet, and began adorning her face with lipstick, rouge, eyeliner, eye shadow, and mascara every time she left the house, so that the woman described in Morris Heller's journal as *meek,* the woman who for years inspired feelings of compassion and protectiveness in those who knew her, no longer projects an aura of victimhood and skittish uncertainty, and as she sits on the banquette along the eastern wall of Balthazar dressed in a black leather miniskirt and a tight cashmere sweater, sipping her white wine and watching Alice come through the door, heads turn when people walk past her, and she exults in the attention she receives, exults in the knowledge that she is the most desirable woman in the room. This revolution in her appearance was inspired by an unlikely event that occurred in February, just one week after Alice and Jake put an end to their tottering romance, when none other than Benjamin Samuels, the high school boy who impregnated Ellen nearly nine years ago in the pavilion of his parents' summer house in southern Vermont, walked into the real estate office where Ellen works, looking for an apartment to rent in Park Slope or one of its adjacent neighborhoods, a twenty-five-year-old Benjamin Samuels, fully grown now and employed as a cell phone salesman in a T-Mobile store on Seventh Avenue, a college dropout, a young man devoid of the intellectual skills required to pursue one of the professions, law or medicine, say, which his parents once hoped would be his destiny, but just as handsome as ever, more handsome than ever, the beautiful boy with the beautiful soccer player's body now ripened into a large beautiful man. He didn't recognize Ellen at first, and although she suspected that the broad-shouldered fellow sitting across from her was the matured incarnation of the boy she had given herself to so many years earlier, she waited until he had filled in the blanks on the rental application form before she announced who she was. She spoke quietly and tentatively, not knowing if he would be pleased or displeased, not knowing if he would even remember her, but Ben Samuels did remember her, and Ben Samuels was pleased to have found her again, so pleased that he stood up from his chair, walked around to the other side of Ellen's desk, and put his arms around her in a great welcoming hug. They spent the afternoon walking in and out of empty apartments together, kissing in the first apartment, making love in the second apartment, and now that Ben Samuels has moved into the neighborhood, he and Ellen have continued making love nearly every day. That is why Ellen cut her hair—because Ben is aroused by the back of her neck—and once she cut her hair, she understood that he would be even more aroused by her if she started wearing different, more alluring clothes. Until now, she has kept Ben a secret from Alice, Bing, and Miles, but with so many changes suddenly afoot, the fourth court order, the imminent dispersal of their little gang, she has decided that this is the day she will tell Alice about the extraordinary thing that has happened to her.

Alice is kissing her on the cheek now and smiling her Alice smile, and as Ellen watches her friend sit down in the chair facing the banquette, she wonders if she will ever be good enough to do a drawing that would fully capture that smile, which is the warmest, most luminous smile on earth, a smile that sets Alice apart from every other person she knows, has known, or will ever know until the end of her life.

Well, kid, Alice says, I guess the grand experiment is over.

For us, maybe, Ellen says, but not for Bing and Miles.

Miles is going back to Florida in three weeks.

I forgot. Bing alone, then. How sad.

I'm thinking ten more days. If I work hard, I should be

able to finish the last chapter by then. Is that okay with you, or would you rather pull out now?

I don't ever want to pull out. It's just that I'm getting scared. If the cops show up, they'll toss our stuff out onto the street, things could get broken, Bing could go crazy, all sorts of unpleasant possibilities come to mind. Ten days is too long, Alice. I think you should start looking for a new place tomorrow.

How many rentals do you have?

Plenty in the Slope, not so many in Sunset Park.

But Sunset Park is cheaper, which means that Sunset Park is better.

How much can you afford to pay?

As little as the market will bear.

I'll check the listings after lunch and let you know what we have.

But maybe you've had enough of Sunset Park. If you want to go somewhere else, I have no problem with that. As long as I can pay my half of the rent, anywhere is fine.

Dear Alice . . .

What?

I hadn't realized you wanted to share.

Don't you?

In principle, yes, but something has come up, and I'm considering other options.

Options?

One option.

Oh?

He's called Benjamin Samuels, and he's asked me to move in with him.

You little devil. How long as this been going on?

A couple of months.

A couple of months? What's gotten into you? A couple of months, and you never even told me.

I wasn't sure enough to tell anyone. I thought it might be just a sex thing that would flame out before it was worth mentioning. But it seems to be getting bigger. Big enough for me to want to give it a try, I think.

Are you in love with him?

I don't know. But I'm crazy about him, that much I do know. And the sex is pretty sensational.

Who is he?

The one.

What one?

The one from the summer of two thousand.

The man who got you pregnant?

The boy who got me pregnant.

So, the story finally comes out . . .

He was sixteen, and I was twenty. Now he's twenty-five, and I'm twenty-nine. Those four years are a lot less important today than they were back then.

Christ. I thought it might have been the father, but never the son.

That's why I couldn't talk about it. He was too young, and I didn't want to get him into trouble.

Did he ever know what happened?

Not then, no, and not now either. There's no point in telling him, is there?

Twenty-five years old. And what does he do with himself?

Nothing much. He has a dreary little job, and he isn't terribly bright. But he adores me, Alice, and no one has ever treated me better. We fuck during our lunch break every afternoon in his apartment on Fifth Street. He turns me inside out. I swoon when he touches me. I can't get enough of his body. I feel I might be going mad, and then I wake up in the morning and realize that I'm happy, happier than I've been in a long, long time.

Good for you, El.

Yes, good for me. Who ever would have thought?

Miles Heller

On Saturday, May second, he reads in the morning paper that Jack Lohrke is dead at the age of eighty-five. The short obituary recounts the three miraculous escapes from certain death—the felled comrades in the Battle of the Bulge, the crashed airplane after the war, the bus that toppled into the ravine—but it is a skimpy article, a perfunctory article, which glides over Lucky's undistinguished major league career with the Giants and Phillies and mentions only one detail Miles was not aware of: in the most celebrated game of the twentieth century, the final round of the National League championship play-off between the Giants and the Dodgers in 1951, Don Mueller, the Giants' right fielder, broke his ankle sliding into third base in the last inning, and if the Giants had tied the score rather than win the game with a walk-off home run, Lohrke would have taken over for Mueller in the next inning, but Branca threw the pitch, Thomson hit the pitch, and the game ended before Lucky could get his name in the box score. The young Willie Mays on deck, Lucky Lohrke warming up to replace Mueller in right field, and then Thomson clobbered the final pitch of the season over the left-field wall, and the Giants won the pennant, the Giants won the pennant. The obituary says nothing about Jack "Lucky" Lohrke's private life, not a single word about marriage or children or grandchildren, no information about the people he might have loved or the people who might have loved him, simply the dull and insignificant fact that the patron saint of good fortune worked in security at Lockheed after he retired from baseball.

The instant he finishes reading the obituary, he calls the apartment on Downing Street to commiserate with his father over the death of the man they discussed so often during the years of their own good fortune, the years before anyone knew about roads in the Berkshires, the years before anyone was buried or anyone else ran away, and his father has of course read the paper over his morning coffee and knows about Lucky's departure from this world. A bad stretch, his father says. First Herb Score in November, then Mark Fidrych in April, and now this. Miles says he regrets they never wrote a letter to Jack Lohrke to tell him what an important figure he was in their family, and his father says, yes, that was a stupid oversight, why didn't they think of that years ago? Miles answers that maybe it was because they assumed their man would live forever, and his father laughs, saying that Jack Lohrke wasn't immortal, just lucky, and even if they considered him their patron saint, he mustn't forget that saints die too.

The worst of it is behind him now. Just twenty days before he is released from prison, then back to Florida until Pilar finishes school, and after that New York again, where they will spend the early part of the summer looking for a place to live uptown. In an astounding act of generosity, his father has offered to let them stay with him on Downing Street until they find their own apartment, which means that Pilar will never have to spend another night in the house in Sunset Park, which scared her even before the eviction notices started coming and now puts her in a full-blown panic. How much longer before the cops come to throw them out? Alice and Ellen have already made up their minds to decamp, and even though Bing went into a rage when they announced their decision at dinner two nights ago, they both held their ground, and Miles believes their position is the only sensible one to take anymore. They will be moving out the minute Ellen manages to find Alice an affordable replacement, which is likely to happen by the middle of next week, and if his circumstances were similar to theirs, he would be on his way out as well. Just twenty days, however, and in the meantime he must not abandon Bing, not when the venture is falling apart, not when Bing so desperately needs him to be here, and therefore he intends to stay put until the twenty-second and prays that no cops show up before then.

He wants those twenty days, but he does not get them. He gets the day and the night of the second, the day and the night of the third, and early in the morning on the fourth, there is a loud knock on the front door. Miles is fast asleep in his downstairs bedroom behind the kitchen, and by the time he wakes up and slips into his clothes, the house has already been invaded. He hears the tread of heavy footsteps clomping up the stairs, he hears Bing shouting angrily at the top of his voice (*Get your fucking hands off me!*), he hears Alice shrieking at someone to back off and leave her computer alone, and he hears the cops yelling (*Clear out! Clear out!*), how many cops he doesn't know, he thinks two, but there could be three, and by the time he opens the door of his room, walks across the kitchen, and reaches the entrance hall, the commotion upstairs has turned into a clamorous roar. He glances to his right, sees that the front door is open, and there is Ellen, standing on the porch with her hand over her mouth, her eyes wide with fear, with horror, and then he looks to his left, fixing his eyes on the staircase, at the top of which he sees Alice, large Alice trying to wrestle herself out of the arms of an enormous cop, and just then, as he continues looking up, he sees Bing on the top landing as well, his wrists shackled in handcuffs as a second enormous cop holds him by the hair with one hand and jabs a nightstick into his back with the other, and just when he is about to turn around and run out of the house, he sees the first enormous cop push Alice down the stairs, and as Alice tumbles toward him, cracking the side of her head against a wooden step, the enormous cop who pushed her races down the stairs, and before Miles can pause to think about what he is doing, he is punching that enormous cop in the jaw with his clenched fist, and as the cop falls down from the blow, Miles turns around, rushes out of the house, finds Ellen standing on the porch, takes hold of her right hand with his left hand, drags her down the front steps with him, and the two of them begin to run.

An entrance to Green-Wood Cemetery is just around the corner, and that is where they go, not certain if they are being chased or not, but Miles thinks that if there were two cops in the house and not three, then the uninjured cop would be tending to the cop he punched in the jaw, which would mean that no one is pursuing them. Still, they run for as long as they can, and when Ellen is out of breath and can go no farther, they flop down on the grass for a spell, leaning their backs against the headstone of a man named Charles Everett Brown, 1858–1927. Miles's hand is in terrific pain, and he fears it might be broken. Ellen wants to take him to the emergency room for X-rays, but Miles says no, that would be too dangerous, he must keep himself hidden. He has assaulted a police officer and that is a crime, a serious offense, and even if he hopes the bastard's jaw is broken, even if he feels no regret about smashing in the face of someone who threw a woman down a flight of stairs, Alice Bergstrom no less, the best woman in the world, there is no question that he is in bad trouble, the worst trouble he has ever known.

He doesn't have his cell phone, she doesn't have her cell phone. They are sitting on the grass in the cemetery with no way to reach anyone, no way to know if Bing has been arrested or not, no way to know if Alice has been hurt or not, and for the time being Miles is still too stunned to have formulated a plan about what to do next. Ellen tells him that she woke early as usual, six-fifteen or six-thirty, and that she was standing on the porch with her coffee when the cops arrived. She was the one who opened the door and let them in. What choice did she have but to open the door and let them in? They went upstairs, there were two of them, and she remained on the porch as the two cops went upstairs, and then all hell broke loose, she saw nothing, she was still standing on the porch, but Bing and Alice were both shouting, the two cops were shouting, everyone was shouting, Bing must have resisted, he must have started fighting, and no doubt Alice was afraid they would push her out before she could gather up her papers and books and films and computer, the computer in which her entire dissertation is stored, three years of work in one small machine, and no doubt that was why she snapped and started struggling with the cop, Alice's dissertation, Bing's drums, and all her drawings of the past five months, hundreds and hundreds of drawings, and all of it still in the house, in the house that is no doubt sealed up now, off-limits, and everything gone forever now. She wants to cry, she says, but she is unable to cry, she is too angry to cry, there was no need for all that pushing and shoving, why couldn't the cops have behaved like men instead of animals, and no, she can't cry even if she wants to, but please, Miles, she says, put your arms around me, hold me, Miles, I need someone to hold me, and Miles puts his arms around Ellen and strokes her head.

They have to do something about his hand. It is swelling now, the area around the knuckles looks bloated and blue, and even if no bones are broken (he has discovered that he can wiggle his fingers a bit without increasing the pain), the hand must be iced to bring down the swelling. Hematoma. He thinks that is the word he is looking for—localized swelling filled with blood, a small lake of blood sloshing around just under the skin. They must ice the hand, and they also must eat something. They have been sitting on the grass in the cemetery for close to two hours now, and they are both hungry, although it is far from certain that either one of them would be able to eat if food were set before them. They stand up and begin walking, moving quickly past the tombs and mausoleums in the direction of Windsor Terrace and Park Slope, the Twenty-fifth Street entrance to the cemetery, the exit from the cemetery, and once they reach Seventh Avenue, they go on walking all the way to Sixth Street. Ellen tells Miles to wait outside for her, and then she goes into a T-Mobile cell phone store to talk to her new boyfriend, her old boyfriend, it's a complicated story, and a few moments later, she is unlocking the door to Ben Samuels's apartment on Fifth Street between Sixth and Seventh Avenues.

They can't stay here for long, she says, just a few hours, she doesn't want Ben to get involved in this, but at least it's something, a chance for a breather until they can figure out what to do next. They wash up, Ellen makes them cheese sandwiches, and then she fills a plastic bag with ice cubes and hands it to Miles. He wants to call Pilar, but it is too early, she is at school now, and she doesn't switch on her phone until she returns to the apartment at four o'clock. Where do we go from here? Ellen asks. Miles thinks for a moment, and then he remembers that his godfather lives nearby, just a few blocks from where they are sitting, but when he calls Renzo's number, no one picks up, it is the answering machine that talks to him, and he knows that Renzo is either working or out of town and therefore does not bother to leave a message. There is no one left except his father, but just as Ellen is reluctant to involve her friend, he balks at the idea of dragging his father into this mess, his father is the last person in the world he wants to turn to for help now.

As if she is able to read his thoughts, Ellen says: You have to call your father, Miles.

He shakes his head. Impossible, he says. I've already put that man through enough.

If you won't do it, Ellen says, then I will.

Please, Ellen. Leave him alone.

But Ellen insists, and a moment later she is dialing the number of Heller Books in Manhattan. Miles is so upset by what she is doing that he walks out of the kitchen and locks himself in the bathroom. He can't bear to listen, he refuses to listen. He would rather stab himself in the heart than listen to Ellen talk to his father.

Time passes, how much time he doesn't know, three minutes, eight minutes, two hours, and then Ellen is knocking on the door, telling him to come out, telling him that his father knows everything about what happened in Sunset Park this morning, that his father is waiting for him on the other end of the line. He unlocks the door, sees that Ellen's eyes are rimmed with tears, gently touches her face with his left hand, and walks into the kitchen.

His father's voice says: Two detectives came to the office

about an hour ago. They say you broke a policeman's jaw. Is that true?

He pushed Alice down the stairs, Miles says. I lost my temper.

Bing is in jail for resisting arrest. Alice is in the hospital with a concussion.

How bad is it?

She's awake, her head hurts, but no permanent damage. They'll probably let her out tomorrow morning.

To go where? She doesn't have a place to live anymore. She's homeless. We're all homeless now.

I want you to turn yourself in, Miles.

No chance. They'd lock me up for years.

Extenuating circumstances. Police brutality. First offense. I doubt you'd serve any time.

It's their word against ours. The cop will say Alice tripped and fell, and the jury will believe him. We're just a bunch of illegal trespassers, squatters, freeloading bums.

You don't want to spend the rest of your life running from the police, do you? You've already done enough running. Time to stand up and face the music, Miles. And I'll stand up there with you.

You can't. You have a good heart, Dad, but I'm in this thing alone.

No, you're not. You'll have a lawyer. And I know some damned good ones. Everything is going to be all right, believe me.

I'm so sorry. So fucking, terribly sorry.

Listen to me, Miles. Talking on the phone is no good. We have to hash it out in person, face to face. The minute I hang up, I'll go straight home. Get yourself into a taxi and meet me there as soon as you can. All right?

All right.

You promise?

Yes, I promise.

Half an hour later, he is sitting in the backseat of a car-service Dodge, on his way to Downing Street in Manhattan.

Ellen has gone to the bank for him with his ATM card and returned with a thousand dollars in cash, they have kissed and said good-bye, and as the car moves through the heavy traffic toward the Brooklyn Bridge, he wonders how long it will be before he sees Ellen Brice again. He wishes he could go to the hospital to see Alice, but he knows he can't. He wishes he could go to the jail where Bing is locked up, but he knows he can't. He presses the ice against his swollen hand, and as he looks at the hand, he thinks about the soldier with the missing hands in the movie he saw with Alice and Pilar last winter, the young soldier home from the war, unable to undress himself and go to bed without his father's help, and he feels he has become that boy now, who can do nothing without his father's help, a boy without hands, a boy who should be without hands, a boy whose hands have brought him nothing but trouble in his life, his angry punching hands, his angry pushing hands, and then the name of the soldier in the movie comes back to him, Homer, Homer Something, Homer as in the poet Homer, who wrote the scene about Odysseus and Telemachus, father and son reunited after so many years, in the same way he and his father have been reunited, and the name Homer makes him think of home, as in the word *homeless,* they are all homeless now, he said that to his father on the phone, Alice and Bing are homeless, he is homeless, the people in Florida who lived in the houses he trashed out are homeless, only Pilar is not homeless, he is her home now, and with one punch he has destroyed everything, they will never have their life together in New York, there is no future for them anymore, no hope for them anymore, and even if he runs away to Florida to be with her now, there will be no hope for them, and even if he stays in New York to fight it out in court, there will be no hope for them, he has let his father down, let Pilar down, let everyone down, and as the car travels across the Brooklyn Bridge and he looks at the immense buildings on the other side of the East River, he thinks about the missing buildings, the collapsed and burning buildings that no longer exist, the missing buildings and the missing hands, and he wonders if it is worth hoping for a future when there is no future, and from now on, he tells himself, he will stop hoping for anything and live only for now, this moment, this passing moment, the now that is here and then not here, the now that is gone forever.

Acknowledgments

Warm thanks to the following:

Charles Bernstein, Susan Bee, and their son, Felix.

Mark Costello.

Larry Siems and Sarah Hoffman of the PEN American Center.

My daughter, Sophie Auster, for her sixth-grade paper on *To Kill a Mockingbird* (1998).

Siri Hustvedt for *the strangeness of being alive.*